KT-418-958

Patricia SCANLAN

A Gift for You

**SIMON &
SCHUSTER**

London · New York · Sydney · Toronto · New Delhi

A CBS COMPANY

First published in Great Britain by Simon & Schuster UK Ltd, 2015
A CBS COMPANY

Copyright © Patricia Scanlan 2015

This book is copyright under the Berne Convention.
No reproduction without permission.
® and © 1997 Simon & Schuster, Inc. All rights reserved.

The right of Patricia Scanlan to be identified as author of this work has been asserted
in accordance with sections 77 and 78 of the Copyright, Designs and Patents Act, 1988.

1 3 5 7 9 10 8 6 4 2

Simon & Schuster UK Ltd
1st Floor
Gray's Inn Road
London WC1X 8HB

www.simonandschuster.co.uk

Simon & Schuster Australia, Sydney
Simon & Schuster India, New Delhi

A CIP catalogue record for this book is available from the British Library

Hardback ISBN: 978-1-47115-072-2
Trade Paperback ISBN: 978-1-47115-073-9
eBook ISBN: 978-1-47115-075-3

This book is a work of fiction. Names, characters, places and incidents are either
a product of the author's imagination or are used fictitiously. Any resemblance
to actual people living or dead, events or locales is entirely coincidental.

Typeset in the UK by Hewer Text UK Ltd, Edinburgh
Printed and bound in Great Britain by CPI Group (UK) Ltd, Croydon, CR0 4YY

READING BOROUGH LIBRARIES	
Askews & Holts	
AF	£14.99

A Gift
for You

Patricia Scanlan was born in Dublin, where she still lives. Her books have sold worldwide and have been translated into many languages. Patricia is the series editor and a contributing author to the *Open Door* series. She also teaches creative writing to second-level students and is involved in Adult Literacy.

Find out more by visiting Patricia Scanlan on Facebook.

Also by Patricia Scanlan

Apartment 3B
Finishing Touches
Foreign Affairs
Promises, Promises
Mirror Mirror
Francesca's Party
Two for Joy
Double Wedding
Divided Loyalties
Coming Home

Trilogies

City Girl
City Lives
City Woman

Forgive and Forget
Happy Ever After
Love and Marriage
With All My Love
A Time for Friends

To Mammy and The Mothers with great love and gratitude. I can never thank you enough.

Acknowledgements

Acknowledgement

To all who gift me with love and kindness. My love for you is boundless, my gratitude immense. You are great Blessings in my life.

Contents

CHRISTMAS

A Gift for You   3
Back Where I Belong   20
Façades   31
The Christmas Tree   65

VALENTINE'S DAY

The Angel of Love   73
A Woman in Her Prime   89
The Seventh Floor   107

MOTHER'S DAY

One Small Step   117
The Unexpected Visit   127

DIFFICULT DAYS

Fairweather Friend   138
True Colours   161
Ripples   177
A Dish Best Served Cold   209
The Judge   223

BIRTHDAY

Life Begins at 40!   243
The Best Birthday Ever   256
A Low Threshold of Pain   272

CHRISTMAS

A Gift For You

Magdalena Dunne was bursting to go to the loo. Her bladder had developed a mind of its own in the last six weeks. Sneezing and coughing were a nightmare. She was practically incontinent, she thought glumly as she struggled against the heaving mass of Christmas shoppers on Henry Street and headed for the Ilac shopping centre. She should pitch a tent in the loos in Ilac, she visited them so often, she reflected, passing through the doors to the crowded concourse as the piped music of *Have Yourself A Merry Little Christmas* assaulted her ears.

Magdalena snorted. Merry Little Christmas indeed! No drink, no ciggies, unremitting heartburn, a leaky bladder, an iffy sciatic nerve and the dread and fear of her first (and her *last,* she assured herself) baby's delivery wasn't exactly a recipe for The Best Christmas Ever. And she was lonely, *sooo* lonely for her parents and sister, Karolina, far away in Eastern Europe. Her mother had emailed her some photos of the family's farmhouse quilted in soft snow, the land a lustrous white tapestry, broken here and there with bare-branched trees bowing low with their winter dressing.

Back in Poland, her father, Tomasz, would be blessing the fields with holy water and placing crosses made of straw in the four corners before hanging the branch of mistletoe above the front door, for luck. Her mother, Zuzanna, would be preparing for the Christmas Eve supper. The house would be sparkling, all the windows shining in the winter sun. Zuzanna would have been preparing for weeks for *Wigilia*, as Christmas Eve was known in her native land. The old belief that if the house was dirty on Christmas Eve it would be dirty all year had been ingrained in her and her sister and she smiled, remembering the hours of polishing and cleaning they'd had to do in the run up to Christmas.

Magdalena knew her mother might not be too impressed to know that she had not done her own cleaning but had hired mini-maids to come in for a couple of hours and blitz the house. It was a one-off. Pregnancy and being hectically busy at work had left her weary, and when she had tentatively suggested it to Michael, her husband, he'd agreed immediately.

'Very good idea!' he declared enthusiastically, relieved no doubt that he wouldn't have to hoover.

'Really? No moans about the cost, no saying we can't afford it?' she teased.

'It's a gift for you.' He grinned, enveloping her in a bear hug, and she'd nestled in against him, loving her good-humoured, kind-hearted Irishman.

There was a queue for the loo and she stood, legs crossed, cursing every occupant of the serried row of cubicles. The relief when she finally bolted a door behind her and peed with abandon was indescribable.

While she retouched her make-up, Magdalena took stock. She still had a few Christmas presents to buy and she also wanted to pop into M&S to buy some of their roast potatoes and pre-prepared seasonal vegetables to go with the turkey. She knew it was cheating, but she was in no humour to peel potatoes and veg when she got home. Michael, too, was up to his eyes at work and he'd told her he wasn't sure when he'd be home. Sometimes she wondered if her husband's desire to work extra hours was a subconscious excuse to escape from her and her pregnancy.

Magdalena sighed. Their lives were changing irrevocably, that was for sure. Part of her didn't want the change. They'd been happy doing their own thing with no one to please, only themselves. The baby was going to make an enormous difference to their lives and their freedom.

Don't think about it now. Focus on what you have to do, she instructed herself as she left the relative haven of the crowded toilets and entered the Christmas fray again. She'd need to get a move on. Her lunchtime was being whittled away and lateness was frowned upon in the busy accounts department where she worked. Magdalena's line manager, Beady Eyes Barrett, as her minions referred to her, was a cranky old cow to work for. She didn't approve of pregnant women getting time off to go for check-ups and the like. If girls wanted to get pregnant and have babies that was their look-out. It shouldn't interfere with their work, according to Dolores Barrett. Just because they were pregnant was not an excuse to be treated differently. Working mothers were the bane of Dolores's life. Looking for days off because they had to bring children to clinics. Rushing out of work because crèches called to say the darlings were sick. Teething problems weren't *her* problems, Beady Eyes was fond of proclaiming.

Magdalena could just see her crabby supervisor mouthing off in the canteen, oblivious that she was causing severe stress to at least half a dozen women under her thumb. Or maybe she wasn't so oblivious. Maybe she knew *exactly* what she was doing and enjoyed it.

Magdalena would be joining those beleaguered unfortunates following her maternity and unpaid leave. She tried not to think about *that* scenario. Soon she'd be free of Dolores for almost the next year. It was a joyful prospect.

She could always leave her job in the big computer software company that she worked for and look for another position elsewhere, but there was no guarantee that she wouldn't end up with another Dolores. Besides, the salary was excellent at Johnson & Johnson and the perks were good. Apart from Dolores, Magdalena liked and got on well with her colleagues so why *should* she have to move? She shouldn't be getting herself tied up in knots; it wasn't good for the baby, she told herself sternly, zigzagging to avoid a harassed mother with a twin buggy.

She looked at her shopping list again and felt a sudden wave of exhaustion. Just this once, she'd get book tokens and gift vouchers. Impersonal, but utterly practical and time-saving. She'd buy a book for herself too, a little Christmas treat. Her favourite Irish author, Ciara Geraghty, had a new book out. She would *immerse* herself in it to keep her homesickness at bay.

The lonesomeness was worse than usual this year, she thought dolefully. Most likely because she was hormonal and apprehensive as the weeks rolled on and the day of her delivery drew closer. Her mother was coming to stay when the baby was born, in late January, and so there would be no Christmas visit from her parents this year. Last year, she and Michael had gone to Poland and it was the happiest Christmas she had ever had. Her family loved her Irish husband and they had pulled out all the stops to celebrate a traditional Polish Christmas with their daughter and son-in-law. Tears blurred Magdalena's brown eyes. What she wouldn't give for a hug from her mother and father and hear them call her *kochanieńka*.

Stop it, you silly girl, she scolded, rubbing her eyes with the back of her hands. *You'll see them in January when your own* kochanieńka *is born*.

Michael Dunne eyed the basket of washing and glanced at his watch. He was under pressure but there was a good breeze blowing and Magdalena had left strict instructions that he was to hang out the clothes before he left for work.

The tumble dryer was on the blink and he was supposed to get that sorted too. Life was all hassle these days and Magdalena was as tetchy as be damned. It was probably because she was petrified of giving birth. He wouldn't fancy it himself, he had to admit. But it was unnerving living with her at the moment. She'd suddenly burst into tears for no reason, weeping that she was homesick for her family and that she was scared of giving birth. He'd try to reassure her and say it was a natural thing for women, wasn't it? Millions of women gave birth. Why was she panicking?

But his stout words sounded hollow to his own ears. He would never forget the pre-natal class where they'd shown the video of a birth. It had been pretty gruesome. If he thought that he had to endure that type of pain, he'd possibly faint. He'd fainted once when he'd broken his ankle playing football. One minute he was feeling woozy and in agony and the next enveloped in total blackness. He'd felt a bit of a wussie when he came to.

Michael had watched the birthing video through half-shut eyes and felt quite queasy. To tell the truth, he didn't *really* want to be at the birth. Not that he'd say that to Magdalena. He was afraid he'd pass out or puke and make a show of himself. He didn't want to see Magdalena groaning in pain for hours on end. He didn't want to feel helpless and in the way. He didn't want to see blood and gore. He just wanted everything to be back to normal and to have his confident, sexy, funny, sweet wife back the way she was and not this weepy, unsure, panicky woman who had taken her place.

It wasn't a picnic for him either. He had fears and worries too. They'd just a few months ago managed to sell their apartment to buy a neat three-bedroom bungalow near the seafront in Raheny and they now had a pretty hefty mortgage. Gone were the days when they could hop on a Ryanair flight to Lodz to visit Magdalena's family in Ksawerów.

Still, they had a house now in a very pretty cul-de-sac, not too far from where his own parents lived. It would be a good place to bring up their child, with the seafront and Bull Island ten minutes from their door. They'd had to cut down on their free-and-easy way of living, for sure, but it would be worth it. They'd had five carefree years together with no one to worry about but themselves. Not many had been as lucky as they were. They had friends who'd bought property at the height of the boom and who were now crucified with massive mortgages. He and Magdalena had escaped that horrendous fate, at least. He grabbed the linen basket piled with clothes and hurried out to the clothesline. He had a hell of a lot to do today, including making preparations for the traditional Polish Christmas Eve meal that he was going to surprise his wife with.

'So! Your last day for months and months and months, you lucky wagon.' Denise Dawson plonked herself on the banquette beside Magdalena and grinned.

'Brilliant, isn't it?' Magdalena grinned back. The office had closed at three and they had all trooped over to the Lord Edward for a drink and nibbles. After which, she was going home to make the stuffing, and the custard for the pudding and that was it. Finito! She had the shop-bought spuds and the veg; Michael could deal with the turkey. Her parents-in-law had flown over to the States to spend Christmas with their daughter in Boston, so she and her husband were on their own and that suited Magdalena fine in her pregnant state.

She was going to plonk herself on the sofa and watch TV and read and relax until the baby was born. She was totally organized and had her bag packed for the hospital, had the baby's clothes and bits and pieces all bought. They were buying the cot, the car seat, the sterilizer and baby bath in the January sales. The baby's room was painted and ready for the precious little person who would soon be coming into their lives. All the hard work that she'd put in had paid off. Magdalena was as prepared as she could be.

The pub was jammers. Employees from the nearby civic offices were celebrating and the atmosphere of festive holiday high spirits was infectious. Magdalena felt herself relax as she sipped a rare glass of red wine. She'd done very, very well. She'd given up smoking and alcohol once she'd found she was pregnant. She'd drunk loads of water and eaten proper food, with lashings of fruit and vegetables, for the first time in years. She'd felt healthy and energized for most of her pregnancy. Only the last few weeks had been a little difficult and that was to be expected.

'I'd love a glass of red.' Sally, one of her colleagues sighed, looking enviously at the glass of ruby liquid that Magdalena was raising to her lips.

'Why don't you have one?' Magdalena was surprised. Sally enjoyed a drink.

'I'm not as far gone as you are,' Sally said, winking.

'*You're pregnant?*' Magdalena exclaimed.

'Shush, don't let Dolores hear, for God's sake, she gives me a hard enough time as it is. I needed to bring Finn, my little fella, to the doctor last Monday and she wouldn't give me a couple of hours off even though I told her that I'd work it back. She made me take a half-day, the old weapon. My annual leave is disappearing so fast I'll have no holidays at all in the summer.'

'Congratulations, Sal! Why wouldn't hatchet face let you work the time back?' Denise interjected.

'She said that it would set a precedent and everyone would want to do it.' Sally speared a garlic mushroom and ate it with relish.

'I suppose she *has* a point,' Magdalena sighed. 'If everyone started asking to pay back time instead of taking leave there'd be chaos.'

'I know that,' Sally agreed. 'But if only she wasn't so inflexible and so unhelpful, she'd get much more out of people. My husband's company is so accommodating, thank God. They have a human resources manager who bends over backwards to help the staff with exactly these types of problems and the productivity there is way over expectations. He was doing a course that he couldn't miss, otherwise he'd have got time off to bring Finn to the doctor, no problem. But I can't keep asking him to take time off, either. I have to do my share . . . even if it means taking half-days. I hope that cocktail sausage chokes her,' she added nastily, glaring in Dolores's direction. 'Would you just look at her in her new red cardigan! She'd give Amy Farrah Fowler a run for her money. *And* she's flirting with Casanova Prior. I think she's a bit pissed on one glass of wine.'

The trio craned their necks towards the next table and giggled at the sight of their supervisor's two pink cheeks as she took a lady-like sip from her glass and smiled demurely at their seedy sales manager.

'What age is she, allegedly?' Denise asked tartly.

Magdalena snorted with laughter. 'What a bitch you are. "*Allegedly.*"'

'Well, you know the way she goes on about being in her mid-forties. She's mid-fifties if she's a day,' Denise scoffed.

'I wonder, has she ever done it?' Sally eyed her boss disdainfully.

'*Sally!*' Denise protested. 'You're putting me off my chicken wings! 'Imagine Dolores with those skinny shanks wrapped around George Prior going, "Ooohh, ooohhh, *OOOHH!*"'

They all guffawed, drawing Dolores's disapproving gaze in their direction. That made them giggle even more.

Magdalena gave a happy sigh. She'd miss the girls, and the craic, and after-work drinks, but she wouldn't miss Dolores Barrett one little bit. Knowing that she wouldn't see her for months on end was nearly the best Christmas present of all.

Half an hour later, Magdalena got up to go home. Normally, she would be the life and soul of the party and wouldn't leave so soon but the pressure on her sciatic nerve was painful and her bump felt tight and uncomfortable. Besides, she'd just had the one glass of wine and was perfectly sober, while all around her, with the exception of Sally, of course, everyone was getting tiddly and it was no fun being sober among a crowd of inebriates, she told Denise, laughing when the other girl protested. 'Ms Dunne, this is *so* not you. I never thought I'd see the day when you'd leave before Batty Barrett! I never thought I'd see the day when you'd leave before *I* got piddly-eyed.'

'Denise, that day has arrived! Deal with it,' Magdalena teased. 'Besides, it's Christmas Eve, I've got chores to do.'

'And I'll have to leave in another ten minutes. I've to pick Finn up from the crèche,' Sally remarked.

'Oh, for God's sake! You married women are all the same. You only think of yourselves. What about us poor singletons that need to be entertained and amused? No wonder Dolores turned out the way she did. She probably had friends like *you* . . .' Denise complained. 'Who's going to pour me into a taxi? I'd like to know.'

'Go up and wipe Dolores's eye with George. He'll look after you,' Sally suggested wickedly.

'Bioch, is there no end to your nastiness? Go home and leave me all alone.' Denise stood up to let her friend out.

'The best of luck, Denise.' Magdalena laughed, as she hugged her, before wishing the rest of her work mates a

Happy Christmas with promises to meet early in the New Year before the baby was born.

It had been a relief to leave the noise and the stuffiness of the pub and breathe in the biting-cold blustery air. The pavements were so crowded with last-minute shoppers, she couldn't face the trek to Tara Street to catch the Dart so, when unexpectedly, she saw a taxi with the yellow light on, she flagged it down impulsively and waddled towards it, puffing slightly as she hauled her bulk into the backseat. 'Tara Street Dart Station,' she said politely, feeling snugly cocooned in the soft leather seat listening to Bing Crosby croon *White Christmas*, while outside on the pavements, shoppers trudged to and fro, laden with carrier bags, and revellers congregated in little knots, forcing pedestrians onto the street to sidestep them. The taxi ride was a little Christmas gift for her, Magdalena decided, damping down her feelings of guilt, utterly relieved she didn't have to face the walk along the windswept quays to the Dart.

The commuter train, when she finally boarded, was jam-packed with shoppers and workers getting off early for Christmas and she'd had to stand, although one frail old lady had offered her a seat. Three men had been sitting in the seats opposite and beside her and not one of them had even looked in Magdalena's direction. Equality didn't mean goodbye to good manners, she thought crossly, as she graciously refused the elderly woman's kind offer, hoping that a seat would become vacant at Connolly. She wasn't that lucky and her hip was throbbing as the train lurched out of Connolly towards Clontarf.

She wondered whether Michael would give up his seat to a pregnant woman. She must ask him, she mused, as the train swayed into Killester and a seat finally became vacant. The second-next stop was hers. Dusk was settling silently, softly onto the city, and the glow from lights on Christmas trees grew brighter, spilling out through windows onto suburban gardens; some long and narrow, others little square postage stamps, most neatly tended, a few higgledy-piggledy with strewn rubbish and household junk. As she sat staring into peoples' homes for fleeting seconds while the train cruised towards the next station, and watched women in their kitchens preparing for seasonal feasts, Magdalena felt the unwelcome shroud of loneliness hovering again, ready to envelop her, should she allow it. *Don't think about it*, she chided, as they passed a garden festooned with twinkling lights strung along the hedges and trees, and a massive Santa atop the chimney.

'Oh, Mammy, look at *that*!' a child in the opposite seat cried excitedly, nose pressed against the cold windowpane, agog! In a few years' time, her own child would be old enough to share in the excitement of Christmas and an unexpected feeling of joy and anticipation suffused Magdalena, lifting her spirits.

Her stop was less than ten minutes from home and as she walked down from the station towards the seafront, she inhaled the salt-laden air appreciatively. She loved living so close to the sea. That was one of the big plusses of living in Dublin. The sea and the countryside were so close to the city. Escape from noise and traffic was always possible. She turned into the small secluded cul-de-sac and felt another sudden surge of loneliness. The twilight was deepening and her neighbours' windows shone with festive iridescence, while her own house was dark and unwelcoming. The first house she passed had lights twined about the undressed branches of a cherry tree, and she thought of home and how her father would have twinkling lights on the hedgerow that led to the farmhouse where she had grown up. Magdalena swallowed hard. She would *not* cry, she told herself fiercely. She was a very lucky young woman with so much in her life. She would focus on that.

She walked up her garden path. Even though the car was parked out at the front, there was no one at home. Her husband also used the Dart to get to work. She'd got a text from him on the train to say he would be home around six. That had made her grumpy. It was Christmas Eve; she had left the work drinks party early, and he could make more of an effort sometimes, she thought crossly. She'd need to get the clothes in off the line so they wouldn't get too damp, then she would turn on the Christmas tree lights and make herself a cup of tea before getting busy in the kitchen.

A welcoming rush of warmth enveloped her when she let herself in; the central heating had a time switch, and the house was cosy after the chill evening air. But Michel had not set the alarm. He was so absent-minded sometimes. He'd probably forgotten to hang out the washing too. Magdalena sniffed. Was she imagining it, or was there a whiff of something cooking? They had decided to follow the Polish tradition of no cooking on Christmas Day and prepare the turkey dinner this evening. Had Michael come home at lunchtime and made the stuffing, and put the bird in to slow cook? She switched on the porch light and the hall lamps. She hated a dark house. The hall, decorated in mint-green and grey, led into a large kitchen–dining-room painted in cheery lemon, cream, and New England blue. She loved her bright, airy south-facing kitchen.

Magdalena opened the kitchen door and dropped her bags of shopping on the floor. The aromas were mouthwatering. The light from the big oven showed a tinfoil-swaddled mound. What a good husband I have, she thought, turning on the main lights, feeling most guilty for her earlier crotchety thoughts about him.

'Aww!' she gave a little cry of delight when she walked further in and saw that Michael had gone to the trouble of setting the table Polish style, with a white tablecloth, and a sheaf of hay. He'd even got *oplatek*, a thin wafer made of flour and water that was a traditional part of the Wigilia feast.

But why was the table set for so many? Magdalena frowned, perplexed, counting the place settings. Six. One was most likely the traditional vacant chair and place setting reserved for unexpected guests. That still left three other places for real guests.

Had Michael invited some of their Polish friends to dinner to surprise her, so she wouldn't feel too homesick?

A rush of love for her thoughtful husband overwhelmed her and Magdalena burst into tears. She was blowing noisily into a tissue when she heard him call her name from the hall. 'Oh, Michael! You are so good to me.' She turned and flung her arms around him. 'You're so, so good to me,' she hiccupped. 'Who's coming? Did you invite Gabriela and Wiktor, and Marta?'

'How did you guess? I didn't want you to be lonely.' Her husband smiled down at her, his blue eyes glinting with love and amusement. 'They're hiding in the lounge. We wanted to surprise you. Come in and say hello.'

'They're here already? Oh, my goodness. I bought roast potatoes and vegetables in M&S. I'd better put them in the oven,' Magdalena said, suddenly feeling flustered, shrugging out of her coat and laying it on a chair.

'Stay calm, all taken care of,' her husband said reassuringly. 'Come and say hello first then we can organize ourselves.' He dropped an arm around her shoulder and they walked through the dining room into the lounge where two women and a man stood beaming with delight.

But it wasn't Gabriela, Wiktor and Marta that greeted her. When her parents and sister launched themselves upon Magdalena with cries of joy, they were echoed by her own.

'Oh, my God! *Oh, my God!* I don't believe this!' she exclaimed, then, when the hugging and kissing were over, enquired 'How? When?'

'When Michael found out you were expecting a baby, he asked would we come to visit for Christmas, even though we will be coming over also when the baby is born. He paid for our tickets and said it was a gift for you. How could we refuse?' Her mother wiped the tears from her eyes.

'I didn't have to spend a fortune,' Michael explained, grinning, 'because I booked them eight months ago and I got a good deal. I took today off work, picked them up from the airport and Zuzanna and Karolina have been busy in the kitchen since they arrived.'

'And I blessed the garden and hung up the mistletoe,' her father added, chuckling, 'and made sure all the lights were out, and kept these women quiet when I spied you coming up the road.'

'I just can't believe it!' Magdalena exclaimed, happier than she had ever been. What a joyful Christmas this was turning into.

'Believe it! With all my love, Happy Christmas, Magdalena,' Michael said, bending down to kiss his beloved wife, his hand resting tenderly on her bump as their child gave a vigorous kick that made them smile at each other with utter delight.

Back Where I Belong

It's a very different Christmas this year, that's for sure, and I'm absolutely *thrilled* with myself. I'm a Christmas Angel and I'm back on top of the Christmas tree! For the last few years, I've languished in a cardboard box under the stairs, while Madame Saundra (plain ordinary Sandra to you and me, check out the birth-cert.) went minimalist and spent a fortune on her 'themed' Christmas trees.

I don't mean to sound bitter and twisted, it's not very angelic, I admit, but I'd been the angel on top of the Christmas tree in Sunnymede Cottage for fifty years and I loved it.

I was always very happy when Lillian, Saundra's grand-mother, would take me out of the soft, creamy tissue paper she folded me in each year, and hand me to Matthew, her husband, who would place me very gently on top of the tree.

I adored Matthew; he was the most gorgeous man, and I don't mean just physically. He was a quiet, reserved, hardworking farmer, who was a great husband, father and neighbour. He was *utterly* kind. He'd keep an eye on the elderly widow across the field and would do bits and pieces around her house for her in the most unobtrusive way. 'A little help is better than a lot of sympathy,' was Matthew's motto.

Lillian adored him. He had a terrific sense of humour and their marriage was rock solid and, for the most part, full of joy and laughter. They didn't have much money but they always had a warm house and good food on the table and what they had they shared with family and neighbours.

I was the first Christmas decoration they bought the year they were married. I always remember it was the 8 December, the Holy Day when country people used to come to Dublin to do their Christmas shopping. I knew they were from the country by their accents. Soft, rolling vowels, compared to the more strident distinctive Dublin twang. I was sitting on a shelf, as proud as punch, in a tizzy of anticipation, hoping against hope that someone would pick me up and buy me and bring me home to do the job I was created to do. A Christmas Angel isn't like a Guardian Angel. I didn't have to 'mind and guard and rule and guide'. My job was to radiate joy and goodwill and peace and serenity as much as I could, for the Christmas Season.

I wondered what sort of a home I'd go to. Would there be children? Would they be careful with me? There was always the danger of getting broken. But if you went to a good home and were taken care of, you could last a long time. That was what I wanted. To last a long time with a family who would take care of me, a family I would get to know and love, a family I would be with for generations. It was the dream of every Christmas Angel.

I'd been picked up and put down a few times. It was nerve-wracking. I'd liked the first lady who picked me up, an elderly woman with white hair, and a kind face. 'Isn't she a lovely little Angel?' she said to her granddaughter. 'If I had the money I'd buy her, but your mammy would give out to me for spending my money on gewgaws.' I didn't like the sound of the mammy.

My friend, Angelica, was bought the day after we were placed side by side on our shelf. A thin, middle-aged woman with short hair and a pinched look about her, picked her up, gave her a cursory look and handed her to the shop assistant. 'Good luck, Angelica,' I said. We could communicate telepathically.

'Thanks, Angelina.' She gave me a little wave and I could sense her nervous excitement as the woman handed over the money – two and six – and the assistant placed it into the tube and it rattled along to the cashier. Things have changed a lot since those days – every so often I gad off to Dublin, once Christmas is over of course. I leave my little glass body and fly free. Anyway, it was just before closing time the following day and I was lonely for Angelica and wondering how she was getting on, when I heard a girl say, 'Ah, Matthew, look! Isn't she gorgeous? Let's buy her for the tree.' I looked up and saw a young woman in her mid-twenties, with long auburn hair and big hazel eyes, wearing a black coat with a wide belt, looking like a young Rita Hayworth. I still think the Forties and Fifties had the most stylish and elegant clothes. I love looking at the old black-and-white films they show in the afternoons around Christmas time, but I digress.

'We'd better buy it quick, Lillian, if we want to get to Amien's Street to catch the early train back,' the young man said. He was a dish. Tall, broad-shouldered, with chestnut hair and blue eyes fringed by long black lashes a woman would die for. 'I'll buy it,' he said, taking a ten-shilling note from his wallet. 'A gift for you.'

'Oh, Matthew, I'll treasure her always,' the girl said, tucking her arm into his, and I could see she was mad about him. I felt ecstatically happy as I was neatly wrapped and placed in a Clery's bag and handed to my new owner. At last! I'd found my family and they had found me.

The city was brimming with pre-Christmas excitement. Couples embraced under the big clock as we left the department store. Carol singers sang enthusiastically, the shop windows shone with festive glitz and the trees, festooned with lights, sparkled and twinkled like the diamonds in Weir's window. The frosty chill turned breath white and reddened cheeks and noses as Lillian, Matthew and I, swinging in my bag, hurried along Talbot Street, weaving in and out of the crowds before running up the steps of the packed train station.

I was bursting with excitement as they made their way through the carriages, laden with cheery bags from all the big stores, Clery's, Arnotts, Boyers and Roches. They found two empty seats and moments later the whistle blew, the doors were slammed shut and we clickity-clacked our way out of Amien's Street, crossed the Liffey, and headed south to my new home, a neat little cottage in a village called Riverside, not far from Brittas Bay.

How proud and happy I was that Christmas Eve, two weeks later, when Matthew reached up and gently placed me on top of their Christmas tree as the fire blazed up the chimney and the aroma of pudding wafted around the cottage as it bubbled merrily on the stove. Outside, snow-flakes drifted down silently dressing the trees for Christmas morning, as my beloved owners kissed under the mistletoe and a slender red candle flickered and flamed in the window, and the house was filled with love and joy as they celebrated their first Christmas together in their own home.

It brings a lump to my throat when I remember Lillian and Matthew. They were a couple whose love remained steadfast through thick and thin, and a couple who would have been horrified had they lived to see what had become of their lovely home, and the way their granddaughter, Sandra aka Saundra had turned out.

A demanding young madam from the minute she was born to Rebecca, Matthew and Lillian's only child, Sandra grew up to have notions about herself and became what Lillian would have described as 'a right little consequence'.

Rebecca left Riverside to study architecture in UCD where she met Hugh Sullivan, a part-time lecturer. They married, built up a successful architectural practice and, after two miscarriages, were ecstatic when their baby girl was born. She was a much loved child and wanted for nothing. As Sandra grew into her teens, visiting her grandparents in Riverside was not high on her list of priorities; she was far too interested in 'chilling' with her posh D4 friends. Spending Christmas in the country was 'boring' and 'like totally uncool', I heard her rant to Rebecca one Christmas day as they had a spat in the sitting room while Lillian and Matthew, now elderly and afflicted by the ailments of cruel ageing, served up the dinner in the kitchen.

That was the last Christmas my beloveds were together. And it was my last Christmas on top of the tree. Matthew had a heart attack the following March as he lifted a bag of feed off the tractor, and Lillian, heartbroken, went to her husband, and our glorious Creator five months later.

For the next few years, I languished in my box under the stairs. Every so often, Rebecca and Hugh would come to visit and heat the house and do a spot of painting but they never spent Christmas there. Sandra became 'Saundra' and married a hotshot financial whizz kid, Theo Carr, in Italy, in a wedding that cost an arm and a leg. It wouldn't have been Lillian and Matthew's cup of tea. It was all designer dresses, a wedding-gift list in BT's and wedding planners. I could just imagine Lillian saying, 'It was far from wedding planners and gift lists she was reared.'

Then, one sunny spring day, I heard the sound of tyres crunching on gravel and minutes later Saundra's D4 accent broke the silence, and a waft of Poison filled the air. I heard her say, 'We could knock the wall between the kitchen and the dining room and make it open plan, and we could knock the wall down that faces south and have it totally glass . . .' and my heart sank.

All that summer, builders hammered and banged and Lillian and Matthew's snug home was turned into a designer show house, with wine-barrel chandeliers, Louis Vuitton steamer trunks for tables, Argentinean leather chesterfield sofas that looked hideously uncomfortable, and mirrors, and picture frames that had cost an arm and a leg for their 'distressed' appearance. Lillian would have been mighty 'distressed' to pay such ridiculous money for such nonsense.

All their posh friends came for barbecues on the newly built deck and that first Christmas, Saundra decided that gold and silver would be her decorating 'theme'. Only two of Lillian's precious Christmas baubles made the grade. I was ignored. She chose a silver diamante bow to decorate the top of her tree that year.

They were all so superficial, those so-called sophisticates, as they boasted about their affluence, their investments, their villas on golf courses on the Algarve, their Jags and Mercs and four-by-fours. They tried to outdo each other in every aspect of their lives and could not hide their envy if one of their crowd stepped further up the ladder of avarice and one-up-manship. Mendacity, envy, selfishness and insincerity seeped into the walls of Sunnymede when those people gathered and it made me weep for the days of straightforward kindness and goodness when Lillian and Matthew were alive.

For three years, Saundra, Theo and their 'friends' used Sunnymeade as their 'country retreat'. Theo would work the room at parties, drawing people aside, telling them of a 'Golden opportunity to make a killing,' on this investment or that bond, or hotels in the States, that was going to *skyrocket* in value. I heard names like ISTC, Anglo, Seanie, 'Fingers', Irish Nationwide AIB, BOI, spoken of in smooth, smug, confidential tones as Theo urged his guests to borrow even more money to fund these 'blue chip' investments. 'You'll have no problem getting a loan, he would assure them, expansively. 'Let me put you in touch with someone.' He had no time for 'cautious people'. He advised many of his guests to place their money 'offshore'; he had 'people' who could look after them. Some took his advice, delighted to have pulled a fast one on the taxman. Saundra would open yet another bottle of 'bubbly' and discuss Botox and fillers and plan trips with the 'girls' to have a discrete nip here and a little tuck there.

And then, last year, everything changed utterly! The theme for that particular Christmas was Swarovski. All crystal baubles that cost a fortune, and blue velvet bows and blue lights, on an artificial silver Christmas tree. It was a hideous look. So cold and stark, a far cry from the twinkling warm hues of Lillian's and Matthew's tree that scented the house with the smell of fresh pine.

It was a far smaller group than they usually entertained on St Stephen's night. An edgy, nervous energy percolated through the rooms as a miasma of uneasiness settled on Sunnymede. The Hendersons didn't come. They'd lost four million in a 'sure fire' investment Theo had convinced them to put their life savings into. The Wentworths lost two million in the same venture. Others had lost high six-figure sums. There was talk of property crashes in Spain and Dubai, and stocks and shares on the floor, pensions decimated, and fortunes owed to the banks. Seanie and 'Fingers' had come crashing down from their pedestals.

Theo, behind the façade of hail-fellow well-met bonhomie, was like a tautly strung violin, and Saundra's Botoxed forehead hid a tension headache that lasted for the entire three days they were in situ. Things turned nasty when Bert Lewis, the worse for drink, cursed Theo and said he'd lost everything because of his advice and what the hell was he going to do about it? Drunk, bitter and angry, he said what everyone else was thinking and the party ended abruptly. The guests filtered out with indecent haste, murmuring awkward goodbyes.

'We've become outcasts,' Saundra wailed, as their 'best friends' drove away and life as they'd known it came crashing around their ears.

Sunnymede and the villa in the Algarve were put up for sale as Theo sought to secure his assets by buying property in New England in Saundra's name. He'd sold most of his stock for top dollar in a company just before it began its steady and inexorable slide to the bottom, a company he continued to urge his 'friends' to invest in even as it went belly-up. There was talk of insider trading. It didn't particularly bother him; business was business. There were always risks. But it did bother him that his reputation was ruined. No one in their circle would ever take advice from him again and slowly, like the tide going out, their former chums withdrew from him and Saundra, and the façade of friendship dropped like icicles melting on the eves.

It was a bad time for selling property. While there were many viewers there were no takers. The steamer trunks, sofas, mirrors and distressed picture frames were gone. The house was quite bare. The price dropped . . . several times. And then, one wintry afternoon, the door opened and a young couple walked in, hand in hand.

'Oooh, I like it!' the girl exclaimed. She had long, wavy brown hair with glints of gold. She reminded me of Lillian.

'Well, thanks to my wonderful grandma, we can just about afford it.' The young man smiled. He was fair-haired with a smattering of freckles and lovely green eyes.

'Mam said we could have her old sofa, the one with the big cushions, and the pine dresser. Oh, Pete, it's perfect for us!' The girl was excited and I felt myself relax. All was going to be well. I just *knew* it.

Five weeks later, I'm sitting atop the tree, and the smell of cooking and the sound of laughter is drifting from the kitchen. Tara, my new owner, found me under the stairs, dusted me down and said to her smiling husband, 'Isn't she *gorgeous!*' I had a delightful sense of déjà vu.

Lillian would approve, I thought, as Pete made sure I was facing in the right direction, perfectly positioned. I was back where I belong.

Façades

'You're coming home for Christmas? Fantastic! We'll have to get together. You'll have to come over for a meal.' Izzy Reynolds injected a note of false gaiety into her voice as she spoke to Mari Clancy, an old schoolfriend who was ringing from Dubai. 'Is Brett coming with you?'

'Er . . . no, not this year. Things are a bit crazy at work and he can't take time off.' Mari sounded glum.

'Oh . . . poor Brett,' Izzy sympathized, privately relieved that the wealthy consultant wouldn't be around to patronize her and Bill with his boastful tales of life in the Emirates.

'So, look, how about the day after Stephen's Day? You know the way the diary fills up, and Mam will have me doing the rounds like nobody's business,' Mari said briskly.

'I'll be looking forward to it,' Izzy lied, thinking that a visit from Mari was the last thing she needed. They talked for another while, swapping gossip and news and Izzy was glad it was Mari who had called. It must be costing a fortune, but Mari was loaded and money wasn't an issue for her. It never used to be an issue for her and Bill, either, she thought dolefully, replacing the receiver.

Later, in the kitchen, she found herself humming 'My heart is low'. To her way of thinking, 'Only A Woman's Heart' was one of the greatest songs ever written for and about women. The writer of that song knew *exactly* what Izzy was feeling at that moment. Low, disheartened, dispirited, depressed and extremely agitated.

She wiped her worktops vigorously. When Izzy was stressed she cleaned her worktops over and over again, lifting the bread bin and matching set of coffee, tea and sugar containers, annihilating any unfortunate crumb lurking in the vicinity. Today the worktops were getting a rigorous going-over, as were the fridge-freezer doors and the top of the cooker.

It was funny, how she headed for the kitchen when she was under pressure. Her sister always attacked the bathroom in her moments of stress. Izzy's best friend would invariably cut the grass.

She sighed deeply. Her husband Bill had been out of a job for the last fourteen months and there was no sign of anything on the horizon. Christmas was just ten days away and her three children were up to ninety with excitement at the thoughts of Santa's impending arrival.

The Christmas shopping had to be done. She and Bill had just had a row about it. Now, to crown it all, she'd had the call from Mari, to say she would be back in town for Christmas. More expense. Normally, she loved having visitors and it would have been a pleasure to see her old schoolfriend, but these days she didn't want to see anyone. She just wanted to shrivel up inside her shell and stay there.

In the last few months, all her hope that Bill would have no problems in finding another job had become harder and harder to sustain. As money got tighter, their savings dwindled and their standard of living noticeably diminished. Izzy increasingly felt like burying her head in the sand like the proverbial ostrich.

She didn't want Mari Clancy coming to her house when she had no oil for the central heating. Izzy didn't want her to know that she'd sold her Fiesta and Bill's Volvo was in the garage because they hadn't got the money to tax and insure it. Mari would have to put up with cheap wine and a simple meal. Izzy just didn't have the money for steaks and champagne. It was months since she'd been able to afford luxuries like that.

Izzy rubbed viciously at a particularly stubborn piece of grit that was embedded between the curved edge of her drainer and the muted beige worktop. To think she couldn't even afford to drive any more. Who would have ever thought it? Who would have ever thought that their family's affluent, comfortable lifestyle would have been so severely shaken and disrupted that gut-wrenching evening when Bill had come home from work, grey-faced and shaken to tell her that the multinational computer company that he worked for was closing its Irish operation in favour of their American outfit, with a loss of five hundred jobs.

'I'm finished, Izzy, I'll never get another job at my age.' Bill sat with his head buried in his hands while Izzy tried to take in what her husband had just told her.

'Don't be daft, Bill!' she said firmly. 'You're only forty-three. That's young, and people are always going to need human resources managers. *Experienced* human resources managers.'

'Izzy, you don't know what it's like out there, I'm telling you, it's cut-throat. They can get fellas half my age with better degrees that'll work for half my salary because they're so desperate to get a job. The Celtic Tiger's well and truly vanished.' Bill had tears in his eyes and Izzy, horrified at the state her usually cheerful and easygoing husband was in, flung her arms around him and hugged him tightly.

'Stop worrying, Bill, we'll manage fine. You'll get a job, I know you will. You're the best there is; you'll be snapped up in no time,' she comforted, absolutely believing every word she spoke. Bill was bloody good at his job. He'd get another job . . . and soon.

Week after week, month after month, she'd said the same thing over and over, trying to keep her spirits up as much as his. Unemployment didn't happen to people like her and Bill with their pretty, four-bedroom semi-detached dormer bungalow in a tree-lined cul-de-sac in Clontarf. They had always been able to afford a fortnight abroad every year and trips to London where Izzy's sister lived. Music and swimming lessons for the kids had been the norm and Izzy had never envisaged that it would ever be otherwise.

When she'd thought about unemployment she'd had a mental image of people whose lifestyles were a million miles from her own. Izzy wasn't a snob or anything like it; she was lucky and she knew it. She'd never thought that unemployment could happen to her family. Bill was a trained professional, for God's sake, with years of work experience. Being a human resources manager for hundreds of employees was an important job. People like him didn't end up on a dole queue. Or so she'd thought.

'Get real, Izzy!' her younger sister, Stella, remonstrated one day several months after Bill had been made redundant, when she had been moaning about their situation. Stella was a community welfare officer and she knew a lot about unemployment. 'Don't kid yourself that it's all people from so-called deprived areas that are on the dole, it isn't. There's a hell of a lot of people like Bill, in middle management, who are out there suffering behind their lace curtains and going to the St Vincent de Paul for help with their mortgage repayments. People who enjoyed a lifestyle just like yours.'

'St Vincent de Paul, but that's for poor people!' Izzy exclaimed in horror.

'These people are heading for poor,' Stella said gently. 'They're living in lovely houses, with no heating and no phones and not enough money to pay the mortgage, and in danger of their homes being repossessed. They need help too.' Seeing her sister's stricken face she said gently. 'Look,

I'm not suggesting you're ever going to need to go to the St Vincent de Paul, but what I'm saying is, start economising. Use some of Bill's redundancy money to whack a bit off your mortgage. Get rid of one of the cars. I'm not saying that Bill won't ever get a job again, hopefully he will, but just don't think that he's going to waltz into a new position just like that. It doesn't happen like that any more, unfortunately. There's a recession out there and it's not going away anytime soon.'

Izzy came away from her chat with her sister more scared than she had ever been in her life. For the first time since Bill had been made redundant she had lifted her head out of the sand and taken a long, hard look at their situation. Stella's words might have been harsh but they had stiffened Izzy's resolve. It was time to sit down and take stock and face the hard facts. Bill was unemployed and likely to stay that way. The future had to be faced.

That night, when the children were in bed, she sat down with her husband and calmly announced that it was time for them to discuss their financial situation so that they could make long-term plans. Bill slumped down at the kitchen table twiddling a biro. She could see his fingers shaking. 'I don't know how we're going to manage,' he muttered.

I'd like to kill the bastards that did this to him, Izzy thought viciously, as she saw her husband's hopes and dreams fade to ashes. He flicked on his calculator and they began to work on the figures he had in front of him. They talked of her going back to work, *if* she could get a job; but then they would have to pay for childcare for the three children, which was so expensive it would take up most of her salary.

Bill said they had to reduce their mortgage by two thirds – that was vital – and at least they'd have the comfort of knowing that their home was safe enough. They'd use his lump sum for that. They'd sell her Fiesta and with the money they'd make from that they'd continue the insurance policies, the most important of which was the policy they had taken out for their children's education. They'd pay the VHI for another year. If Bill didn't get a job after that there'd be no more private health insurance.

They went to bed subdued.

Izzy began to take her calculator to the supermarket. Before, she had never considered the cost of food that much. Whatever she felt like had gone willy-nilly into the trolley, as had make-up, books, magazines, and a couple of bottles of wine. But those days were gone. Every cent counted now. It was coming up to the second Christmas of Bill's unemployment and her money was cut to the bone. Any saving, no matter how small, was welcome. Thank God for big impersonal supermarkets, she thought one day as she stood at the cash desk with her trolley full of Yellow Pack and Thrift. It would be a tad mortifying if the neighbours saw her, or the girl at the check out knew her. That was always a little worry. Silly, she knew, but she couldn't help it.

It wasn't that Izzy normally gave a hoot what people thought of her, it was just these days she seemed to be a bit more vulnerable. Only the other day, her seven-year-old son, Keith, had come in, his little face scarlet with emotion. 'Mammy! Jason Pierce says that Daddy's got no job an' that we're going to be poor an' that you can't afford to bring us to Disneyland in Paris. He's a big liar, isn't he? I told him to put his dukes up an' I gave him a puck in the snot an' he went home bawling,' her son added with immense satisfaction.

'Say "and", Keith, not "an"',' Izzy corrected automatically, hoping that Jason Pierce's nose was well and truly bloodied. Little brat! Since the Pierces had moved in next door, six months ago, there had been nothing but fights with the youngsters in the cul-de-sac. It wasn't really Jason's fault; it was that obnoxious father of his, Owen. Owen Pierce was the most bigheaded, boastful, superior individual Izzy had ever had the misfortune to encounter.

Owen was a tax consultant, who had begun to make good money. On the way up, he revelled in his yuppie lifestyle. He and his wife Nicole and their two children, Jason and Diana, had moved in mid-summer, and had proceeded to make themselves thoroughly unpopular with their neighbours.

At first, the ten other families in the cul-de-sac had welcomed them and been friendly and chatty, but gradually Owen's thoroughly bumptious ways had begun to grate. It was his hail-fellow-well-met 'I'm a tax consultant. What do you do for a living?' carry-on that got under people's skin. Owen had the biggest satellite dish, the biggest barbecue pit, the most expensive shrubs and the flashiest car. He loved boasting and always made sure that when he was telling Izzy or Bill something, the rest of the neighbours could hear as well. Izzy normally did not make snap judgments about people, but she knew very soon after she met him that he was someone she couldn't stand.

Nicole had invited Izzy in for a cup of coffee about a month after they had moved in. Nicole, with her heavily made-up face and her perfectly manicured nails, had made sure to let Izzy know that she had a woman who came in to clean twice a week. She had timed the coffee invite with the arrival of the woman who did her ironing. Nicole's daughter, Diana, was the same age as Jessica and as they sat drinking their freshly ground coffee, the other woman paused in their conversation and said meditatively, 'I wonder if I have anything I could give you for Jessica. She and Diana are the same age and Diana has *so* many clothes. She gets so many presents. I've got lots of stuff that she's never worn.'

Izzy was flabbergasted. She'd only met the woman twice, for heaven's sake, and here she was offering her clothes for Jessica. Did she think the Reynolds were on their uppers and needed charity, just because Bill was unemployed? Izzy had assured her new next-door neighbour that Jessica had *plenty* of clothes and hastily finished her coffee and made her escape. Even if Jessica had to go around in *rags*, she wouldn't accept such impertinent help from the superior Pierces.

You weren't very neighbourly, she accused herself silently, glad to get back to the comfort of her own kitchen Was she being so prickly because her pride was hurting and she didn't want to seem like the poor man at his better's table? If Bill had been working and she'd been free of all her financial worries would she have handled Owen and Nicole differently and felt more gracious towards them? Was she, in fact, just indulging in a fit of extremely large sour grapes?

'Definitely not. Most definitely not, Izzy!' Jill, her other next-door neighbour, retorted emphatically when Izzy, shame-faced, put this scenario to her one day when they were waiting at the school gates to collect their children.

'He's a pushy shagger!' Jill exclaimed irritably, 'and she's a stuck-up madam with notions about herself.'

Izzy had laughed and didn't feel so bad knowing that it wasn't just her straightened circumstances and envy of her neighbours that had put her off Owen, Nicole and their offspring.

'Mammy, can we go to Disneyland sometime?' Keith's big blue eyes stared up into hers, wide and innocent, as blue as two cornflowers, as he shovelled the last of his macaroni cheese into his mouth.

'Well . . . um . . . some day, please God, we'll get to Disneyland. We'll just have to say a prayer that Daddy gets a job soon.' She smiled down at her son, who had gone trotting off, saying, 'Dear Holy God, please let my daddy get a job soon so he can bring us to Disneyland before scummy Jason Pierce goes.'

As Izzy cleared away the dirty dishes, she thought ruefully that it wasn't a prayer that was needed to get them to Disneyland . . . it was a miracle.

She walked into the sitting room and gave a little shiver. The house was *so* cold. She felt thoroughly resentful and frustrated that she could no longer just flick a switch and have instant heat. Even though they had tried to conserve oil by turning on the heat later in the evenings, because winter had come early they had run out of that precious dark liquid a week ago. Since then, Izzy had been lighting the fire and, because they were economising on fuel, the back boiler was never hot enough to give off more than lukewarm heat from the radiators. Because of Christmas and all its expenses, they wouldn't be able to afford oil until well into the New Year. If even then.

I'm sick of this, Izzy thought bitterly as she walked over to the floor-to-ceiling window and stared out at the lowering sky that threatened snow. Snow! That was all they needed to make life even more miserable. Come the New Year, she might go looking for a part-time job that would enable her to be there when the children came home from school. She'd been a clerical officer when she had married Bill. Maybe she should have stayed working instead of taking her lump sum. Then they wouldn't be so hard hit now. If she got a part-time job, though, it could affect Bill's means-tested dole money. There was no point in her working if it meant a reduction in his income, Izzy thought glumly, straightening the folds in her lace curtains. She had washed them yesterday and they were pristine. Most of the other houses in the cul-de-sac had roller blinds, net curtains being rather old fashioned, but Izzy had always liked 'proper curtains', as her grandmother called them. She hated the idea of people being able to see through her front window. Her home was her haven, not a showpiece for the neighbours to view every time they walked by.

Owen, whose latest foible was practising his putting shots on the front lawn, was always trying to gawk in the window and it gave Izzy no small satisfaction to know that he couldn't see in. Her curtains were her protection from his prying eyes.

He was out now, strimming the edge of the grass, despite the fact that it was a bitterly cold winter's day. She grinned as the catgut broke and flew across the lawn. She knew she was being petty but she didn't care. He just got on her nerves. She had got so fed up of him strolling in front of her windows and playing rugby with Jason on the front lawn that she had asked her brother, a horticulturist, what she could put down to separate the gardens and keep her unwanted neighbour out. A large thorny orange-berried pyracantha trained along a white wooden picket fence now formed a border between numbers 7 and 8 Maple Wood Drive, curtailing Owen and Jason's sporting activities somewhat.

Jason was driving poor old Keith around the twist about the new computer he was getting for Christmas. It was going to be 'the best computer in the world', with better games than the old Dell one that Keith had, according to Jason. Every mother in the cul-de-sac could cheerfully have wrung Jason Pierce's neck, as their own envious offspring demanded 'a best computer' as well.

Bill and Izzy had been arguing that morning about what to buy the children for Christmas. Bill, as sick of penny-pinching as she was, wanted to borrow a couple of hundred quid from the credit union to splash out on Christmas, and to hell with it. Izzy had argued that they needed oil. The house insurance was coming up and all of the children needed new shoes. If there was one thing Izzy was very particular about, it was about getting good shoes for her children and nowadays a pair of decent shoes for a three-year-old could cost the guts of fifty euros. Paying out fifty euros each for the three of them would leave her fairly skint.

'We can't afford it and that's that,' Izzy asserted. Bill's face darkened with impotent fury.

'Don't rub it in, for Christ's sake! I know we can't, I just want to give the kids a decent Christmas. Is that too much to want?' he snarled. A red mist descended in front of Izzy's eyes. It wasn't *her* fault that they had no money. She was only trying to keep them out of debt.

'Listen, mister, you can do what you damn well like. I was only trying to help. Do you think *I* don't want to give them a good Christmas? I'm trying to do my best for all of us and it's not easy. So don't you take it out on me, Bill. It's not my fault you're unemployed. It's not me who can't get a job.' Izzy was so angry her voice was shaking as months of suppressed rage, fear and frustration fuelled her outburst.

'God, you really know how to put the boot in, don't you?' Bill raged. 'You should have married someone like bloody Superdad over there, not a loser like me.' With that, he'd picked up his anorak and strode out of the front door, slamming it hard behind him. Sick at heart, Izzy sat down at the kitchen table, put her head in her hands and bawled her eyes out. She had never felt so sorry for herself in her life. What had she done to deserve this? she sniffled. After a good twenty minutes of alternate cursing and sobbing, she felt somewhat better. A good cry was just the thing sometimes; it helped to get it all out of your system. Fortunately, the children had spent the previous night on a sleepover with their cousins so they hadn't witnessed the row. She didn't want them being upset as well.

It was almost 3 p.m., Izzy noted, and still no sign of Bill. She wondered what he was doing. It had got even darker outside, the clouds so low they seemed almost to touch the rooftops. The frost, which hadn't thawed all day, cast a silvery sheen to the lawns, the flaming orange of the pyracantha berries a startling contrast. The stark silhouettes of bare-branched trees encircled the cul-de-sac protectively; a robin nestled in the shelter of an evergreen shrub. Normally Izzy would have enjoyed the picturesque, wintry scene outside her big window but today it just seemed bleak and cold and again she shivered.

'To hell with it,' she muttered crossly, and, with a determined set to her jaw, she walked over to the fire and struck a match, watching with pleasure as the flames caught the firelighters and roared up the chimney, the kindling flaming, spitting and sparking and scenting the room with the freshness of pine. The glow of the orange-yellow flames casting their shadows on the walls soothed Izzy. She sat cross-legged on the rug in front of the fire and pulled two large carrier bags overflowing with presents, in front of her. This was the ideal time to sort out the Christmas present situation. It was something she had been putting off all day, but she might as well do it while Bill and the kids were out of the house. If she were quick and organized, she'd have her task complete before he was home. Then her husband wouldn't have the added indignity of seeing her selecting presents they had received last year, to be given to their relatives this year. If only she could remember who had given her what. It would be a disaster to return a gift to someone who had given it to them in the first place.

Izzy gave a wry smile as she unloaded the bags on to the floor. The only other time in her life when she had had to recycle presents was that first year she had moved into a flat with her two best friends and they had all been practically penniless. It had been fun then though, not like this.

She eyed the assorted collection surrounding her. Tablemats, they could go to Aunt Sadie. A basket of Body Shop soaps and shampoos. Now who had given her them? She cast her mind back, was it Stella? No, it was Rita, her sister-in-law. Well, Stella could have the Body Shop basket and Rita could have the lovely red angora scarf that her godmother had given her. Izzy fingered the scarf, enjoying the feel of the soft luxurious wool between her fingers. It would have been nice to have been able to wear it herself, she thought regretfully, but needs must and Rita would like it.

She wanted to give her sister-in-law a nice present. Rita was very good to them, as indeed were all of their families. That was why Izzy wanted to give them presents at Christmas. And she wanted to show that she and Bill were not completely on their uppers.

Foolish pride, she thought ruefully. They *were* on their uppers. This year, she decided, she would keep a list of who gave what, so that next Christmas if Bill were still unemployed, it would be easier for her to match up presents. If people saw her this minute, no doubt they would think she was dreadfully mean, but it was the best she could do under the circumstances.

She spent a peaceful hour sitting in the fire's glow sorting out the presents and wrapping them. She had just stood up and was trying to get rid of the pins and needles in her feet when she saw Bill marching into the cul-de-sac. He was lugging the biggest, bushiest Christmas tree she had ever seen. A broad grin creased her face. Bill was a sucker for Christmas trees. The bigger and bushier the better.

She flung open the front door as her husband struggled up the path with his load. Panting, he stood looking at her. 'I'm sorry, love. I didn't mean it.' Their eyes met and a flicker of happiness ignited briefly. 'You're the best wife a man could have and I know I'm dead lucky.'

'Oh, Bill, it's all right, I didn't mean what I said either.' Izzy, happy that their tiff was over, flung her arms around him, ignoring the prickly tree and was rewarded with a one-armed bear hug. 'It's brilliant, where did you get it?' She eyed the tree admiringly.

'Up near the Castle from a fella on a lorry, much cheaper than that lot outside SuperValu. Look at the width of it and look at the fullness up top and the symmetry is almost perfect.' Bill, who was a connoisseur of Christmas trees, enthused about his find. 'It's the best ever.'

'You say that every year.' Izzy laughed. 'Come on in. I have the fire lighting. It was cold, so I lit it early to make the place warm for when the kids get home,' she added a little defensively.

'You did right, Izzy, it's bloody freezing out today,' Bill declared stoutly, and they smiled at each other. 'Hey, what do you think if I rang Rita and asked her to keep the kids for another hour or two and we decorated the tree for them as a surprise?'

'Oh, yeah! Just imagine their faces!' Izzy felt her previous despondency lift as a rare lightheartedness enveloped her. 'Do you think Rita would mind?'

'Naw.' Bill shook his head. 'Say we'll take her gang if she wants to go shopping or anything.'

'Right,' Izzy said briskly, 'you ring her and I'll put the kettle on and we'll have a cup of coffee and get going,' Unemployment, be dammed, they were going to have the best Christmas tree ever.

Rita obligingly agreed to keep the children for another couple of hours and gratefully agreed to Izzy's offer to take her own children the following afternoon so she could do some Sunday shopping in peace and quiet. For the next two hours, Izzy and Bill thoroughly enjoyed themselves as they transformed the six-foot tree into a magical delight adorned with twinkling lights and glittering ornaments and frothy tinsel.

They laced the ceiling with garlands and Izzy prepared the crib, decorating it with black papier-mâché to give the impression of mountains, and twining ivy across the top and down the sides. She arranged a little light in at the back and laid the straw that she kept year after year, on the floor of the crib. Bill hung up a sheriff's star from an old cowboy set that he had had as a child and it glittered in the firelight as bright as any star of Bethlehem. They would have a little ceremony when the children were home. Jessica, being the youngest would solemnly place Baby Jesus in the Crib.

They stood back to admire their handiwork. 'It's lovely,' Bill declared, as Izzy fussed at a piece of ivy wanting to have it just so.

'So is the tree.' His wife smiled. 'Definitely the best ever.'

'It's a biggie all right.' Bill grinned.

'Bigger than Superdad's,' Izzy murmured wickedly. Bill caught her knowing gaze and laughed.

'And real, as well; poor Jason has to make do with an artificial yoke, even if it is the biggest and most expensive one there is. It's just not the same, sure it isn't?' His eyes twinkled.

Owen and Nicole had put their tree up over a week ago. They had been the first in the cul-de-sac to put one up.

Great wreaths of holly hung on their doors and windows and Jason and Emma were bursting with pride. Each day, Keith enquired anxiously if they were going to put their tree up and Izzy reassured her young son that indeed they would. She was dying to see his face when he saw the six-foot giant that now reposed all alight in their front window.

Ravenous after their exertions, they decided they deserved a rare treat and ordered a Chinese. They ate it sitting in front of the fire, thoroughly enjoying their spare ribs in barbecue sauce, and the crispy duck and prawn crackers. The twinkling lights of the Christmas tree and the amber luminescence of the fire enveloped them in a cocoon of golden warmth as rain and sleet lashed against the windows and the wind howled like a banshee as it swirled and eddied around the cul-de-sac. Izzy and Bill enjoyed their fireside meal, all their troubles put behind them for the precious few hours they had to themselves. Later they made slow, tender love in the firelight. It was the nicest time they'd had in ages and Izzy, renewed in spirit, felt she could face anything.

That evening, the dishes tidied, the lights of the tree switched off and the sitting room in darkness, they heard Rita's car in the drive. The children, tumbling out of the car door ran to greet their parents and shelter from the sleety rain. 'I won't come in!' Rita yelled, sticking her head out the window. 'I'll see you tomorrow around two with my gang.'

'Fine, Rita, thanks a million,' Izzy called back as Bill helped the trio divest themselves of coats and hats. Waving at her sister-in-law as she reversed down the drive, Izzy was glad to close the door and shut out the wintry night.

'We have a surprise for you. You've got to close your eyes and no peeping,' Bill warned, as he led Rachel, Keith and Jessica to the sitting room door.

'What is it? What is it?' Keith was hopping from one leg to the other with impatience.

'Keith, they're not going to tell you 'cos it won't be a surprise then,' Rachel said sagely, doing her big-sister act, but Izzy could see her eyes sparkling with anticipation.

'Huwwy on,' Jessica had her fingers up to her eyes and was peering anxiously through them. Watching the capers of the three of them, Izzy experienced a rare frisson of happiness and knew that whatever happened in the future, no one could ever take these precious moments away from her.

'Keep those eyes shut,' Bill warned, as Izzy took Jessica by the hand and led them into the darkened sitting room illuminated only by the firelight and the little red lamp in the crib. 'Open up!' Bill ordered as he plugged in the lights. He hugged Izzy as the children squealed with delight and excitement.

'Oh, Daddy, it's *COOL*!' Keith was beside himself.

'Oh, Mammy, isn't it *beeeautiful*?' Rachel breathed. Jessica stood speechless, her big blue eyes getting rounder by the minute. Hesitantly she stretched out a chubby little hand and touched one of the ornaments.

'Tanta Plause,' she exclaimed triumphantly, stroking the little fat Santa, her eyes as bright as the Christmas tree lights.

'Oh, look at the crib, Mammy. Can we put Baby Jesus in?' Rachel beseeched.

'Daddy and I were waiting until you came home so we could say a little prayer to welcome Baby Jesus into our family,' Izzy smiled and hugged her eldest daughter. She wanted her children to appreciate the special spirituality of Christmas and the crib ceremony was one of their most important family events.

With great solemnity, Rachel placed the infant Jesus in his manger in her younger sister's hands and guided the toddler to the correct spot in the centre of the straw, between Mary and Joseph. 'Welcome, Baby Jesus,' they all chorused reverently.

'And we hope you'll be very comfortable in your manger,' Rachel added as she patted the straw down. Jessica planted a big wet kiss on the newly installed infant.

'I bet he *will* be comfortable, our crib is *much* nicer than Jason Pierce's an' they don't have a light or straw either,' Keith declared with satisfaction as he took a bit of straw and placed it in front of the two little sheep on the mountainside. 'In case they're hungry,' he explained to his parents who were having a very hard time keeping their faces straight.

The following Monday morning, Bill arrived upstairs with a cup of early morning tea for his wife. 'What kind of a day is it?' Izzy murmured sleepily. She and Bill were going shopping for the Santa toys. They had decided on a compromise and decided to borrow 150 euros from the credit union and use 100 euros out of the 250 euros that Izzy had managed to put by for expenses. Through a chink in the curtains she could see a sliver of daylight. The wind and sleet of the previous two days had died down.

Bill drew back the curtains and peered out. 'I don't believe it,' she heard him say. 'Izzy come here, you've just got to see this!'

'What?' she asked, intrigued, wrapping the duvet around her to protect her from the early morning chill. She followed her husband's pointing finger. And burst out laughing. 'What a prat! What a prize prat,' she said, chortling as she viewed an outsized Noblis fir decorated with multicoloured lights, standing in a tub in the centre of the Pierces' front lawn.

All in all, it hadn't been a bad Christmas, Izzy decided, as she put the finishing touches to the creamy homemade vegetable soup she was serving as a starter for lunch with Mari. It was made with the stock of the turkey bones and there'd be plenty for tomorrow, she thought with satisfaction.

It was the day after Stephen's Day and Bill had taken the children on the Dart into Dublin to go to the pictures, so Izzy and her friend could have a bit of peace. Izzy had lit the fire early and had piled on the coal and briquettes so that the back boiler was boiling and the radiators were fine and hot. They were going through coal at an awful rate. Once the children were back at school, it would be back to lighting a fire in the evening. Still, at least the house was warm for her guest today.

A Gift For You

It had been two years since Mari had last been home. Izzy had known her since they were in their teens. They'd gone to secondary school together and worked in the civil service before Mari had fallen in love with a young doctor. They had married and gone to live in Dubai ten years ago. Izzy and she kept in touch by email, Facebook, and the occasional phone call. Mari had come back home several times over the years and Izzy had marvelled at how glamorous and sophisticated her friend had become.

She had, by all accounts, a glittering lifestyle out in the Emirates. A life full of parties and shopping and exotic travel. Her husband, Brett, had become a successful heart specialist and now they had a very affluent lifestyle. Brett and Owen would get on well, Izzy reflected, grinning. In fact it would be hilarious to listen to the pair of them trying to outdo each other.

She lifted the lid of another saucepan and added some chopped chives to the flaked salmon that was poaching in a cream and white wine sauce. Her mother had made a Christmas pudding and trifle for her and her mother-in-law had baked a Christmas cake, so at least she had dessert and afternoon tea taken care of. She also had a decent Chardonnay chilling. Someone had given it to them ages ago and she had put it aside for a special occasion. This was just such an occasion.

It was just as well Mari had picked the day after Stephen's Day because there was precious little left in the kitty, and what was in the fridge was going to have to do them for the rest of the week. Still, Rachel and Keith had been thrilled with their new bikes and Jessica was playing her ABC computer morning, noon and night. It had been a good idea putting those few euros from the children's allowance aside over the year. It had gone a long way towards paying for their Santa gifts.

Izzy turned down the salmon and went to give a last look over the house. She had hoovered and dusted thoroughly that morning and the house was fragrant with polish and pot pourri. A thought struck her and she ran upstairs to her bedroom and slid open her Sliderobes. On the bottom shelf of her make-up area there was a three-quarters full roll of soft floral toilet paper. Izzy took it and went into the main bathroom to replace the cheap, rough off-white thrift roll that was in the toilet roll holder. Maybe she was being daft but she badly wanted to keep up appearances. She always kept the expensive roll for when there was visitors. There was no need for Mari to know anything about Bill being unemployed. She couldn't explain exactly why she didn't want her friend to know of their plight. Mari wouldn't look down her nose at them in the least; she wasn't a bit like that, for all her wealth. She'd be very sympathetic if anything. It was just her silly pride, Izzy decided. But Bill's being unemployed seemed almost tantamount to failure in the light of Brett's success. It was a horrible thing to think, she scolded herself shamefaced, but even so . . .

Just for good measure, she produced a box of matching tissues, which she was also keeping for 'good wear', out of her wardrobe, and placed them on the shelf under the mirror. They gave a nice co- ordinated touch to the bathroom, and satisfied, Izzy went back downstairs to await her guest.

She paused in front of the mirror to check her appearance. She'd got her hair cut and blow-dried on Christmas Eve and it still looked good and a bit of make-up did wonders. The last year had added a few grey hairs to her chestnut curls, she thought ruefully, and the fine lines around her wide hazel eyes had deepened perceptibly. Still, she didn't look too bad considering, and the black trousers and amber blouse looked very well on her. A ring on the doorbell made her jump and she glanced at her watch. Mari was early.

'Happy Christmas,' came the cheerful greeting as Izzy opened the door and was hugged warmly by her friend who was certainly dressed for the weather in a magnificent, expensive fur coat. Mari had no problem wearing fur. Izzy tried not to think of the poor animals that had been slaughtered to make it.

'Come in, come in,' she urged. ' Now that Mari was here, she was delighted to see her.

'God above, I'm freezing.' Mari grimaced as she shut the door behind her.

'I've a blazing fire lit; come in and sit down beside it,' Izzy urged, leading the way into the sitting room.

'I've been cold since I came home,' Mari explained. 'The heat thins your blood and I know the animal lovers won't approve of the coat but it really stops me from freezing to death.' She looked tired, Izzy thought, despite the fact that her make-up was perfectly applied and her blonde, high-lighted hair in its classical chignon, the height of chic.

'Well, how are you, Izzy? How are the gang?' Mari smiled as she shrugged out of her coat, and handed it to Izzy. She sank into the big armchair in front of the fire and held out her hands to the blaze.

'I'm fine, we're all fine,' Izzy said cheerfully. 'Sit down there and relax . . . and what will you have to drink?'

'I have the car, Izzy, so I'll just have the one glass of wine,' Mari replied, and Izzy gave a mental sigh of relief. The good wine would last through lunch and she wouldn't have to open that awful bottle of plonk she'd bought on special offer. She should have remembered: Mari always hired a car when she was home. She hung the coat on the hallstand and went to the kitchen to pour the wine, which was chilling in the fridge. 'There's a lovely smell.' Mari followed her in. 'What's for lunch?'

'Salmon and pasta and a side salad.' Izzy answered as she did the business with the corkscrew.

'Oh, yum, you always made great pasta dishes, Izzy,' Mari lifted the lid of the saucepan and sniffed appreciatively. 'I've really been looking forward to seeing you and catching up on the all the craic and the gossip. Where's Bill and the children?'

Izzy handed her a glass of wine. 'He took them into Dublin on the Dart, for a treat. They've gone to the pictures.' Mari's face fell.

'I will get to see them, won't I?'

'Oh, indeed you will,' Izzy laughed.

'Oh, good. I've brought them a few presents and I've a bottle of brandy for yourself and Bill.'

'Mari, you shouldn't have!' Izzy exclaimed. Her friend was terribly generous and knowing that she wouldn't come empty handed, Izzy had wrapped up a hardback copy of best-selling author – Philippa Gregory's brand-new novel that her Aunt Patti had given her. She'd been dying to read it herself but she knew that Mari, who was an avid reader, would thoroughly enjoy it and a brand new hardback book was a decent present to give her old friend.

'I suppose I won't recognize the children.' Mari sipped her wine appreciatively. 'Jessica was only a baby the last time I was home.'

'She's well and truly a little girl now, marauding all over the place and up to all kinds of mischief,' Izzy grinned. Mari had no children but she always took an interest in Rachel, Keith and Jessica and always brought them something on her trips home from Dubai.

'Will I serve up our lunch now?' Izzy cocked an eyebrow at the other woman.

'Why not, if it's OK with you? I haven't eaten all morning and I feel a bit peckish,' Mari agreed.

'Go on in to the dining room and sit down and I'll bring in the soup,' Izzy instructed. She had set the dining table with the good silverware and crystal and her best linen tablecloth and napkins. And she had a lovely centrepiece on the table made up of holly and ivy, that she and Bill had picked in the woods. She lit the candles and served the soup and garlic bread and the pair of them sat down to a good natter.

Although Mari had said she was peckish she didn't do justice to the meal and Izzy was terribly perturbed that perhaps she hadn't liked the dish. Her friend always ate like a horse and never put on an ounce, unlike Izzy who only had to look at a cream cake to put on weight.

'Was it OK? Maybe it was a bit rich? 'Izzy said apologetically.

'No, no! It was fine. Really!' Mari assured her. 'I just wasn't as hungry as I thought.'

They had their coffee in at the fire, chatting about inconsequential things and somehow, Izzy, listening to tales of the glamorous life in the Emirates, just couldn't bring herself to tell Mari that Bill was unemployed.

He and the children arrived home around six and they were full of excitement about their jaunt on the Dart and their trip to the cinema and McDonald's. 'It's lovely and warm in here,' Keith said appreciatively, and Izzy, being extra sensitive on the day that was in it, prayed that her son would keep his mouth shut and say nothing else. She didn't want her affluent friend thinking that the house wasn't always this warm.

When Mari produced their presents, there was as much excitement as when Santa's gifts had been discovered on Christmas morning. Mari was in her element as they all vied for hugs and kisses before Bill took the three of them out to the kitchen to get some hot, nourishing soup into them. Rachel, en route to the kitchen, sighed, and said wistfully, 'I wish it was Christmas every day of the year so we could *always* have this gorgeous food.' Izzy nearly died. Her face actually flamed as she stood waiting for her child to say something like she was sick of beans and mince and fish fingers, but she said nothing else and followed her sister and brother.

'Turkey and ham and Christmas pud always seems so exotic when you're a child, doesn't it?' Mari remarked innocently, quite unaware of her friend's angst.

'Hmm . . .' agreed Izzy distractedly. God only knew what the children were going to come out with next to land her in it. She should have been honest with Mari at the beginning and told her about Bill being unemployed. There was no shame in it. It could happen to anyone, but it would look a bit odd to go suddenly blurting it out now, especially when she had led Mari to believe that everything was normal in the Reynolds' household. She was going to be on tenterhooks for the rest of the evening. She must excuse herself for a minute and grab Bill and tell him to say nothing about being unemployed. She'd tell him she'd explain later. He'd probably be annoyed with her and feel that she was ashamed of him. By trying to keep up a façade she'd made a right mess of things, she thought miserably.

'They're just gorgeous, Izzy. You're so lucky,' Mari said, enviously, interrupting her friend's musings.

'I know that,' Izzy agreed, carefully folding up the expensive wrapping paper and mentally reflecting that it would come in handy next year.

'Mammy, I did wee wee all by myself.' Jessica appeared at the door with her dress caught up in her little panties.

'You're a good girl!' her mother exclaimed. 'Come here until I tuck in your vest.' Jessica cuddled in against her as Izzy adjusted her clothing.

'There's lobely soft toilet woll in the bathwoom, it's nice and soft on my bum bum,' Jessica announced, staring at Mari.

Jesus, Mary and Joseph! Izzy thought in mortification. Next, she'll be saying we're poor people or something. Heart scalded, flustered, she told her daughter to go back out to the kitchen to finish her soup. Jessica wrapped her little arms around her neck. 'I lobe you, Mammy. The next time, will you come to the pictures?'

'Of course I will, lovey.' Izzy hugged the little girl to her before she went trotting out to the kitchen.

'She's so beautiful,' Mari said, and her voice sounded terribly sad. Izzy caught her friend's gaze and to her dismay saw that Mari's eyes were bright with tears.

'God! What's wrong, Mari?' Izzy exclaimed, closing the door and rushing over to her side. 'What is it? Tell me what's wrong.' She put her arms around her friend as Mari began to cry.

'Brett and me, we're finished. He's been having an affair with this American bimbo half his age and now she's pregnant and he wants a divorce. He wouldn't let me come off the Pill, he kept saying to wait another year and then another and now this tart's pregnant and it's fine by him. I hate him, the bastard,' Mari sobbed. 'I didn't want to tell you, I was just too ashamed.'

Izzy couldn't believe her ears. What a shit Brett was. She knew Mari had always wanted children.

'You've nothing to be ashamed about,' she said outraged, 'He's the skunk. I can't believe he did this to you. He's not worthy of you, Mari. Don't you *dare* feel ashamed.'

Mari lifted her head from Izzy's' neck. 'I don't know why *I* feel this way. *I* did nothing to be ashamed about. It's just . . . Oh, you know what I mean, Izzy, my poor mother will be mortified. The first divorce in the family. What will the relations say?' she hiccupped.

'Don't mind the relations or anyone. It's your life and your business,' Izzy snorted.

'I've been on my own for months. I just couldn't tell you. Can you understand?' Mari managed a wry smile.

'I understand *exactly*,' Izzy said slowly. 'Actually, Mari, I've been keeping something from you as well.' She met her friend's tear-stained gaze. 'Bill's been out of work for over fourteen months and it's a bit of a struggle. Like you, I just couldn't bring myself to say it out straight. I wanted to keep up appearances. I'm sorry it was just silly pride,' she admitted ruefully.

'Oh, Lord. That's awful for you and Bill,' Mari exclaimed. 'You should have told me!'

'I know, and you should have told *me*!'

'He'll get another job,' Mari soothed. 'And at least the pair of you are as crazy about each other as ever. You can spot that a mile off. God. You can face anything when you're together. I was so gutted when I found out about Brett and that . . . that pea-brained, simpering idiot who's got her claws into him. The thing that hurt most of all is that she's pregnant. Every time I suggested trying for a baby he said to wait another year. He didn't want his cushy life-style disrupted by crying babies. I'll probably never have a child of my own now.' Her voice wobbled and she burst into tears again.

'Of course you will; you'll meet someone new. You're still a relatively young woman,' Izzy reassured her, shocked by what she had just heard. Her own circumstances might not be the best but they were a hell of a lot better than Mari's. No wonder the poor girl couldn't eat her lunch. No wonder she'd seemed so on edge for the afternoon.

'I haven't told the family yet. Mum will have a fit.'

'She'll get over it.' Izzy assured her.

'It's such a relief to tell someone, Izzy,' Mari confessed, wiping her eyes with the back of her hand. 'It's been so hard being at home trying to pretend everything's normal. I told them Brett couldn't come home because of work commit-ments. A bit feeble, I know, but no one's questioned it. It's bloody hard trying to keep up the façade.'

'Of course it's been hard, Mari, but you've got to tell them. You can't go around keeping that to yourself. You'd crack up. And I know your family – they'll be very supportive; it's amazing how kind people are when the chips are down. I know,' she added wryly.

'Oh, Izzy, what idiots we've been, trying to put on brave faces. If we can't tell each other our problems, then who can we tell?' Mari said.

'*Exactly!*' Izzy agreed. 'Now, look, why don't you phone home and tell them you're staying the night and we'll open the brandy you brought and we'll have Brandy Alexanders and have a really good natter about things.'

'Oh, Izzy, that would be *lovely*,' Mari said, sighing, beginning to feel better already.

'I'll just run up an put the heat on in the spare bedroom, and fish out some towels and a nightdress for you.' Izzy patted her on the shoulder.

'Now don't go to any trouble,' Mari remonstrated.

'It's no trouble for an old pal,' Izzy said firmly.

She turned on the radiator and laid a clean, long-sleeved nightdress on Mari's bed. That would keep her snug, she thought, and she'd put the electric blanket on later. To hell with the electricity bill for once. Mari was undergoing a bad enough trauma without spending the night shivering.

Izzy stood at the bedroom window, staring out into the night. A sliver of new moon hid behind a wisp of cloud. The lights of the Christmas trees in her neighbour's window spilled out into the darkness, adding festive illumination to the cul-de-sac. Owen's Noblis stood proudly on his front lawn. Owen had got a new four-wheel drive for Christmas and had spent a lot of time sitting in it making calls on his car phone. 'He'd got it cheap because it was an end of year model,' Bill remarked, grinning when he'd seen it.

Izzy smiled. Her neighbour was pathetically childish, really. Maybe there was some reason for his juvenile behaviour. Maybe he'd had a terribly deprived childhood. Who knew? Who knew what went on in people's lives? Who knew what went on behind the façades? Look at poor Mari. Who would have believed it?

She and Bill were lucky; they had each other and they had the children. She could hear the three of them laughing and chattering in the kitchen. Closing the curtains, Izzy straightened the folds, switched off the light and went downstairs, where Bill took the opportunity to kiss her soundly under the mistletoe, before she went back into the snug, warm sitting room to rejoin her friend.

The Christmas Tree

I couldn't make up my mind whether or not to put up a Christmas tree this year. It seemed a lot of trouble when I was going to be here on my own. Don't get me wrong, I'd had invites to spend Christmas with family, but did you ever just want to stay at home in your own house and sleep in your own bed?

I could understand of course, why my son and daughter didn't like the idea too much. When I was their age, if my own widowed eighty-year-old mother had refused *my* invite to spend Christmas with us, I'd have been upset and worried at her being alone on Christmas Day.

I've spent the last decade trotting between their houses, for the festive season. And while I love them, and my five grandchildren, and have spent many Christmases with them since my much-loved husband, John passed away; this year, I had a yen to stay at home.

I didn't buy a turkey. I don't really care for it. The only part I like is the dark meat under the legs. Instead, I bought a fillet steak to have with fried onions and fried potatoes. A tasty dinner, with little fuss. I'd cooked a ham, though, so I'd have meat to make sandwiches for visitors.

As I say, I'd dithered about putting up a tree. But then, when I saw the gleaming, twinkling lights in windows in the village, I was sorry I'd told my daughter not to bother.

It came up in conversation with my new neighbour, Sarah. She and her husband, Simon, had bought the bungalow next door at the end of summer. I was worried about who would move in after old Mr Kelly died. When I heard a young couple had bought the house, I won't deny I was apprehensive. I wondered whether they would have loud and frequent parties, but to my relief I couldn't ask for nicer neighbours.

I met Sarah at the post office, when I was collecting my pension, and complimented her on the lovely Christmas lights she had laced around the fir tree in the front garden. They're delightful to look at, especially when the dusk is settling. That was how we got into conversation about the Christmas tree and I told her I regretted not putting one up this year.

Well, an hour later, there was a knock on the door and it was Simon. Now, between you and me, if I was fifty years younger, he's exactly the type of man I'd have fallen for. He's the tall, broad muscular type. Like my own dear John. A manly sort of man, not like these young chaps today who have too much to say for themselves and spend half their lives sitting at computers, with their nets and their twitts, and emails and the like.

Simon is an electrician. He has his own company and is doing well, even in the recession. His father is a farmer and Simon helps out on the farm. He has the look of it, a real outdoors type with a strong face and the brownest of brown eyes, with a tan that is most certainly not out of a bottle.

'Mrs Kenny,' he said, standing at my door with his thumbs hooked into his jeans, 'Sarah told me that you can't decide about your Christmas tree. If I can be of any use at all, I'd be delighted to help out.'

'That's very kind of you,' I said, 'but I left it too late to buy one now. There'll only be rubbish left. I've always put up a real tree. My late husband had no truck with artificial ones. When I saw the one you have lit up in your garden I got a little nostalgic for one, that's all. But thank you very much for offering, Simon.'

'No trouble at all.' He smiled. He had a lovely lopsided smile, just like John had. He waved from the gate and I waved back, warmed by his and Sarah's kindness. Just before tea, there was a knock at my door. Simon was there, with *the* most beautiful, perfectly shaped Christmas tree. The scent of it brought back such memories. I felt a terrible pang of loneliness for my beloved husband. The passing years have not eased the sense of loss; at times like Christmas I miss John more than ever. But Simon looked so pleased with himself I hid my sadness from him and opened the door wide.

'I have some lights too, in case all yours aren't working,' he told me eagerly, all ready to start decorating.

I was overwhelmed as he set to, positioning it in the bay window, turning it this way and that for the best angle to show off its glory. Sarah came to help and between us we decorated it from the big box of baubles I had in the attic. They devoured the slices of the baked ham I served them, on thick Vienna roll slathered in butter, which we ate under the luminous glow of the tree, with the fire crackling and flickering in the grate.

The tree was magnificent, the soft reds, blues, silver and greens of the lanterns reflecting on the baubles as they glistened and shimmered. Despite my feelings of loss and sadness, I was delighted to have a decorated tree and very touched by my young neighbours' kindness. I sat up until late, admiring it after they had gone. And only when the glow of the embers had dulled to dusty grey did I go to bed.

'Nana you have a *real* tree!' My grandchildren were ecstatic when they called on Christmas Eve. They have an artificial tree at home. My daughter has neither the time nor the patience to vacuum up pine needles. The children oohhed and aahhhed, their joyful faces reflected in the shining decorations that swung gaily from the branches. I was reminded of my own children when they were young. Simple pleasures are still the best.

'Mum, I would have put it up for you,' Charlotte, my daughter, chided.

'I wanted to surprise you,' I fibbed. 'Simon and Sarah from next door got it and we put it up together. It was a nice way of getting to know them.'

'How kind!' she exclaimed. 'It's beautiful, just like the ones Dad used to put up.' We squeezed hands as grief shadowed us momentarily. 'I was thinking, I could cook dinner here, if you'd like?' she'd offered. 'Then we'd all be together. And we could enjoy the tree.'

'Perfect!' I was *delighted* with the suggestion. Christmas in my own home after all these years. What could be nicer? I slept like a log that night in my own comfy bed, and looked forward to going to Mass on Christmas morning with my grandchildren, and seeing the crib.

'Mum must have had an inkling,' I hear Charlotte say to Sarah and Simon. 'She was so insistent on staying at home this year.' I gaze down at them as they follow the coffin into the church. My darling John is by my side here, and we watch together as relatives and friends crowd into our small village church.

I have never been happier. I am young and carefree again. The New Year is one day old. The Christmas lights shimmer in windows around the village, incandescent in the deepening, snowy gloom. My tree glows brightest of all. Charlotte was determined to have it lit for me.

They've given me a terrific funeral. It's the hymns that have started them all crying. *Here I am, Lord, it is I, Lord. I have heard you calling in the night.* It nearly makes *me* cry as the soloist's pure voice floats from the gallery, the notes dipping and soaring over the heads of the large group of mourners that are kneeling in this small country church where my funeral Mass is being held.

My funeral! How strange to think that I am 'dead' and about to be buried beside my husband, when the reality is that I'm *not* dead at all.

It all happened so quickly, really: one minute I was sitting in the armchair by the window doing my crossword, as I did every morning after breakfast, and then I felt a pain in my chest. But even as I crumpled, my mother and John came and held out their hands to me and I felt myself sort of float out of my body as I reached for them. It was the most indescribable feeling. I felt young again. I had no aches, no pains, my eyesight was perfect. I felt reborn almost. I turned to look and got quite a shock I can tell you when I saw myself sitting in the chair. Who was that old woman with the grey hair, head tilted sidways, glasses a little askew, paper slipping out of lifeless hands. Then I realized it was me.

'Am I dead? I must be if I'm with you and John,' I said to my mother.

'Not a bit of it. There's no such thing as death; you've just passed beyond the veil of forgetting' she said laughing, hugging me tightly, and I felt such joy to be with her. My husband smiled at me, held out his arms to me, and my heart melted as I snuggled into his embrace. 'It was a lovely tree, this year, not as good as mine, but good enough,' he teased. 'Next year, we'll put up the Christmas tree together.'

VALENTINE'S DAY

The Angel Of Love

It was definitely the most comfortable bed that she had ever slept in, Irene O'Shaughnessy decided sleepily, as she snuggled into her cosy hollow and pulled the patchwork quilt, which she had made herself, up over her ears. She would make herself a cuppa in a while. There was no rush to get up. She could lie in bed all morning if she chose. She could do just what she liked. It was pelting rain, drumming on the Velux window in the ensuite in an angry tattoo. She had a great new detective novel to read; what better day than today for a laze in bed with a book.

The sound of an ambulance siren coming closer followed by a blue flashing light illuminating the grey morning gloom gave her a start. It must be Mrs Andrews again, she thought in dismay, as she slipped out of bed and padded over to the window. Her elderly neighbour, who lived across the road, was in very poor health and had been whisked off to hospital by ambulance just a month ago, a few days after Irene had

73

moved into her new house. How different it was, she mused, living in the city with your neighbours so close to you that you could know what was going on as it was happening rather than hearing about things second-hand at the village post office.

Irene peeped through the curtains as the drama unfolded and watched as a figure was stretchered into the ambulance, followed by an agitated middle-aged woman sheltering under an umbrella. Irene recognized her as Mrs Andrews's daughter. The poor woman never had a minute's peace with her ailing mother. Moments later, the ambulance was gone, siren wailing, and peace descended once more on the small circle of houses known as Sea View Close.

Irene shivered. She was so lucky to have her health and to be able to enjoy life, unlike her poor stricken neighbour who couldn't make the most of her lovely new home and pretty garden. She let the curtain fall back into place again and hurried back to the warmth of her bed. She switched on the electric blanket and arranged the pillows cosily around her. The rain battered the windowpane relentlessly, the wind moaned and wailed under the eaves but she was as snug as a bug in a rug with nowhere to go and no one depending on her. It was the greatest feeling in the world, Irene thought with satisfaction, as she stretched languidly and curled her feet up under the hem of her winceyette nightie. She knew that friends and relatives felt sorry for her, thinking that she was lonely living by herself but her widow-hood had liberated her. She was as free as a bird.

A Gift For You

Irene sighed. That was a terrible reflection on her marriage. But the truth was, she'd been just as lonely when her husband, Jim was alive. Jim had been a hard worker, a good provider. He'd left her well looked after. There was no denying that. Her lovely new home was proof that her late husband could not be faulted for looking after her material well-being, but the same could not be said for the way Jim had dealt with her emotional needs.

Her marriage had been such a disappointment, she reflected drowsily. She had started out with such hopes because she really had loved Jim. And at the beginning, she'd felt that he'd loved her. He'd wooed her in his quiet, shy way, taking her for long walks along the winding country roads of Waterford, where they'd both grown up. They'd known each other since childhood but it was only when Jim had become an apprentice to a carpenter in Wexford and left their small village, that Irene had realized how much she missed his quiet, stalwart presence.

When he'd asked her to go to the pictures with him, one weekend that he was home, she'd been delighted. Jim O'Shaughnessy was a challenge and she wanted him. She was going to bring down those barriers and get under his skin and find out what made him tick. During the following weeks, she'd drawn him out of himself, got him talking about his work, made him laugh and felt slowly but surely that she was getting through his reserve. His grey eyes with their incredibly long, curling lashes would light up when he saw her and the shy smile that curved around his firm, well-shaped mouth always lifted her heart and made her feel incredibly happy.

When Jim kissed her for the first time, Irene kissed him back with a passion that surprised him.

'I love you,' she whispered, burying her face in his neck.

'Do you?' he whispered back, holding her tight against him. 'What do you love me for? Sure, you could have any man you wanted. All the fellows in the village are mad for you.'

'I don't want any of the fellows in the village. I want you. I'm happy when I'm with you.'

'I'm happy when I'm with you, too. You're beautiful, Irene.' Jim blushed a dull red as he said the words with bashful shyness.

Irene was over the moon with happiness. He loved her as much as she loved him; it was just that he found it hard to say the words. His kisses were passionate and hungry. The kisses of a man in love. What more could she want?

She would have gone the whole way; it was Jim who'd drawn away and said that he didn't want to do anything to dishonour her. He respected her too much and besides he didn't want her father after him with a shotgun, he'd murmured as his breathing returned to normal. Girls who went all the way were considered loose and beyond redemption but, at the time, Irene didn't care. She just wanted to make love and be as intimate as she possibly could with the strong, virile young man who'd taken over her mind and soul.

Jim fascinated her. She loved watching him work with his hands, his long fingers caressing a piece of wood as gently as they caressed her. He made beautiful ornaments for her and when he'd given her an intricately carved sandalwood jewellery box with a heart in the middle of the lid, on Valentine's Day, she'd known that she was loved, even if he had yet to say the words. Irene waited patiently for his proposal. Eighteen months went by, and not a word, until finally, in complete frustration, she'd asked him, 'Are we going to get married?'

'I suppose so, if that's what you want.' He looked away, embarrassed.

'Don't be too enthusiastic,' she snapped.

'Don't be like that, Irene,' he muttered.

'Do you love me?' she demanded.

'Ah, for heaven's sake, woman, don't be asking me questions like that.'

'Well, do you, Jim? You've never said it,' Irene said heatedly.

'Calm down like a good girl.' He jammed his hands in his jeans pockets and stared at her.

'Is it so hard to say?' She couldn't understand his reticence. She'd tell him that she loved him twenty times a day, except that she knew that it embarrassed him. 'Is it so hard to say, Jim?' she repeated when he remained stubbornly silent.

'Yes. For me it is. It's not my way.' He paced the floor agitatedly.

'I need you to say it,' she pleaded.

He remained stubbornly silent, his jaw jutting out aggressively.

'Do you love me, Jim?'

'I suppose I do. Now are you satisfied?' he demanded but he took her in his arms and his kiss was tender.

She'd asked him many times during the first years of their marriage, especially in the precious moments after their lovemaking when she held him in her arms and felt that no one else but them existed in the universe. But he always shushed her and lay silently with his head against her shoulder stroking her long, black hair. Getting him to open up emotionally, to say endearments and to tell her that he loved her was like drawing blood from a stone.

He worked long hours at his trade and when he came in from work, tired, he'd eat the dinner that she put in front of him and then stretch out in his favourite armchair and fall asleep. Irene would be as mad as hell. She'd be dying to talk, to tell him the news of her day. She worked as a legal secretary in Waterford and she loved meeting the clients. She'd want to ask him about his day and who he'd worked for making kitchens or wardrobes or stairs, or bespoke furniture, but all that she would get was a low rumbling snore as he slept in the armchair. Around nine, he'd wake up and head off to the village pub for his nightly pint. He wasn't a heavy drinker, she never had a problem there, he'd just nurse a pint for an hour or so and then he'd come home and be in bed by half ten, ready for an early start the following morning.

Gradually, over the years, resentment began to eat her up. Why couldn't he make the effort, she'd ask him again and again? Why did he not take her needs and feelings into consideration? What was the point in being married if they didn't share and talk and do things together as a couple?

'Oh, for God's sake, woman! Don't be bothering me with all this romancy stuff. Don't we go walking on Sunday afternoons? Don't I give you every penny I earn? What more do you want?' was his retort.

'You never tell me that you love me. You never say anything nice to me. Is it so hard, Jim? All I want is for you to talk to me and tell me that you love me now and again.'

'I married you, didn't I? Let that be the end of it.'

'Yeah, but I had to ask you. You didn't even have the guts to ask me yourself,' she'd blurted out one day when she was particularly afflicted with her monthlies.

'And aren't I sorry I did, if this is the way you're going to carry on,' he'd snapped back at her and she'd nearly died. He hated it when she nagged him and he would take off to his shed at the end of the garden where he'd hammer and saw to his heart's content while she'd be left fuming in the kitchen.

When she'd found out that she was pregnant after two years of marriage she'd been over the moon.

'That's nice,' Jim said when she'd told him the news.

'Oh, Jim! Can't you be a bit more enthusiastic! We're going to have a *baby*!' She'd been desperately disappointed at his reaction.

'I *am* enthusiastic. It's good. I'm glad for you that you're having the baby,' he'd replied, leaving the unspoken words, *it will give you something to keep you occupied and you won't have to be bothering me* hanging in the air between them.

Her daughter, Beth was the most placid, beautiful baby and she had become the focus of Irene's attention, a situation that suited her taciturn husband down to the ground. He was as emotionally guarded with Beth as he was with Irene and any hopes she'd had that their little daughter would break down his reserve soon faded as he left the rearing of her to his wife, and life went on as before, only now, Irene gave the love she'd had for her husband to her blonde little beauty and this time it was returned in full.

Irene felt sad listening to the rain and wind, as the heat from the electric blanket warmed her and the sound of car engines starting signalled the exodus of the Close's inhabitants to their jobs in the city. Jim should never have married. He wasn't cut out to be in a relationship. He had controlled her for a long time by withholding his love and affection, until she'd wearied of the game and ceased to play it. Resentment had turned to indifference. She'd stopped banging her head against the brick wall of his emotional selfishness. If it weren't for Beth she'd have been a very lonely woman.

When her daughter had left home at the age of eighteen to go and work in Dublin, Irene was bereft. She missed her bright, sparky daughter and longed for her infrequent visits home. Beth married a lovely man who had no trouble telling her that he loved her, and they bought a beautiful home in Blackrock after the birth of their first child. Irene visited frequently.

She adored Dublin. It was a whole new world and she would sally forth into the city and spent the day shopping and exploring to her heart's content. Jim never minded her sorties to the big smoke. She knew quite well that he was as happy as Larry on his own once she left a few meals prepared for him. He would rarely accompany her, although he got on well with Derek, Beth's husband.

Jim had died as he had lived, quietly, unobtrusively, collapsing in his beloved shed three days before their fiftieth wedding anniversary, sanding down a piece of wood for a cabinet that he was making. She had given up asking him to slow down and retire. But even though he promised he would, he was in thrall to his work and even in his mid-seventies he had worked in his shed every day except Sunday. She had found him slumped over his workbench, a small smile curving his mouth. It had been so shocking and unexpected that Irene couldn't take it in. It had been the grace of God that her best friend, Eileen, happened to cycle past just as she ran out onto the road to run the quarter mile to her nearest neighbour. Eileen had phoned the doctor and the priest and taken charge, while Irene went back to the shed to Jim, to wait for the undertaker to arrive.

As she'd sat with his body when he was waked, her strongest emotion was anger. They could have had such a lovely life together if only he'd nurtured the love that had been there at the beginning. Instead, he'd let it fade until there was nothing but a wasted lifetime of resentment and regrets on her side and God only knew what on his, because *she* surely did not know. Her bitterness was stronger than her grief in those early months of widowhood and she had cursed Jim and God for her misery.

'You can come and live with us if you like, Mam,' Beth had offered kindly in the weeks following Jim's death. Irene was tempted. But she valued her independence and she didn't want to be a nuisance to her daughter. There was nothing in the world to stop her moving up to Dublin and buying a place of her own, though, she thought with mounting excitement. She would be close to her daughter and beloved grandchildren but she wouldn't be a burden to them. Jim had left her very well provided for. He'd inherited his parent's farm and leased it to a local farmer. It was worth a lot of money and it was hers now, as was their own house and the acre of land that it stood on. In fact she was a relatively wealthy woman now at the age of seventy-four.

Over the following months, she and Beth had scoured the property pages and estate agents' windows looking for just the right place. And then, one day, she'd seen an advertisement for a small, exclusive, housing development off the Strand Road in Sandymount. Eight detached houses, a mixture of two-storey and dormer bungalows. Sea View Close. It was perfect. Five minutes from the Dart. Across the road from the sea front, yet in off the main street, and protected from the noise of the unremitting pounding of the traffic. Best of all, Beth's house was just a mile or so up the road.

Irene had bought from the plans. A two-bedroomed dormer, with a fitted kitchen and dining room that led into a conservatory which opened onto a patio and small private south-west-facing garden.

The sitting room to the front of the house looked big and open, even on the plans, compared to the small square parlour of her home in Waterford. The main bedroom was ensuite, an undreamt of luxury.

Beth was as excited as she was and they read magazines on decor and interior design and visited fabric and furnishing shops, changing colour schemes every second day. Over the months that followed, as Irene put the farm and her house on the market, she travelled regularly to Dublin to see the progress of her dream home.

Her whole life was changing completely and she felt exhilarated and optimistic as she was carried along on the tide of excitement that swept through her the first time she put the key into her new front door. The house smelt so fresh and new, even if outside was still a mucky, dusty building site.

She had the downstairs rooms painted a warm, buttermilk yellow and as the sunlight poured in through the big bay window of the sitting room, gleaming on the shiny polished maple floor, Irene felt a rare surge of happiness. This was going to be a house of joy, she decided. A bright, light happy home for her. It was time to let go of all the unhappiness of the past and start afresh. She was still hale, hearty and sprightly, she had a few good years left, and she would make the most of them.

She had stood at Jim's grave and said firmly, 'I'm going up to be with Beth and the children, there's nothing to keep me here. You were happy to be left alone when you were alive, and now that you're gone I'm sure it won't bother you one bit not to have me here. I'm paying Gerry Reilly a stipend to maintain the grave. I haven't decided yet whether to join you or be buried in Dublin when my time comes. Rest in Peace, Jim.' She emphasized the 'peace' her tone tinged with bitterness as she turned on her heel and marched out of the small, well-tended graveyard, her shoes crunching on the gravel path, breaking the ethereal silence. She wondered if he had heard her. Wondered how he would feel at her threat to be buried in Dublin. He had told her once that his father had proposed to his mother not by asking her to marry him but by asking if she would 'like to be buried with his people'. It was no wonder, Irene supposed, that Jim hadn't a romantic bone in his body if that was what he'd been reared to. Well, eternity was a long time to be in a grave and she wanted to be at peace. There had been no peace in her marriage, but there would be peace and a happiness of sorts in Dublin, she assured herself as she closed the iron gate of the graveyard with a resounding, defiant, clang.

And she *had* been happy since moving to Dublin, Irene reflected, as she lay, drowsy and warm, in her bed. Her three grandchildren were the joy of her life, her bond with her daughter could not be stronger, her son-in-law was a kind man, and she bloomed in the shelter of their love. She had recently joined the local active retirement group and she was on nodding terms with all her new neighbours. It was a good life, Irene acknowledged, as her eyes closed and she fell into a dreamless, contented snooze as thunder rumbled out to sea and great flickers of lightening streaked the leaden horizon.

'I'll stay put today, pet,' Irene said to her daughter on the phone as the Angelus bell rang at midday. She was sitting at the breakfast counter eating scrambled eggs on toast, with a few fried mushrooms and tomatoes on the side, watching the rain sluice down the French doors that led out to the patio.

'I'll pop in with the girls on the way home from piano practice,' Beth said kindly.

'Right then, I'll bake a cream sponge for us and we'll have a cuppa.' Irene said happily.

'Mam, I've put on half a stone since you came to live in Dublin,' Beth protested, laughing.

'Good, you were too scrawny, miss,' her mother retorted as the doorbell rang. 'There's a ring at the door. I'll see you later,' she said, hopping down off the stool and hanging up.

'A parcel for you, ma'am. Sign here, please,' a young man said, thrusting a docket at her, impatient to be gone. So different from home, she thought, remembering how the chat would be had at the back door when the postman called. Dublin was home now, she chided herself, closing the door and wondering who would be sending her something in a thick padded envelope that wouldn't fit in her narrow letterbox. She saw Denis Finlay, her solicitor, named as the sender and, perplexed, she opened the large brown envelope and drew out a bubble-wrapped parcel and a letter:

Dear Mrs O'Shaughnessy,

The new owner who purchased your house found this down behind Jim's workbench in the shed and he asked me to forward it on to you.

I hope you've settled in well in your new home in Dublin.

Kind regards,

Denis.

She unwrapped the parcel and gave a little gasp when she saw the perfectly carved figures of an angel enfolding a woman and a man in his embrace. It was smooth and polished, the grain of the wood rich and textured as she studied it, stunned. Her breathing quickened as she turned it upside down and saw that Jim had inscribed the base:

To My Dear Wife, Irene, on our Wedding Anniversary. The Angel of Love has held my love for you always and will hold it for all eternity. Love Jim.

'Oh, Jim, Jim!' Irene cried, as an ache twisted her heart and she held the carving close. 'Oh, Jim, you did love me in spite of the distance between us,' she wept, filled with sadness, regret and a strange kind of joy.

She walked back into the kitchen and sat down beside the stove, the flames dancing orange and yellow around the logs burning in the grate, brightening the gloom of the winter's day.

Her husband had not been gifted with eloquence and she had never been able to accept that, Irene thought with an unwelcome deep sense of shame. The more she'd nagged him, the more he'd withdrawn; she was as much to blame as he was. She stood up and went to a drawer in her dresser and took a tissue-wrapped square from underneath a pile of folded tea towels. She unwrapped the layers of tissue and gazed at her wedding photo. They had been married on Valentine's Day and the crocuses and snowdrops had lined the pathway to the little country church, great splashes of colour after the gloom of winter. They'd been married surrounded by family and friends and had a wedding breakfast in the local hotel before getting the train to Dublin to spend their honeymoon in the Gresham Hotel. Three days of absolute joy and happiness as she and her new husband ravished each other after all the months of pent-up longing. She studied the photo of herself and Jim, beaming with delight, and remembered how happy she had been on that special day of love. Getting married on St Valentine's Day had been a good omen, she'd felt. Irene sighed. She hadn't displayed the photograph in her new home, unwilling to be reminded of the past.

'I'm sorry, Jim,' she murmured, tenderly polishing the glass until it sparkled. She placed it gently on the mantle, and stood the angel carving beside it. '*And* I'll be buried with your people,' she said to her husband's image, and felt a great relief as the angel seemed to smile at her and a peace and contentment took the place of the anger and resentment that had blighted her life for so long.

A Woman in Her Prime

'Mummy, my bottom pirped,' seven-year-old Andrew Finn announced matter-of-factly, as he, his mother and his elder sister stood on the coast road at Clearwater Bay, talking to a glamorous blonde who was leaning nonchalantly against her BMW coupé, twirling her keys.

'Andrew!' exclaimed Ella Finn glaring at her son.

'But it *did*, Mum, it went *pirp, pirp, pirp*,' he informed her gleefully.

Ella groaned silently as she noted a flicker of distaste trying to create a wrinkle across Paula Nolan's Botoxed forehead.

'I guess I should be going,' the blonde said crisply. 'I'll see you at the bash?' One perfectly plucked eyebrow arched as she paused from the key twirling momentarily.

'Sure,' Ella agreed, glad the encounter was over.

'Is Maggie coming to the Lifeboat Fundraiser?'

'As far as I know.'

'And . . . er . . . is Daniel coming, or will he be milking cows?' The tone was acerbic.

'It was his dad that used to have cattle. We own a stables,' Ella murmured, thinking, *You haven't changed, you sarky mare.*

'Of course. I'd forgotten. My mother regales me with the village gossip when I phone but I never remember *any* of it.'

'Really?' Ella smiled sweetly as a breeze blew her copper curls around her face. 'I suppose the goings-on of us boggers wouldn't be of the slightest interest to a City Slicker like you. Anyway I'd love to stop and chat but Daniel's meeting us for lunch so we must get our skates on.'

'We're having a picnic with my dad; do you want to come?' Andrew invited gaily.

Oh, hell! Ella thought. She didn't want her husband's ex-girlfriend joining them for lunch, now or ever.

'I don't think Paula's quite dressed for the beach; it would be a bit hard going down the ninety-nine steps in those high heels,' she pointed out to her kind-hearted son.

'What happens if it rains? Does your car get flooded?' Andrew enquired, staring at the convertible.

'Err . . . no, I put the roof up.' Paula gave him a supercilious glance.

'Do you have to build it?' he persisted.

'No, you press a—'

'Andrew, we have to go. Daddy will explain it to you,' Ella said firmly.

'Give Daniel my regards. I expect I'll get to see him; I'm here for a few days,' Paula purred silkily.

'I'm sure he'll be delighted to see you.' Ella kept her tone neutral, as a burst of jealousy swept through her. She wanted to smack the cold-eyed woman in front of her. How Daniel had ever had a relationship with Paula was a mystery to her. 'Bye.'

'Cheers,' drawled Paula as she slid gracefully into the cream leather interior of her sports car. She started the engine and roared off with a nonchalant wave.

'Cool car, Mum. Let's tell Daddy about it.' Andrew grinned up at her, the sprinkling of freckles across his nose so endearing she wanted to lift him up in her arms and smother him in hugs and kisses. There would have been uproar had she done so. Andrew did not care to be kissed in public any more and she had to restrain her urges to cuddle him until bedtime, when he endured them . . . and, she hoped, secretly enjoyed them. But he wouldn't admit it; he was a 'big boy' now was his constant refrain.

'Let's go and meet Dad.' Ella smiled down at him. 'Lead on Macduff.'

They walked along the winding path until they came to the ninety-nine steps that led down to a golden slice of beach that curved in the direction of a small pier further on, where fishing boats danced up and down on the rippling, glittering sea and nets and lobster pots lay strung along the quay, and old anchors lay rusting in the sun. Gulls wheeled and circled and swooped and dived. cawing raucously. The chugging and throbbing of a boat's engine added to the seaside cacophony, melodic on the breeze.

She saw her husband waving and her heart lifted. She loved Daniel Finn with all her heart and always had done, even as a spotty teenager, and even through the heart-stinging days when he'd romanced the beautiful Paula and then been left high and dry when she'd shaken the dust of Clearwater Bay off her stilettos and headed for the bright lights of New York.

Ella had gone to work in Dublin and share a flat with her best friend, Maggie; and one weekend, when she'd come back home for the annual Lifeboat Fundraiser Dance and Barbecue, Daniel had asked her to dance as the evening drew to a close. To her surprise, she'd found him very easy to talk to. He'd confided that he was thinking of buying land to open a stables and she'd offered to help out in the yard on the weekends she was home. She was mad about horses and mad about Daniel. And soon, it became clear that he was equally keen on her. They'd married two years later and built up a livery and horse-riding business, which was now thriving.

Paula had come back to Dublin the previous year and had secured herself a top-notch job in PR, but she'd never come back to Clearwater Bay to visit, until now.

How chic and sophisticated she'd looked in her sports coupé, her taupe linen trousers crisp and sharply creased, her cream, figure-hugging vest showing off her toned, sculpted body.

Ella sighed as she followed her children down the wooden steps. Typical of her luck to be caught in her faded-denim

A Gift For You

shorts and the black V-top that was speckled with white paint. It had splashed on her earlier when she'd been white-washing the yard. She hadn't even a slick of lipstick on, she thought, glumly, as she remembered Paula's full, glistening lips. Her husband waved and loped towards them in his rangy, long-legged stride.

'Come on, dear woman, what vitals have you got for your starving hunter-gatherer?' Daniel planted a firm kiss on her unlipsticked lips, before kissing their daughter, Sally, and swinging Andrew up in the air.

'*Am* I your dear woman?' She looked up at him, drinking in the sight of him, so lean and rugged, his blue eyes crinkling up in the most attractive way when he smiled, his teeth white and even against his tanned weather-beaten face.

'Of *course* you're my dear woman, especially if you brought me some of those scrumptious cherry-and-walnut buns that I *adore*,' he replied grinning, dropping Andrew onto the fine, hot sand and taking the picnic basket from her.

'I made egg and onion sandwiches for you.' She slipped her hand into his and his warm fingers closed over hers in a loving clasp.

'What have I done to deserve such a banquet?' he teased, as they reached their favourite spot – a small hollow surrounded by green spiky marram grass and with a soft bed of mossy fern to sit on. She spread out the green-checked-tartan rug, and he knelt beside her, taking plastic plates and cups out of the basket, while she unwrapped the sandwiches and buns, and the children raced down to the shore and screeched in delight as a frothy surge of white spray played around their bare feet.

'Paula's home,' Ella blurted.

'Aahaa!' Her husband's eyes narrowed as he stared at her, comprehension dawning. 'Hence the "Am I your dear woman" question?'

'Daddy, Daddy, come on into the sea, it's warm, honest, Dad.' Andrew pranced around them, scattering damp sand all over the rug.

'Andrew!' Ella exclaimed, exasperated.

'Sandwiches always taste better with sand, 'Daniel assured her, standing up to follow his son, who had gone tearing back to join his sister.

He leaned down and kissed her. 'My dear woman now and always,' he said tenderly, stroking a finger along her cheek before he sprinted down to join his children at the water's edge.

Paula Nolan paced around the small bedroom chewing the inside of her lip. She felt terribly restless. Her mother was fussing and fluttering and making her numerous cups of tea and proffering apple tart and homemade shortbread and telling her she was far too skinny. It was driving her mad.

She sat down on the faded, pink candlewick bedspread draped over the narrow divan bed that sagged in the middle, and remembered how caged and frustrated she'd felt living in this godforsaken backwater. A tsunami of long-forgotten feelings were back, threatening to submerge her. Why she'd let her mother persuade her to come to the annual Lifeboat Fundraiser Dance and Barbecue she had no idea. Well, she had, she supposed. She'd wanted to show off the new convertible; she'd wanted Daniel to see just how well she'd done for herself by leaving this little sleepy seaside village and making a life for herself.

Meeting Ella today had rattled her, though. It was years since she'd last seen her. Then she'd been a spotty teen with greasy hair and braces. The woman she'd met today had a glow of health and happiness that shone in the gleam of her copper curls and bright, sparkling eyes that were devoid of make-up. Her arms and legs were golden from the sun and even though Paula had the most expensive all-over fake tan, it looked faintly orangey compared to Ella's natural colour.

She frowned, remembering the stomach-lurching sense of shock when her mother had told her that Daniel Finn had married Ella Russell. What could he have seen in the gawky teen who'd been so shy she'd blushed every time he looked at her?

Shyness was not a trait she could attribute to herself, she thought wryly, remembering how she'd made all the running to get Daniel to date her. She'd been brazen, flaunting herself at him, and the more he resisted, the more she persisted until eventually he'd agreed to go to a dinner dance with her and they had become an item.

Skinny, lanky, black-haired, Daniel with the piercing blue eyes had been the only man she'd dated whom she totally respected. Daniel, even at twenty, had always been his own man. When she hadn't been able to persuade him to come to New York with her, she'd told him it was over. He'd shrugged and said, 'Suit yourself. Good luck.' And she'd hated him for not even making *some* effort to persuade her to stay. She'd tried to put him out of her head and slowly purged him from her thoughts, until her mother rang her in New York a few years ago to tell her that he was getting married. She'd been shocked. Even though she was dating a high-flying hedge-fund manager, she'd never forgotten Daniel and his rejection of her.

Life in New York had got tough as the recession hit and her job in a high-end interiors-and-design magazine had evaporated when the publishers went belly-up. Being unemployed in NY was not for the faint-hearted, and she didn't want to live off her hard-earned nest egg. Reluctantly, Paula had decided to move back to Ireland. She'd spoofed her way into a PR job in Dublin that was right up her alley, and had bought a penthouse apartment overlooking the seafront in Clontarf. She'd got it for half the price she would have paid for it in the boom years, so, all in all, she hadn't done too badly.

How had Daniel fared in the intervening years? she wondered, irritably waving away a wasp that had flown in the open window. He was probably florid and balding now, she thought nastily, as she stood up and unzipped her trousers and stepped out of them. She pulled her top over her head and studied herself in the long cheval mirror and smiled with wry satisfaction. A woman in her prime, she decided, as she turned sideways and saw her toned, supple body with not an ounce of spare flesh. Her highlighted-blonde hair was cut in a sharp bob and she looked every inch the sophisticated, successful career woman.

'Eat your heart out, Daniel,' she muttered, posing in front of the mirror, wondering how would he feel when he met her at the barbecue. She'd wear her black, strapless Karen Millen dress that clung to every curve of her body and his eyes would follow her every move, she vowed.

But why wait until the party? She'd drive around the winding roads that lead to his stables. Her mother had told her that the Finns had bought Twelve-Acre Field from the Corrys. He might be mucking out his horses or what ever he did with them. If Ella could look wholesome in her denim shorts, *she* would look sexy and alluring, she decided, eyes sparkling with anticipation as she opened her suitcase. She was going to rub Daniel's Finn's nose in it. Let him see what he could have had, if he hadn't been such a stick-in-the mud.

'Aw, Maggie, it's great to see you. Hello, darlings!' Ella hugged her best friend warmly and swooped on the two adorable six-year-old twins who tumbled out of Maggie's beat up Focus.

'Thank God I'm here. The M50 was a car park and the N11 wasn't much better,' Maggie groaned, hugging Ella back. 'Thanks so much for having us, it was unfortunate that Mam's got the builders in; she said the house is a tip. Mind, my house isn't much better,' she added, following Ella into the bright, homely kitchen and gazing around enviously.

'It's so tidy.' She sighed. 'Mine's a breeding ground for MRSA.'

'Stop – your house is lovely,' Ella chided as she filled the kettle and spilled a packet of chocolate gold grain onto a plate.

'Is Paul coming later? I put his name in the pot, I was going to make a steak and kidney pie?'

'Oh, yum!' Maggie exclaimed, plonking herself in the chair and stretching.

The girls raced into the kitchen. 'Mam, can we go with Sally to—'

'Go where you like . . . do what you like, just let me talk to Ella for twenty minutes. We've a lot to catch up on.' Maggie waved them away.

'Thanks, Mam!' They couldn't believe their luck as they galloped back outside to join their friends.

'OMG! Look at my legs; they look like I slashed myself.' Maggie stared in dismay at her long skinny legs that had streaks of dried blood on them. 'I decided I better shave them, it was worse than the Forest of Arden, and the razor was blunt,' she explained dolefully, and Ella giggled. It was great to have her friend staying for a few days. It would be just like old times when they'd shared a flat in Dublin.

'Paul?' she queried again, wondering if Maggie's husband was coming down from Dublin later.

Maggie shrugged, and threw her eyes up to heaven. 'Don't know, is the honest answer. He's installing some new software at work and the computer has to run all night. I'm hoping he'll make it for tomorrow evening but I'm not banking on it.'

'Oh,' Ella murmured. She knew the other couple had issues about Paul's workaholic tendencies.

'Mam, can we change into our swimming togs?' Maggie's twins burst in thought the door.

'What did I say? Twenty minutes for Ella and me.'

'But—'

'Aw—'

'Out! Out! *Out!*' Maggie pointed her finger, and they left, grumbling loudly.

'God Almighty, I brought you into the world; isn't that enough for you?' she declared after their retreating backs. 'What do you want me to do . . . rear you?'

'Maggie, you're incorrigible.' Ella laughed, as she handed her a mug of tea.

'Well, we've more important things to be dealing with. I got your text about Paula. Tell me all. What does she look like? Is she as glam as ever or, by any stroke of all that's fair and wonderful, has she put on a stone and got batwings, and roots that need doing, just like me? Sit down and tell me everything . . . now!'

Ella did as she was bid and sat down at the table to indulge in a long-awaited, deeply satisfying gossip with her old pal.

She saw him before he saw her and couldn't help her sharp indrawn breath as she watched the lean, broad-shouldered man canter a chestnut gelding around the edge of a field. Skinny and lanky he most emphatically was not. Daniel Finn had turned into a real hunk.

He saw her at the three-bar gate and slowed the horse to a trot. Paula swallowed and slid her Moschino sunglasses on to her nose.

'Hello, stranger,' came that familiar slow, lilting drawl.

'Hi, Daniel.' She stared up at him, noting the set of his jaw, the strong aquiline nose, the firm lips that were curved into a grin at the sight of her. She saw his strong muscular arms and long fingers that held the reins so easily and firmly. Her eyes trailed up to the hint of chest hair curling at the open neck of his checked shirt. Old memories came roaring back and she felt a lusty, longing desire for him that shocked her.

He jumped athletically from the saddle, a man at ease with himself and at one with his environment. Most of her boyfriends since Daniel had been sharp-suited business types, who wouldn't know one end of a horse from another. One had even begun dying his hair when the grey started appearing at his temples. Daniel's short black hair had a sprinkling of grey that made him look even sexier, she thought wistfully, as she remembered how he used to kiss her slowly and sensually and—

'Nice set of wheels,' Daniel said admiringly, and she felt more than a tad piqued to realize that he was staring, not at her, but at the car, with a glint of appreciation in his blue eyes.

'Work hard, play hard, I'm worth it,' she asserted, perching her glasses on her head so he could see her expertly made-up eyes.

'I'm sure you are.' He grinned at her, his eyes sliding over her in a long, admiring gaze. 'Are you here for the fundraiser? Didn't think it would be your scene,' he said, easily leaning against the gate that separated them.

'Thought I should come back and see the old home town,' she said lightly.

'And has it lived up to expectations?' His eyes twinkled as he studied her intently.

'We'll see.' She slanted a sultry gaze at him and turned to walk to the car.

'See you at the party, then,' he called, as he mounted the horse, and before she had even turned back to look at him, he was gone, racing across the meadow without a backward glance.

Paula's eyes narrowed and her lips pursed. By the time she was finished with him, he'd be panting for her, she promised herself. And then she'd drop him all over again.

'Oh, my God! Look at her – she thinks she's on the red carpet!' Maggie muttered, as Paula made her entrance into the crowded marquee. 'She looks fabulous. Is there no justice?'

'Great chassis, for sure,' Daniel remarked admiringly, watching the other woman sashay over to some of the lifeboat crew at the bar and start talking to them.

Ella smiled sweetly at him. 'You think so?'

'I do.'

'Really?'

'But not as great as *yours*.' He grinned, swatting her ass.

'Good answer, buster. Now go and get us gals a drink.'

'Yes, ma'am,' replied her husband, who was looking particularly handsome in a pair of cream chinos and a maroon Lacoste short-sleeved shirt.

'OK, look, there's Paul!' Ella announced, as she saw Maggie's husband standing at the entrance, peering around.

Her friend's face creased into a grin. 'Brilliant. Divorce averted for another week,' she declared, as she made her way through the throng towards him.

Two hours later, the marquee heaved to couples dancing to the strains of Elvis singing 'Love Me Tender'.

'You should go and ask her for a dance and put her out of her misery,' Ella murmured against her husband's shoulder. 'She keeps looking over at us.'

'I want to dance with you,' he retorted, nibbling her ear.

'Stop. My mother's looking.' Ella elbowed him in the ribs and he laughed.

'Just for that, I'll dance with Paula; she might appreciate me more than you do,' Daniel announced, before making his way over to his ex, who smiled seductively up at him and slipped into his arms, draping her own around the back of his neck.

As they danced, Daniel winked at her over Paula's shoulder, and Ella smiled back. She was his dear woman and nothing and no one, especially not Paula Nolan, would change that.

Her plan wasn't working. He'd only danced with her once and he'd seemed quite unmoved by her sensual, undulating body as they'd moved around the dance floor.

A new strategy was called for, Paula decided, as she lay in her soft, saggy bed, listening to the sound of a cock crowing and the racket of early-morning bird-song under the eaves. 'Noisy buggers,' she swore, burrowing her head under the pillow.

The car! That was it. She'd offer to take him for a spin in the car. He'd never be able to resist that.

'Sorry, I've a mare in foal and I'm waiting for the vet. I bet Andrew would love a spin, though. Just a quick one. Would you mind?' Daniel asked later that morning when she'd driven over to the yard.

'I've no car seat,' she pointed out, utterly relieved that she could legitimately get out of that request.

'Ah, don't worry about that, just drive up to the house and back, it's on private land so you're fine.' He pointed up to the impressive ivy-clad stone house beyond the paddock. Paula tried to hide her dismay. She didn't want a little brat, who never shut up, in her car. What on earth would she say to a seven-year-old?

She needn't have worried, she thought wryly: he did enough talking for the both of them. Yap, yap, yap . . . Why hadn't Daniel come with her? She'd worn a sexy mini and a low-cut halterneck top. What did it take to get a response from her ex? Paula fretted, driving up the long tree-lined drive that led to the house where Daniel now lived.

'Are your lips not real?'

'What?' she demanded, coming out of her reverie.

'It's rude to say *what*,' Andrew explained kindly.

'Sorry . . . *pardon*!' Paula growled.

'Are your lips not real? Do they come off?'

Paula eyed the little monster in the back seat with venom. 'Why do you say that?'

'My dad said your lips aren't real. They're bigger than they used to be.'

'Your dad said *that*?' She couldn't hide her shock. She'd thought the silicone job was quite discretely done. The boy was unaware of her consternation and prattled on.

'Yep, he said it to my mam. And he said your boobies aren't real, either. He called them *Barbie* boobies!' Andrew guffawed. 'My Dad's really funny sometimes.'

'And what did your mam say?' Paula probed, horrified.

'She laughed and she told him to stop saying that and then my Dad said, "Let me kiss *rea*l lips," and they did *yucky* kissing stuff. Uugggh! Are they real?' he persisted.

Tears smarted Paula's eyes. How *dare* they. How dare that stay-at-home little hick and that bog-trotting clodhopper laugh at *her*.

'Spin's over,' Paula responded sharply, as she spun the steering wheel and did a turn that would have put Lewis Hamilton to shame.

A few minutes later, she pulled up outside the stables, listening to Andrew plead for another chance to put the roof up. Daniel was leaning against a wooden fence, one long, blue-jeaned leg resting on the middle bar, listening intently to something Ella was saying to him. They both looked up as she jumped out and opened the passenger door to evict her young tormentor.

'Have to go,' she said curtly, as Andrew raced over to them and climbed onto the gate.

'Thanks for giving him the spin.' Daniel lifted his son over the top bar.

'A pleasure,' she said, drily, getting back into the car. She raised her chin, waved casually, and gunned the engine. She glanced back in the rear-view mirror and saw, with a lurch, that they weren't even looking at her. Both were looking down at their son, laughing as he gesticulated, and she wasn't even in their consciousness.

Fake lips, fake boobs, fake life, she thought bitterly. There was nothing for her in Clearwater Bay. There was no point in staying.

Later that evening, as Daniel and Paul cooked thick juicy steaks on the barbecue, Maggie and Ella sipped chilled chardonnay and watched the sun set over the gold-glazed sea.

'It was a great weekend, wasn't it?' Maggie raised her glass and inhaled the salty tang of the sea and the aromatic smell of barbecue that wafted along on the breeze.

'Terrific,' agreed her best friend. 'We're so lucky. What more could we ask for?'

'Wouldn't mind a night with Hugh Jackman.' Maggie grinned. 'You?' she asked a little tipsily.

'A night with my darling hubby will do me just fine.' Ella smiled as her husband looked over at her and winked.

The Seventh Floor

'Thank you, Saint Anthony,' she murmurs with heartfelt gratitude, manoeuvring into a tight spot between two cars in front of the terraced red-bricked houses on Leo Street. Mostly, thanks to her entreaties to her favourite saint, and driving into town early, she is lucky on Saturday and Sundays to find a space where there is free parking. On St Joseph Street, across the road, parking has to be paid for 24/7. She has often seen people caught out, and ticketed, and felt sorry for them, They are usually unfortunates in cars with country registrations, who don't know the ins and outs of parking in Dublin.

She only brings the car at the weekend because she can't afford the weekly all-day fees in the Mater Hospital car park. The costs are prohibitive and money is tight now. Have the authorities *any* idea of the added hardship that is inflicted on people who have to visit a seriously ill patient day after day, month after month? she wonders. Not that they care. No one cares for the likes of her.

She sighs, leaning across the passenger seat to haul her tote bag off the floor. Beaumont Hospital is the worst, she decides. A walk to a ward that takes fifteen minutes from the car park, and fifteen minutes back, leaves precious little time for a visit. The queues at the pay stations tip you over the hour, and it all costs a fortune, she thinks crossly, remembering how she would go from three to six euros in the blink of an eye.

Life is harsh, cruel now, post-Celtic Tiger, and ordinary people are ground down, paying for the immoral gambling of bankers, developers and greedy, corrupt politicians. White-collar criminals that lied through their teeth and broke many laws. It enrages her that so many of the perpetrators of heinous crime against the citizens of this benighted isle of so-called Saints and Scholars, continue to live in their big houses, and enjoy their foreign holidays and play golf in their posh golf clubs, scorning the notion that a 'personal guarantee' really applied to *them*. The judges, far removed from the hardship of the hoi polloi, have put none of these gurriers behind bars. And why would they? They're all in the same clique, playing golf and enjoying fine dining and giving each other the nod about stocks and shares and when to buy and when to flip. You scratch my back, I scratch yours.

She is grumpy this morning, she acknowledges, heartily sick of the daily trek, and the effort to be positive and supportive. How *she* would love to be the one being nurtured and cherished and supported, she thinks sorrowfully, easing her arthritic body out of the car.

'Stop it!' she chides herself aloud. She cannot afford to give into weakness. She has to be strong. At least she will have the luxury of coming out to her car, and not having to wait for a bus to get her home this evening, she comforts herself, double-checking that the door of the Yaris is locked.

Leo Street is quiet, resting in the early-morning pale wishy-washy October sunlight. A black cat is sitting outside a crimson door, vigorously licking herself clean – the only sign of life. Curtains and blinds are still drawn, shutting out the day as people take their Saturday morning lie-in. A puff of wind tosses crispy golden leaves in the air and they frolic down to her feet, reminding her that autumn has arrived and she needs to get her gas geyser serviced. More money. She is considering installing a wood-burning stove. Gas-heating is so expensive now and their savings are dwindling.

She stifles a yawn. She would *love* a lie-in, she thinks wistfully, rounding the corner to the NCR and making her way to the automatic doors of the new Whitty Building, opposite Mountjoy's women's prison.

The Mater Misericordiae Hospital. *Misericordiae,* meaning 'mercy' or 'pity' in Latin. *Misery* in her vocabulary, she thinks wryly, holding her hands under the sanitizer and rubbing the gel onto her palms and between her fingers. She would like a cup of coffee and a cookie but the prices charged by the small café are unbelievably exorbitant and she has her flask of tea and a sandwich in her bag. She steps onto the escalator and ascends slowly to the first floor.

The hospital is eerily quiet, unlike weekdays when patients, visitors and medical personnel throng the corridors. All the services are pared back at the weekend. People are only allowed to be sick and have needs fulfilled from Monday to Friday. Her husband will get no badly needed physio or doctor visits, no X-rays, tests, *nothing!* It is a five-day hospital, thanks to cutbacks. Her eighty-five-year-old brother was thrown out of a private hospital, with undiagnosed pneumonia, on a Friday morning, due to ward closures for the weekend because of pressures from health-insurance companies. He ended up at death's door and in hospital for another six weeks because of a crazy, dangerous and short-sighted strategy that cost the private-health-insurance company thousands more than his original hospital stay should have done.

It's all about 'beds' now, not patients. If only the nuns were in charge of the HSE, it would be a different kettle of fish, she ruminates. The hospitals went to pot once the nuns withdrew from running them and 'managers' took over. She gives a delicate snort. Bad scran to the 'managers'. They needed to spend a few days lying on a trolley in A&E and it might change their tune.

She walks along the deserted corridor, lined with empty clinics, that leads to the lifts, and becomes aware of footsteps echoing behind her. Not a doctor, or a consultant, she decides. They walk with brisk strides. Always in a hurry. Places to go, people to see. Don't get in my way, please. Not a nurse in squeaky soled shoes, or an administrator click-clacking along in high heels. She knows the distinct types after all these months.

It's a man and he's gaining on her as she turns right and crosses to the bank of lifts. He overtakes just as the steel doors open to one of the lifts and she follows him in. He jabs his finger on the seventh floor button and glances at her enquiringly. 'The same,' she responds. He leans against the handrail and she rests against the opposite one.

'Doors closing,' the automated voice says and then they are cocooned in their steel box with the big glass wall that looks out onto the new hospital complex, and the unexpected vista of the green purple smudged Dublin mountains in the distance.

Will the man chat? she wonders. Some people do, some people don't. He's not a doctor. He's a tired, careworn, middle-aged man in a crumpled suit, and if he's going to the seventh floor, life is hard for him, she reflects.

'Not a bad day,' he says politely, making the effort.

'No,' she agrees, injecting a false note of cheer into her voice, 'not a bad day at all.'

'We did well this year,' he observes, as the lift glides slowly upwards and the sun spills over the autumn-dabbed mountains, a backdrop to the massive glass link corridors to the old hospital.

He has a West of Ireland accent. Connemara, perhaps, she guesses.

'It will shorten the winter.' She tries to be as positive as he's been.

'True.' The lift judders to a halt and he courteously stands back to let her out.

'Thank you,' she murmurs, unconsciously taking a deep breath, as they walk towards the entrance to the seventh floor, mentally preparing herself before passing through the big grey doors that lead to the oncology wards.

He inhales too and they smile at each other. 'Hard, isn't it?' she says.

'*Very*.' He exhales a gale force sigh. 'How long have you been coming?'

'Eleven months. You?' They slow down to talk.

'Three,' he says. 'You're a veteran.' His eyes crinkle in a smile. They are cornflower blue like her husband's.

'You could say that.' She smiles at his droll humour.

'My son is very ill,' he volunteers hesitantly. 'And you?'

'My husband,' she says, passing through the door he holds open for her. There is no need for histories, descriptions and comparisons. They are on the seventh floor, that is enough.

'Hard,' he says again. 'Very hard.'

'It's the anxiety.' She grimaces. 'The constant, grinding anxiety and getting the phone calls that make you think this is it!'

'*Exactly!* We've had a few of those, too.' He nods empathically as they walk along the entrance hallway towards the long corridor that houses the wards. 'There's nothing worse than being called in.'

They stop at the intersection. 'I'm this way.' He indicates right.

'I'm the other.' She smiles at him.

'Where there's life there's hope,' he says, and, as if it was the most natural thing in the world he reaches out spontaneously to pat her back.

She gives him a hug and they stand there, two strangers comforting each other. They give each other one last smile before they go their separate ways. 'God go with you,' he says, raising his hand in farewell.

'And with *you*,' she responds fervently. 'And with you.' She hears his footsteps, solid and determined, fade away and she turns left.

'Come on, old girl, chin up,' she encourages herself, walking past the nurses' station. Her knees ache, as does her neck, a creaking jagged unforgiving pain that keeps her awake at night. She is bone weary.

She stops at the green door behind which her husband lies in a bed that puffs and blows, surrounded by bleeping machines, and tubes and drips and lines, and grey cartons for vomit, and rubber gloves and pill cups, all the accouterments of the very ill.

She takes another deep breath and pastes a smile on her face as she has done, day in, day out, week upon week, month upon month, for all of this long, exhausting year.

She glances to her right, there is no one else around, the man is gone from sight, but further along the corridor she knows that he is doing the same as her, putting on the brave face, showing courage, being kind and adapting to a world that has narrowed to this, the seventh floor of a hospital, where the most part of their life is now spent.

Nothing has changed, but this day *is* different, she acknowledges. Two strangers have brought comfort to each other because they understood the silent suffering of the other. This brief, enriching encounter will keep her going for a while. She has been bolstered and uplifted just when she had begun to wilt.

She opens the door. 'Good morning, love. How are you today?' She greets her husband as she always does, remembering her fellow traveller's words: 'Where there's life there's hope.'

MOTHER'S DAY

One Small Step

I need assertiveness classes, I think to myself, as simmering with irritation as I stuff a turkey that I do not want to stuff, let alone eat. I'm *really* annoyed at myself. Once again, I've let my older sister walk all over me and behaved like an absolute doormat. Mad as I am at her, I'm even madder at myself.

I do beg your pardon. How rude of me to launch off like that without even introducing myself. My name is Jessie Barnsley. I'm a forty-year-old wife, mother of two, freelance copy editor, palm-curling PMT sufferer and, right now, doormat. Let me fill you in before we go any further. Monica, my eldest sister, married to flashy git Kenneth, who likes to be called Ken, is having her annual family barbecue.

Because it's family and we are very definitely B list, she doesn't bother with caterers, not when the rest of us can turn to and bring an assortment of grub. I get a phone call from her four days before the big event: 'Bring the turkey over as soon as it's cooked so I can carve it and plate it up before the others arrive. Lia [sister-in-law] can do up the salads, I'll sort out the ribs and burgers for the barbecue.' Monica issues her instructions like a sergeant major.

'Do we really *need* a turkey? I don't like cold turkey,' I say, a tad irritably, it has to be said. PMT is beginning to kick in and besides, I have a deadline that is fast looming. I'm way behind schedule. I don't have *time* to cook turkey! I tell my sister this.

'*What?*' Monica is clearly taken aback by my lack of enthusiasm. 'Of course we need a turkey. We *always* have a turkey. All you have to do is bung it in the oven. You know Gran and Granddad won't eat barbecue food. You know how conservative they are. And neither will Marcus after getting the trots . . . no, sorry . . . "*salmonella*" last year at Suzy Carter's charity barbie.' Monica drips with sarcasm – she doesn't like Marcus, her brother-in-law. Mind, I'm not mad about him myself. Apart from being a hypochondriac of the highest order, he gives me the creeps. His hugs are gropy sort of hugs, if you know what I mean. You just don't want to be left in a room alone with him. He sneaked up behind me one Christmas and I get the shivers just thinking about it.

Monica is rabbiting on. 'He's such a wussie, honestly. He doesn't just get a headache, he gets a brain tumour, and as for . . .' I tune out and let her at it. Why does she bother going to such trouble when it's clearly an ordeal? It's become a sort of family tradition now, though, Monica's barbecue. She had the first one six years ago and, between yourself and myself and I know this is a bitchy thing to say about my own sister, but it wasn't for the love of us all. It was only to show off her posh new house in Malahide with the fabulous sea views and landscaped garden. The first year, she and Ken looked after the cooking, but the following year, when she decided to have one again and get all the family entertaining out of the way 'in one fell swoop' as she rather crassly put it, Lia, our sister-in-law, kindly suggested we all bring a dish.

That wasn't too bad. I did three dozen savoury vol-au-vents; but since then, I've ended up cooking a twenty-five pound turkey for the past couple of years and it's a nuisance. I mean, it's *her* decision to have a family barbecue, not mine. So why should *I* have to suffer? Why does she do it year after year, if it's such a drag? I suppose she feels she has to now. It's expected of her. Everybody groans at the thought of going, but we usually end up having a bit of a laugh at the end of the day.

'I could do a salmon,' I say now, interrupting her anti-Marcus diatribe.

'Orla's doing salmon, you do the turkey as usual and bring a bottle of gin or vodka . . .'

I feel my blood boil – Monica and Ken like spirits, Ronan, my long-suffering husband, and I prefer wine. 'Monica, Ronan and I aren't mad about spirits; we prefer to drink wine,' I explain.

'Oh, for God's sake!' Monica can't hide her exasperation. 'There'll be plenty of wine here. Look, I have to go, Ken's entertaining some colleagues from London and I have to have a manicure and get my hair done. Bye.' She sounds distinctly tetchy, huffy even. My heart sinks. Monica in a huff is not for the faint-hearted. She does huffy better than anyone else I know and can stay frosty for weeks.

So that's how, this Sunday morning, I'm up at seven-thirty, stuffing a huge, fat, white-skinned, blue-veined turkey, with extreme bad grace. This year, I've cheated. I've bought ready-made apricot-and-walnut stuffing instead of making my own. I rub the skin with lemon to crisp it up, lace the breast with streaky bacon, swaddle it in tinfoil and manoevre the roasting dish into the oven. I still feel hard done by. Resentment has multiplied in the four days since my conversation with Monica. That turkey is proof positive that I do not count in her eyes. She did not listen to one word that I said to her.

A) I don't like cold turkey.

B) I'm tied for time and am under pressure with my work. I was up until 1 a.m. this morning, editing, and am bog-eyed with tiredness.

C) Although I don't drink spirits, I am still expected to bring a bottle of gin or vodka.

What is it about Monica that makes her feel that what she wants is far more important than anything I might want? Why are my feelings and desires of no consequence and why do I put up with her bullying? Because frankly, that's what it is. Bullying and a lack of respect. Monica doesn't rate my copy editing as a job at all. As far as she's concerned, I'm at home all day, so I don't 'work.' She feels perfectly free to ring up and ask me to collect her children from the crèche, because she's been delayed at a very important 'strategy planning session'. She works as PA to a stockbroker and likes to think she's at the cutting edge of high finance.

Don't think that I mind helping someone when they're stuck. That's not it. It's just, week in, week out, I'm expected to drop everything and run to her assistance. What really bugs me is that she expects it of me and I find it so hard to put my foot down and say no. Enough is enough. Ronan, my kind and lovely husband, tells me that I have to make a stand.

Am I being super-sensitive? I ask myself over and over. I don't think so and, today, I've made a decision: this is the last turkey I cook for Monica's damn barbecues.

Bits of stuffing are caught under my rings so I rinse them under the tap and gaze out at my garden. It is a lovely late-summer's morning, Monica is always lucky with her weather. Sweet pea and roses scent the air and my damson tree is heavy with ripening fruit. Soon, I'll pick them and make pots of ruby red jam that my children will spread on thick chunks of bread slathered with butter.

I hear the pitter-patter of feet down the stairs and my two-and-a-half-year-old daughter, Millie, bursts into the kitchen, blue eyes wide and clear, golden curls dancing, ''Allo, Mammy. I'ss hungry,' she declares. I bend down and sweep her into my arms, nuzzling her neck, inhaling the delicious baby scent of her. I adore her, and my four-year-old son, Adam.

I'm very lucky really, in case you think my life is all gloom and doom. I have a really happy family life. Sometimes I think Monica is a little envious. She might have loads of money, a big house and 'high-flying' career, but Kenneth aka Ken is not the ideal husband – his career is everything. He's a pilot, and I think he plays away. Monica is very insecure about his fidelity. I know I'm being judgmental here, but I wouldn't put it past him. He thinks he's God's gift to women.

'I'ss hungry, Mammy,' Millie repeats indignantly, and I kiss her again and open the fridge to get her an Actimel and milk for her cereal.

The aroma of roasting turkey fills the kitchen as the hours pass, reminding me of Christmas. My mouth waters as I eventually lift the crisp golden bird from the roasting dish four and a half hours later. 'Looks good, Jessie,' Ronan approves as he slides the big plate underneath it and carries it to the table for me. He and Adam dive on the crisp streaky bacon.

'Yummy yum yum!' Adam grins, grease dripping down his chin. 'You're a brill cook, Mam.' Ronan and I smile at each other over his head and I feel a moment of happiness. How lucky I am to love and be loved. They are going to play football in the park, my precious husband and son. I warn them to be back before two. We are expected at Monica's for three. Millie is having her nap.

My men leave the house, still chomping on crispy bacon, and absent-mindedly, I pick at the stuffing that is overflowing onto the big oval serving plate. It's scrumptious. And I'm starving. A wild, reckless madness overcomes me. I grab the carving knife and fork and slice into the smooth, perfectly cooked succulent breast. Juices ooze out. I carve again and lay the steaming white slices onto a plate. I pull some of the rich dark meat from under the wings and lay it neatly beside the breast. My fingers are sticky and I lick them, teasing myself with the taste of what is to come. I spoon out stuffing and take a jar of cranberry sauce from the cupboard. I dress the slices of meat with rich red cranberries and shake pepper and salt over my feast. Exhilarated, I pour myself a glass of chilled white wine. Sitting at the kitchen table, I cut a white piece of hot meat, add a dark piece, press some stuffing on top and ease my fork into the steaming, succulent food. I eat slowly, savouring the contrasting moist flavours. It is *delicious*. I have surpassed myself this year. I congratulate myself, taking a sip of cool, tart wine. Tension evaporates. I feel perfectly at peace as the silence of the house wraps itself around me. This is the life.

We arrive half an hour late at Monica's. We got delayed playing a game of skittles with the children.

My sister is doing her nut. 'You're late. Bring the turkey into the kitchen until I carve it,' she hisses at me as she ushers Ronan and the children ahead of her. She looks the height of elegance in her red linen trousers and black sleeveless DKNY top. I carry the tinfoil-wrapped plate carefully, reverently. Ken is out on the deck in a chef's hat and apron, presiding over his smoking barbecue. He hails us in his faux-hearty tones, reserved for lesser family mortals and those he feels superior to.

'Jamie Oliver, eat your heart out,' Ronan murmurs, giving me a wink.

I laugh and Monica turns and glares at me. That makes me laugh even more. I'm a little tipsy. The two glasses of wine I've already had have gone to my head. I'm not used to drinking in the middle of the day. I follow Monica into her state-of-the-art kitchen and place the turkey on the island. Monica is all business-like. Impatiently, she pulls away the tinfoil, anxious to get carving. Her jaw drops.

'What's happened to the turkey?' she squawks.

'Oh, I had mine hot. It was delicious,' I say off-handedly as I pull a couple of bottles of wine out of the tote bag on my shoulder. 'You might want to put these in the fridge to chill for later,' I add calmly. I even smile at her before stepping out through the patio doors to join my husband and children.

DIFFICULT DAYS

The Unexpected Visit

My granddaughter, Isobel, has come to visit me today. When I hear the knock on the door and open it to find her on the step, I'm surprised but, nevertheless, delighted to see her.

It's been a while since she's called to see me – Christmas, actually – and it does my heart good to see her all rosy-cheeked and windswept, her glorious black hair tumbling from its topknot as the wild easterly wind gives a gusty howl and nearly blows the door off the hinges.

'Come in, pet,' I urge, ushering her into the hall before closing the door on the melancholy, wintry afternoon.

'Oh, Nan, it's so warm and cosy in here!' Isobel exclaims, bending to kiss my cheek. A cloying sweet scent from one of the designer perfumes she so favours wafts behind her as she walks ahead of me into the sitting room. She unwinds the scarf from around her neck and unbuttons the fashion-able belted black woollen coat she wears and drops both onto the sofa, before hurrying to stand in front of the fire, hands out to the blaze.

'I love a real fire,' my granddaughter enthuses. 'I wish I had one in the flat, or even better, a stove with lots of glass. They heat the place brilliantly,' she burbles away, words tumbling out in that breathlessly animated way she has of speaking. 'My friends . . . remember Clare, who married Leo?' She cocks an eye at me. 'They have a wood burner in their house. They're so lucky!' Isobel frowns, eyes darkening with sulky disgruntlement. 'I never thought Clare would be married before me. She never went out with fellas until she met Leo. And now she's married, and has her own house and I'm manless and renting an apartment I can't afford!'

I'm very fond of Clare; she and Isobel have been friends since childhood. She is the giver in their relationship. Shaded and diminished by Isobel's shining effervescence. It has always been so.

I give an inward sigh. Isobel's grand romance ended unexpectedly six months previously and I know I'm in for an afternoon of whiny self-pity. It shocks me to think, in spite of so-called women's liberation and feminism and the like, if a girl hasn't got a man on her arm, she considers herself a failure.

I'm eighty now, and it was the same in my day! Spinsterhood was the greatest fear for my friends and me. Spinsterhood might have been preferable for some of them, I reflect, remembering several of the unlucky ones who made bad marriages and suffered physical and emotional abuse, or in one case, poverty because of gambling. Two friends had husbands who weren't faithful, another found out her husband was gay and the marriage was his cover. I was lucky in my marriage, although like most couples, we had our ups and downs.

'Sit down and I'll make a pot of tea.' I put on a bright smile. I had been about to watch an old black-and-white Bette Davis film on one of the movie channels and had been rather looking forward to it, but it behoves me to make some sort of effort at entertaining. I wait to see if my granddaughter will tell me to sit down and offer to make the tea, but I should know better. She sprawls herself in the armchair opposite mine, kicks off her high heels, wriggles her toes in front of the flames and settles in to be pampered.

'Have you any of your to-die-for cream sponge?' she wheedles, her brown eyes glinting in anticipation, a smile curving her crimson rosebud lips. Isobel is beautiful. She reminds me of Ava Gardner. That wild, ripe luscious beauty that is at its best in the late twenties and thirties, before it gets blowsy.

I leave my granddaughter to toast by the fire and put the kettle on and get down china plates, cups and saucers. Old-fashioned, I know, but tea from a china cup is the only way to drink it. I have no cream sponge today, but I know Isobel will enjoy a slice of my cherry-and-walnut cake. The kettle sings as I stand looking out at the sleeting rain that has begun to fall, and the sullen leaden sky grows even more oppressive, threatening snow. It has been a hard February this year, with very little hint of spring.

I wet the tea and pop a tea cosy over the pot to let it brew. Is Isobel on or off the milk, I wonder. Probably off, seeing as it's after Christmas and she could be doing one of her 'detoxing' carry-ons.

'Are you still taking your tea black?' I bring in the tray with the cups and plates of cake. She has her head bent to her phone, thumbs flying over the keys.

'No milk, thanks,' she murmurs without raising her head. What is it with people today that they are so addicted to these yokes? They can hardly go for a pee without texting or taking photos of themselves and Facebooking and Twittering. I have never seen such self-absorption. They need the world to know the boring minutiae of their shallow lives. It mystifies me. I saw Isobel and her ex taking a photo of themselves with her phone! 'It's called a selfie,' my granddaughter explained, having made sure that the angle was right, and the light, and so on and so forth. Me, me, me! The selfie generation, and they call this progress!

'So, to what do I owe the pleasure of this unexpected treat?' I ask lightly, smiling down at my granddaughter as I pour her tea and hand her the cup and saucer.

'Oh, I had to take a flexi day or I'd lose it, so I decided to come for a visit. It's been ages since I've seen you,' Isobel says, before biting into the buttered cake.

'Hmm, it *has* been a while.' I try to keep the tartness out of my tone. The last time Isobel had dropped in, she'd needed money for her car insurance. Don't get me wrong, I love my grandchild. She and her younger brother, Richard, were a great source of joy to Dara, my late husband, and me, when they were young. We loved them as our own and spent many happy hours spoiling them and loving them as only grandparents can. But as they grew older and began to lead more independent lives, the visits grew less frequent.

'Eaten bread is soon forgotten,' Dara had growled grumpily when Richard once told him he couldn't come and sweep out the yard and cut the grass because he was going hiking with friends. He'd promised he'd do it the next weekend he was free. It never happened, of course, and in the end, we got someone in to cut the grass and do a few odd jobs, twice a month because Dara's failing health meant he wasn't able to look after the garden, which had been his pride and joy.

I'd hoped my son, Eamonn, might urge Isobel and Richard to help us out a bit more as old age clipped our wings, but he was so busy with his financial-services business, we weren't on his radar either. I was disappointed, to tell you the truth. Had our rearing of our son contributed to his self-preoccupation? I was worse than Dara for spoiling Eamonn, I have to admit. I treated him like a little prince, so proud of his academic success that I would let him off his chores so he could study or spend time with his friends.

I expected more of my daughter, Emily, and indeed she was, and is, a good and dependable girl who takes excellent care of me now that her father has passed to his eternal rest and I am on my own. Emily, a primary-school teacher, works hard and has reared two sons who have both emigrated to Canada. They are loving it and Emily has been over to visit them in Toronto several times. Emily lives in a midland town and she drives up to Dublin every Saturday to shop for me and do whatever chores I need doing. It was Emily who persuaded me to get a woman in to 'do' for me every morning.

'You can well afford it, Mam,' she urged. 'Spend your money on yourself, you've worked long and hard enough, there's no pockets in a shroud,' my daughter said firmly when I protested. I felt guilty at the thought of spending some of my nest egg employing someone to clean and iron, as though I was the landed gentry and too lazy to do my own housework. Though I put it off for a long time, protesting that I was well able to look after myself, my arthritis slowed me down terribly, and when Lily, the woman Emily found for me, came to do the few hours every morning, I wondered how I'd ever managed without her. I love hearing her key in the door, and her cheery, 'Are you up, love? I'm here. I'll put the kettle on,' roar up the stairs. Lily is a fount of news and information and, at this stage, I know as much about her family as I do about my own. What I love most about her is her authenticity. There's no side to Lily. What you see is what you get. A genuine salt-of-the-earth soul with a great heart. I always feel Dara is minding me from beyond the grave and that he sent Lily to me to help fill the aching gap his going has left in my life.

'How much do you pay her?' my daughter-in-law, Gina, asked me bluntly when I told her I was getting someone to clean for me. Gina is Isobel's mum, and Eamonn's wife. We get on well enough, but Gina is nosy and I don't like that in a person.

'That's between Lily and me,' I'd said firmly, and she hadn't asked again.

Isobel picks up the remote control and starts to flick the channels. 'Oohh, *The Big Bang Theory*, I love that. You aren't watching anything, Nan, are you?' She takes a gulp of tea and settles back comfortably in the chair. Now, I do rather like *The Big Bang Theory* myself – the characters and dialogue make me laugh – but I'm a tad annoyed at madam's appropriation of the remote control, as Bette Davis disappears off the TV screen.

'I thought you came to visit me, not watch TV.' I give her the eye over the top of my specs.

'Sorry, I never get to see TV in the afternoon; it must be lovely to be retired and be able to do whatever you want.' She gives a deep, peeved sigh but mutes the sound.

'It's wonderful,' I say drily. 'Especially now that I can't drive any more and can't go to all the places I used to go to, like the library, and into town to visit art galleries, or for a walk on the seafront, or even to visit your grandfather's grave.'

'Oh! I must bring you sometime,' she says airily, not meeting my gaze.

'So what's new in your life? How's work? Any new fella on the scene?' I don't want her to think I'm giving broad hints to get lifts to the grave, even though I am. I miss my weekly visit to change the flowers and keep the plot tidy.

'Nope, no man. I'm not going down that road again, Nan. That Gary Finlay toad was two-timing me big time! And he took half the Egyptian cotton bed linen and two of my Orla Kiely bath sheets when he moved out of the apartment. My lease is up at the end of February, and the landlord is looking to increase the rent. I'll have to let it go. I won't be able to afford another decent flat unless I share with someone and I so don't want to do that!' Her pretty face darkens into a glower and I think to myself how spoilt her generation is with their posh sheets and designer towels and sense of supreme entitlement.

Dara and I bought our bed linen and towels in Denis Guiney's in Talbot Street – the same as half of Dublin – and only then when we could afford them. No such thing as credit cards. It was the HP in our day. But I never bought anything on the hire purchase; I was too afraid of getting into debt.

'Will you move back home?' I throw a log on the fire and watch the sparks fly up the chimney, before it catches and yellow flames lick and curl around the sides.

'That's such a backward step, Nan,' Isobel sighs. 'I'm nearly thirty. I can't go back to living with Mum and Dad. I've got used to my independence.'

'Well, we have to cut our cloth to suit our measure.' I trot out my mother's favourite saying. 'You'll surely find someone compatible to share with. With all these rent increases, there are plenty of young people in the same boat as yourself.'

'Hmm. All I need is a good-sized room to get me over the hump until I find somewhere I can afford,' she says with studied nonchalance, giving me a smile that doesn't quite reach her watchful eyes.

And then the penny drops.

Isobel wants to come and live upstairs in the big front room that used to be Dara's and my bedroom. It's a beautiful room with a bay window – bright, airy, high-ceilinged. It would make a very nice bedsit indeed.

Two years after my husband passed away and as my mobility lessened, at Emily's urgings, I renovated the house so that the small box room is now an ensuite with a walk-in shower. It adjoins the second bedroom, at the back of the house, where I now sleep. It too is a sunny, serene room overlooking the copse of trees at the end of my garden and I love the way the sunlight filters through the foliage, even in these dark days of winter when the thin bony branches are skeletal and undressed.

'A bedsit sounds just the thing,' I say non-committally but, inside, I'm raging. Only the other day, Gina had casually mentioned how much she enjoys not having to kill herself doing housework now that Richard and Isobel no longer live at home. Eamonn has turned Isobel's bedroom into an office, she declares. It's ideal for him.

Gina and Isobel are in cahoots. They have it all worked out. Lonely, afflicted Nan would be only delighted to have her granddaughter come to live with her for a while. Rent-free too, I bet. So there *is* an ulterior motive behind this unexpected visit. Just like my granddaughter's last one when her car-insurance money was needed and she was broke. I'd paid up, to a gushing flood of thanks and promises to drive me wherever I needed to go.

Anger and hurt swell and swirl inside. I am being used again, made a convenience of by my own kith and kin. My grandchild that I used to cuddle and kiss and spoil and romp with now sees me as an easy touch, as I'm beginning to fear, does her mother.

Well, madam, you'll not be getting your feet under my table now or in the future, I think coldly.

Don't get me wrong, if Isobel was in trouble or homeless, she could have that room with a heart and a half, but she's not getting it like this. Sneakily. Opportunistically. I will not be her or Gina's doormat.

I'll be keeping a wary eye on Miss Isobel and Master Richard. I've been thinking about updating my will for a while now. I want to make it more in Emily's favour; after all, she is the one who does all the running around for me, and my son is happy to leave her do it. I want to leave a decent bequest to Lily, too. 'Kindness is as kindness does.' Another favourite quote of Mother's. Isobel, Richard and Gina will weep and wail at my funeral, and be the first to read my will, but Emily and Lily are the ones who will truly grieve me.

I am nobody's fool. I still have my marbles. I know a set-up when I see one.

I silently thank God for these mercies.

'Have another slice of cake, Isobel,' I say briskly. 'And turn up the sound on *The Big Bang Theory*. I have today's paper here; we might as well have a laugh before we go looking for your new abode.'

Isobel's jaw drops! Her eyes widen in dismay as I casually flick through the paper to find the apartments-to-let section.

'*Bazinga!*' As Sheldon would say!

Fairweather Friend

'Why do you bother going on holiday with Melissa Harris? She's such a cow. She only uses you, you know,' Denise Irvine said crossly, as she forked chicken korma into her mouth and took a sip of white wine.

Sophie glowered at her sister. 'She's not *that* bad!' she snapped irritably, dipping a piece of naan bread into her tikka masala sauce.

'Oh, come on, Sophie, she's a walking bitch and always has been. She drops you like a hot potato as soon as there's a bloke on the scene and then you don't see her for dust until she's ditched and needs a shoulder to cry on. You're too soft with her and always have been. It's time you told her where to get off. Remember last year, you were supposed to go on holiday with her and then she dropped you at the last minute because she met Mister Wonderful, and took off to Ibiza with him?' Denise pronged a stuffed mushroom and ate it with relish.

Sophie looked at her younger sister with envy. Denise could eat and drink all round her and not put on an ounce. She'd be up two pounds at least on the scales after this pig-out.

'What happened to Mister Wonderful, anyway?' Denise topped up their wineglasses. 'I thought they were going back to Ibiza.'

'She found out that he was two-timing her. She's in bits, really she is, Denise. I've never seen her this bad,' Sophie said earnestly. 'She was crazy about Tony, really nuts about him. He was the love of her life.'

'Don't be daft, Sophie!' Denise scoffed. 'How could *he* be the love of her life? She's so passionately in love with herself, there's no room for anyone else.'

'Oh, leave her alone,' Sophie muttered.

'Well, *I* would have told her where to get off, if she'd asked me to go on holiday with only a week's notice after her behaviour last year,' Denise retorted, helping herself to a portion of aloo saag.

It's all right for you, Sophie thought glumly, as she studied her bright-eyed, immaculately groomed, supremely confident younger sister. Denise had friends to beat the band and men fell over themselves trying to get a date with her. She breezed through life with not a care in the world, the epitome of the career woman about town. She thrived in her busy job as a publicist in a large publishing company and at the age of twenty-two, drove her own company car.

Sophie, two years older, drove an ancient Fiesta that she'd had for the last six years. She was a paediatric nurse and while she enjoyed her job, she felt that her life lacked the glamour and excitement of that of her sister's.

Sophie's two closest friends had got married within six months of each other and in the last two years she'd had no one to go abroad with. The idea of going on a singles holiday filled her with dread. Hence the acceptance of the offer of two weeks in Majorca with Melissa Harris. Sophie sighed and took a slug of her Australian Sauvignon. She'd known Melissa since her school days. Blonde, blue-eyed, bubbly and indescribably self-obsessed, Melissa was the centre of the universe in her own eyes, or, as Denise cruelly christened her, *The Queen of the Me, Me, Me Planet*. An only child, spoilt by doting parents, Melissa swanned through life accepting adoration as her due.

In Sophie, she had the perfect handmaiden. It had always been so, from the moment in junior choir when Melissa decided that she preferred Sophie's little black velvet bow to the red ribbon that adorned her golden ponytail. Sophie had handed over the bow unquestioningly, mesmerized by the baby-blue eyes batting perfect long black lashes at her and thrilled beyond measure at the invitation to join Melissa's gang. Although the entire class aspired to be a member of Melissa's entourage, only the chosen few were given the honour.

The honour was withdrawn regularly according to Melissa's mood and whim, and Sophie would find herself on the outside of the golden circle until Melissa had need of her services again. This was the pattern of their friendship, through childhood, teens, and while Melissa studied to become a beauty therapist and Sophie was a student nurse.

Weeks could go by and Sophie wouldn't hear a peep from Melissa and then some crisis would occur and Melissa would arrive at Sophie and Denise's flat in search of TLC, and sympathy, while she sobbed over her latest heartbreak and declared that 'All Men Were Bastards'.

Tony Jenkins was the most recent addition to the AMWB's list. He and Melissa had been scheduled to take Ibiza by storm again until Melissa had discovered him in a steamy clinch with a beautician colleague at a friend's engagement party. It seemed they were having a rip-roaring affair.

'I really loved him,' Melissa wept. 'I just don't understand what he sees in her, Sophie. She's an awful airhead and she's got cellulite! When I think of all the times I did electrolysis on her – she has a terrible hairy lip – I should have let the needle slip and scarred the bitch for life.'

Sophie made a mental note *never* to have Melissa do electrolysis on her. Not that Melissa ever did beauty treatments for her, now that she was qualified. It had been a different kettle of fish when she'd been training and needed guinea pigs. Sophie had been manicured, pedicured and French polished, not to mention tweezed and waxed within an inch of her life. *That* had been painful!

'That tart is going to Ibiza with him. Can you *believe* it?' Melissa was incandescent with rage, her usually flawless porcelain skin mottled red with temper. 'Soph, you simply have to come on holiday with me. I'm damned if Jayne' – the cellulite afflicted 'other woman' – 'is going to come into the salon sporting a tan and showing off photos of her and The Rat.

'We'll go somewhere and get the best tan ever and find the most gorgeous hunks to take care of us and our photos will make that two-timing toad pea-green with jealousy. I'll make sure he gets to see them. I'll post them on Facebook. Bet he still looks at my page. But even if he comes crawling on his hands and knees, he's history, Soph. I'll go straight to the travel agent's tomorrow and book a holiday for us.'

Melissa assumed automatically that Sophie would drop everything and be thrilled to go on holidays with her.

'I don't know, it's very short notice. I wasn't planning to go abroad,' she'd protested. 'I'm a bit skint.'

'Don't be silly, Sophie. What do you mean, short notice? You're not doing *anything* are you? You weren't planning on going away, were you?' Melissa scowled. 'I'm skint too. When I found out about The Skunk and that phony so-called friend, I went out and blew a fortune on this gorgeous Dolce & Gabbana dress. It's to die for, Sophie, but my Visa card is having a nervous breakdown, so it will have to be a cheapie for me too. But who cares? We'll strut our stuff on the beach and we won't have to spend a penny,' Melissa retorted confidently, her eyes beginning to sparkle at the thought of her next conquest.

A fortnight in the sun would be nice, Sophie thought dreamily. Lazing on a lounger with a big blockbuster Jackie Collins novel and a Piña Colada or a dressed Pimm's, while Melissa strutted her perfectly toned and sculptured stuff. Sophie would be quite content to lie on her lounger, her flabby bits not being at all suitable for strutting.

Two weeks later, they were sitting in a bar at the airport, waiting to board a TransAer flight to Majorca. They'd been delayed for three hours and Melissa was frothing at the mouth. 'This is bloody ridiculous. The plane hasn't even left Palma yet. We're going to be here for hours. That's a whole day wasted. It will be the middle of the night before we get to . . . Portal . . . Portal . . . wherever that place we're going to is.'

'Portal Nous,' Sophie murmured.

'I hope it's going to be a bit lively. It's three miles from Palma Nova. It was all I could get at such short notice,' Melissa fretted.

'It will be fine, Mel, stop panicking,' Sophie placated. 'Now let's have coffee and a sandwich, I'm hungry.' Her nerves were frayed. Three hours of Melissa whingeing and moaning about their delayed flight and the devastating betrayal she'd suffered at the hands of The Unmentionable was doing her head in.

'Oh, no, not coffee. Let's go and get pissed.' Melissa flung back her golden hair and uncoiled herself from the hard chair she'd been sitting on, quite aware that every male's eyes in the vicinity were upon her. She undulated towards the bar in her skin-tight white jeans and tightly fitting black halterneck.

Sophie's heart sank. If Melissa went on the sauce, she was in for a load of hassle. Melissa, unfortunately, could not drink, and always needed looking after when she was the worse for wear. Many were the times Sophie had hauled her into loos, or shoved her head out taxi windows as she threw up all round her.

'Now, Melissa, go easy, you've already had three tequila slammers,' she warned.

'Oh, quit it, Soph! You're not my mother!' Melissa snapped as she ordered another drink. 'Do you want one?' she asked ungraciously.

'OK, I'll have a Bud,' Sophie agreed. It might shut Melissa up for a while. Personally, she'd be happy enough to sit in the boarding area and read one of the six books she'd brought with her. She couldn't decide which to start with. The Ciara Geraghty or Philippa Gregory novels Denise had given her. She was so looking forward to getting into them.

Three hours later, Melissa was well and truly plastered and had upchucked twice. She was draped across a tall, dark, arty type, who was waiting on a flight to Crete. 'We should shange our flight and go to Schrete . . .' she slurred gaily.

'Off you go,' muttered Sophie, utterly pissed off.

Two hours later, they finally boarded their flight. Melissa promptly fell asleep and snored loudly for the duration, her head lolling on Sophie's shoulder. Sophie couldn't believe her luck. She pulled *Saving Grace* out of her travel bag and chuckled her way across France and Spain as Melissa's musical snores drowned out the roar of the jet engines.

Unfortunately, a bumpy descent into Palma Airport revived both Melissa and her stomach and, for the third time that day, Sophie resisted the urge to drown her in a toilet bowl.

It took another hour to collect their luggage and find the coach that was to bring them to their apartments. Sophie found it hard to keep her eyes open as the air-conditioned coach finally sped along the motorway towards their destination. She half listened to the forced jolliness of the rep as she reminded her clients to use lots of sun factor and not to imbibe too much San Miguel.

Melissa, green-faced, once again found refuge in sleep.

By the time the coach pulled into the small, two-storey apartment block, Sophie was whacked. It didn't look ultra modern, she noted, as they stopped outside a building that had white flaking paint and two pots of dried-out wilting flowers at the entrance. She was too tired to care as a sullen receptionist took their passports and handed her the key to room 103. They were the only passengers to get off the coach so at least the check-in was quick, Sophie thought, wearily, as they click-clacked their way along a tiled floor, dragging their luggage behind them.

'It's a bit kippy,' Melissa moaned as Sophie struggled to get the big black key to turn in the lock.

Basic, was how Sophie would have described it, she reflected, as she surveyed the white-painted room with a shabby sofa and two chairs, a pine table and chairs and an alcove that housed a two-ring cooker, sink and fridge. The bedroom had a built-in wardrobe whose doors didn't close properly, two divans and a small bedside locker each. The bathroom, decorated in mustard tiles, was not a place she'd spend too long in, she decided. It was 3 a.m., she was exhausted and Melissa's shrieks of dismay were the last thing she needed.

'Let's go to bed. You chose the apartment, Melissa. It's not my fault. I've had a long day. I don't want to hear any more about it. I've had enough, so zip it!' she exploded tetchily, as she pulled off her T-shirt and jeans and dived into the nearest divan.

'There's no need to be like that,' Melissa sniffed huffily as she undressed. 'Can I have some of your bottled water to wash my teeth. My mouth tastes horrible.' Melissa, of course, would never be so organized as to have bottled water. That's what Sophies were for.

'Help yourself.' Sophie yawned as she pulled the white sheet over her and buried her head under the long thin pillow on the narrow divan. At least the sheets were crisp and clean she thought drowsily. Minutes later, she was fast asleep.

She awoke, she had no idea how much later, to high-pitched screeches emanating from a frantic Melissa in the other bed.

'*Getawayfromme! Getawayfromme!*'

Dazed, Sophie sat up trying to remember where she was. Melissa was shrieking like a madwoman, arms and legs flailing in the dark. The unmistakable *bzzzzz* of a mosquito gave a clue to the cause of the drama. 'Oh, for God's sake, Melissa, it's a mosquito. Spray some stuff on yourself and go to sleep,' she snarled, finding the light and snapping it on.

'I think it's a bat!' wailed Melissa.

'It's *not* a bat. It's a mosquito. Here.' She sprayed mosquito repellent over the distraught Melissa, then over herself, and switched off the light.

'You've got really grumpy, these days. You used to be much nicer,' Melissa said in her little girl voice.

Spears of guilt prodded Sophie. She was being a bit of a bitch. Melissa had a fear of insects. 'Sorry!' she apologized. 'PMT,' she fibbed.

'We're going to have a good holiday, aren't we?' Melissa asked anxiously.

'We're going to have a *great* holiday. You're going to get a MEGA tan and find a hunk for your photos, and The Skunk is going to be the sorriest idiot in the world.'

'Yes, he is an idiot? Isn't he? But I'm not taking him back. Definitely not.'

'No, you're not. There's a much nicer man waiting for you out there,' Sophie said kindly.

'Yes, there is. A millionaire, possibly,' Melissa agreed. She always thought big. 'There's a marina around here some-where, where the crème de la crème of the Mediterranean park their yachts.'

'Berth,' Sophie corrected, sleepily.

'What?'

'Berth their yachts, not park,' Sophie explained.

'Oh! Right, I'd better remember that.' She leaned on her elbow and stared over at Sophie. You know Majorca is still very "in". Don't forget Princess Di used to come here years ago. The Spanish royal family comes here and Michael Douglas brought Catherine Zeta-Jones here. He has a huge villa in Deya, but I think it's up for sale. I bet the ex, Diandra, isn't too happy about that. I've read about it in *Hello!*. Maybe we should go there for a day. We'll hire a car.' Melissa was always up to date on celebrity gossip.

'Fine,' murmured Sophie, wishing Melissa would go back to sleep. 'Imagine, if I met a millionaire, I might even invite Tony and Jayne to the wedding,' she fantasized. 'That would really rub their noses in it. Wouldn't it, Soph?'

Silence.

'Sophie?'

But Sophie was asleep. A deep and dreamless sleep.

She came to, to find sunlight dancing through the green shutters and Melissa standing on the patio, arms akimbo as she surveyed the scene in front of her.

'We can't possibly stay here, Sophie!' she declared, aghast. 'It's in the sticks. We don't even have a sea view, which I specifically asked for, and the swimming pool – if you could *call* it a swimming pool – is no bigger than a *bath*!'

'Beggars can't be choosers, Mel, and, after all, it was a cancellation, we might not have got anywhere at such short notice.' Sophie scrambled out of bed and went to join her friend on the postage-stamp patio. The sun was shining. That was all that mattered!

She gazed around at the dry, barren scrubland that backed onto a scree-filled cliff, dotted with pine trees. They were perched on a small hill. Below, she could see other apartment blocks nestled among trees and, in the distance, the glittering, silver blue sparkle of sunlight dancing on water.

'There's your sea view,' she grinned, stretching and breathing in the warm scented Mediterranean breeze.

'This is the pits! The pits!' Melissa moaned. 'And look at those kids jumping up and down in the pool. Horrible little beasties. Urrgh.' Melissa was not at all the maternal type.

'Well, it did say suitable for families and it did say this was a quiet area in the brochure,' Sophie pointed out reasonably.

'I wonder, would they move us to Palma Nova if I kicked up a fuss?' Melissa asked, hopefully.

'Let's give it a chance for a day or two, until we get our bearings. It's only ten minutes by taxi to Palma Nova, anyway, the rep told us last night when you were asleep.'

'Oh, OK, then. But if it's dead quiet, were moving and that's it,' Melissa declared, as she marched back into the bedroom. 'Let's go and see what they serve for breakfast in that snack bar by the pool.'

'Yes, let's. I'm starving. And I'm dying for a cup of coffee. Let's explore.' Sophie didn't care if the apartment wasn't exactly the Ritz. She was in Majorca, the sun was shining and the beach beckoned.

They breakfasted on fresh coffee, croissants, crusty white rolls and jam and fruit. Even Melissa had to admit that it was tasty. 'Let's go to the marina and see if we can nab a millionaire,' she suggested gaily. Her humour was improving by the minute.

Sophie heaved a mental sigh of relief. Maybe they *were* going to have a great holiday.

'*This* is where we're going to breakfast from now on,' Melissa announced joyfully an hour later, as they strolled along the sea front. A fifteen-minute walk from their apartment block had brought them to a completely different world.

'*This* is where I was born to be.' Melissa was giddy with excitement.

Yachts filled with beautiful people bobbed up and down on the gentle waves. The chic, designer boutiques oozed sophistication. There were no prices on display. It was that kind of place.

Melissa sashayed along in her tight white shorts and bikini top, black glass hiding her eyes, for all the world like a film star. Sophie in her denim shorts and black T-shirt felt lumpy and frumpy beside her.

'Let's go to the beach. It's getting hot. I'd like to go for a swim,' she ventured.

'Don't be silly, Soph. We have to do some serious strutting here!' Melissa smiled enticingly at a tanned, gigolo type in a cream Armani suit.

Gigolo smiled back.

'See,' Melissa whispered.

'Mel, you can strut. I'm going to the beach over there and I'm flopping.'

Gigolo was ogling Melissa from head to toe.

'See you on the beach. I'll get a lounger for you,' Sophie offered.

'Fine,' Melissa said snootily. 'If you want to miss the chance of a lifetime to go and slob out on a lounger do it! I'm staying here.'

'Have fun,' Sophie said dryly, as Cream-Suited-Gigolo flashed a toothy grin at Melissa.

Melissa smiled saucily back.

Sophie left her to it.

The beach was a golden, curved crescent of paradise. Pine trees fringed the edge of the cliffs. White-crested wisps of waves lapped the shore.

Off the beaten track, it wasn't crowded like the big resort beaches with their serried rows of white loungers. This beach was a little jewel dotted with coconut umbrellas and delightful green loungers that could be hired for the day. A small island lay about a mile offshore. There were no motorboats or hang-gliders or pedalos in sight. It was a most peaceful place. Sophie choose two loungers, lay her towel on one, stripped to her black M&S bikini, lay down, closed her eyes and breathed deeply. She was in heaven. It was too relaxing even to read. A balmy little breeze whispered around her; the sea murmured its soothing, rhythmic lullaby. Sophie fell asleep.

Melissa joined her several hours later. She was on a high.

'Remember that guy?' she asked excitedly. 'He asked me if I would like coffee. His name is Paulo and he's *absolutely* loaded! He's staying on a yacht with friends; they're cruising around the islands for a month. Imagine! He asked me out to dinner tonight. What will I wear, Sophie? It will have to be something ultra sophisticated. Do you think the little black silk D&G dress I bought would be OK?'

'It will be fine.' Sophie tried to sound enthusiastic. Melissa hadn't wasted any time. It looked like Sophie would be dining alone tonight. Her heart sank. Just as well she had plenty of books to read.

'I'd better get some serious sunbathing done before tonight.' Melissa unhooked her bikini top and slathered on some Hawaiian Tropic. 'Sophie, it's great that we came to this place. I'd never have met anybody like Paulo in Palma Nova. That marina is ultra posh.' She gave a positively beatific smile as she slid elegantly onto her lounger, stretched out and closed her eyes.

Sophie tried not to feel envious as she surveyed her friend. Melissa had everything: looks, fabulous figure, bubbly personality. No wonder she was never manless for long. A deep sigh came from the depths of her as she looked at her own tummy, which was not flat and taut like Melissa's, but curved and rounded with a little soft, jelly sort of bulge, no matter how tight she held her muscles in. Her thighs were dimpled at the top, unlike Melissa's firm, toned, satiny-skinned ones. And there was no denying that she had thick ankles, Sophie thought glumly, as she surveyed Melissa's shapely turned ankles and perfectly pedicured feet.

She felt disgruntled . . . and hungry.

'Will we have some lunch?' she asked.

'Oh, God, no! I couldn't eat a thing, I'm so excited.' Melissa yawned. 'Besides, Paulo bought me a gorgeous cake with the coffee, earlier.'

'Well, I've had nothing to eat since breakfast. I'll just go and get something myself.' Sophie pulled on her shorts and T-shirt, grabbed her bag and flounced off.

'Enjoy it,' Melissa called airily after her. She hadn't even noticed that Sophie was annoyed. *Bitch!* thought Sophie, simmering with resentment. Denise was right, Melissa was so self-centred she thought the world revolved around her. Barely their first day on holidays and Sophie had to eat alone. She climbed, the curving wooden steps up the side of the cliff and tried not to pant. She was so unfit it was a disaster. Still, there was nothing she could do about it now. She might as well treat herself to something tasty for lunch, she decided. Food was always a great comforter. Besides, it would be quite nice to sit at a shaded table outside the cliff-top restaurant and tuck into deep-fried squid in batter, with a crispy, crunchy side salad, and sip ice-cold San Miguel beer.

It was her fifth day alone. She might as well have come on a singles holiday after all, Sophie reflected, as she lay on the lounger in her favourite spot on the beach. Melissa had spent two days with Paulo after the first momentous dinner-date.

'You don't mind, lovie? He's such a pet. You should hear the gorgeous things he says to me and he's *such* a gentleman. He's really smitten, Soph,' Melissa twittered, as she changed into yet another outfit for a shopping trip to Palma. That night she arrived back at the apartment, eyes aglow.

'You'll never guess, Soph? Paulo has asked me to go to Ibiza on the yacht. I'm *so* excited.'

'How long are you going for?' Sophie demanded. She was furious.

'Don't be like that, Soph,' Melissa muttered defensively. 'This is the chance of a lifetime. Paulo is just what I need after The Rat.'

'Look, Melissa, you asked me to come on holiday with you. So far, we've had one breakfast together and I've been left to my own devices ever since. You're being really selfish and I don't think much of your behaviour!' Sophie exploded.

'No, *you're* being selfish!' Melissa rounded on her. 'This could be the best thing that's ever happened to me, and if you were truly my friend you wouldn't be so mean.' She took her case from the wardrobe and began to pack. Sophie felt like thumping her. How typical of Melissa to turn the argument to her advantage.

They didn't speak for the rest of the night. The following morning, Sophie kept her head under the pillow until she heard Melissa leave the apartment, dragging her case behind her.

So much for the gentleman; he didn't even come to collect the cow, she thought grumpily, as she heard the click-clack of Melissa's white high heels fade away.

Surprisingly, once her anger and resentment had abated somewhat, Sophie had actually enjoyed herself. She spent her days on the beach, reading, swimming and watching the incredibly confident, effortlessly stylish young Spaniards who congregated after school. It was an entertainment in itself. At night, she took a taxi to Palma Nova, ate at one of the beach-side restaurants and then browsed around the myriad of shops, before going home to sit on her terrace with her book and an ice-cold Malibu. The days melted into one another and Sophie realized that being on holiday alone was not half as daunting as she'd imagined. It was a liberation of sorts to know that she was perfectly capable of enjoying herself alone.

She was soaking up the late-afternoon rays, immersed in her historical novel, when a child's piercing scream rent the air. Sophie looked up to see a little Spanish girl of about four howling in pain as her elderly grandfather tried to comfort her. She had seen them come to the beach every afternoon and thought they were so sweet. The grandfather doted on the little girl and made magnificent sandcastles to entertain her. Sophie jumped up and hurried over. 'Can I help?' she asked. 'I'm a nurse.'

'Oh, thank you very much. Maria has been stung.' The man spoke perfect English.

Sophie soothed the little girl. 'Could you get me some vinegar from the restaurant and I'll remove the sting and put some cream on it.' She turned to the grandfather. The man spoke in rapid Spanish to a young student nearby, who raced off up the steps towards the restaurant.

Sophie kept talking in calm, soothing tones to the little girl who has stopped screaming but whimpered pitifully.

She squealed again as Sophie applied the vinegar and removed the sting but, once the balm of antiseptic cream had done its trick, she was soon playing again, the incident forgotten.

The grandfather was effusive in his thanks.

'My daughter is pregnant and Maria's nanny had to return to Madrid as her mother is very ill. So I've been looking after her in the afternoons,' he explained. 'I am Juan Santander.' He held out his hand.

'Sophie Irvine,' Sophie reciprocated. They chatted easily for a while. It was nice to have someone to talk to.

'Your friend has not come back?' Juan remarked. 'She was here with you just one day.'

How observant, Sophie thought.

'She went on a cruise to Ibiza.'

'Did you not want to go?' Juan enquired.

'I wasn't asked.' Sophie laughed.

'I see.' His eyes were kind. 'You will be here tomorrow?'

'Yes.'

'We will see you then.' Juan gathered up his granddaughter's bits and pieces. 'Tomorrow.'

The following afternoon, Sophie smiled as she saw the pair make their descent down the steps. Maria raced over to proudly show off her bandage.

Juan winked. 'For such an injury, a bandage was necessary. May we join you?'

'Please do,' Sophie invited.

'I wonder, would you consider something?' Juan asked. 'I told my daughter what had happened and that you were a nurse and that your friend had left you alone. We wondered if perhaps you would like to come and stay with us for a few days in our villa up in the hills? We have a pool and lovely grounds and it is most comfortable. My daughter is looking for someone to mind Maria and the new baby for at least six months. Maybe you might be interested in the position. If you spent a few days with us, you would know if it is something you would like.'

Sophie's eyes widened. It sounded like a fantastic proposition. Leave dreary, humid, stuffy old London and spend six months in this paradise. It sounded like a dream.

To her amazement, she heard herself say, 'I'd love to.'

'Excellent. Can you come today?'

'I'll just go up to the apartment and get my things.'

'We'll collect you. Just give me the address,' Juan instructed. 'We will pick you up in an hour, won't we, Maria?' He spoke in Spanish to his little granddaughter.

'Si, si.' She hopped up and down with excitement.

'See you in an hour, then.' Sophie couldn't believe how impulsive she was being. But this was a chance of a lifetime.

She had just packed her books when the door of the apartment burst open. Melissa appeared, red eyed and on crutches.

'Thank God I'm here. That bastard was so callous. I broke my leg in Ibiza and he couldn't get rid of me quick enough.

I even had to get a taxi at the marina. They let me off and then they sailed away. Can you believe it?' Melissa burst into tears. 'My luggage is in reception – can you collect it for me?' She sniffled.

'Sure.' Sophie's heart sank as she headed off to reception. Trust Melissa to do something dramatic and break her leg. She saw a big silver Mercedes drive up to the entrance. It was Juan and Maria. She couldn't really go with them now and leave Melissa.

She'd leave you, a little voice said. Sophie stood stock-still. What kind of a fool was she? Melissa wouldn't think twice about putting herself first. It was time Sophie did the same. For once in her life, she was going to do something spontaneous. She lugged Melissa's case back to the apartment.

'Why is your bag packed? Where are you going?' Melissa demanded, as Sophie wheeled the case into the bedroom.

'To stay with friends?' she said jauntily.

'What friends? You don't have friends here.' Melissa snorted.

'Yes, I do. Look out of the window. See that silver car over at reception?'

Melissa's jaw dropped. 'Who are they?'

'Sorry, I can't stay and explain, Mel. Have to go.'

'But you can't go!' Melissa was incredulous. 'You *can't* leave me! My leg is broken. I'm on crutches. How will I manage?'

'You'll be fine. We're on the ground floor. You can eat by the pool. You can sunbathe. The rep will bring you to the airport. No worries.' Sophie was enjoying herself.

'But you're a *nurse*. You have a *duty* to sick people!' Melissa raged. This wasn't the Sophie she knew. 'You can't leave me here on my own!' she fumed.

'Watch me,' Sophie drawled as she lifted her bag from the bed.

'Goodbye, Melissa. Enjoy the rest of your holiday. I know I'm going to enjoy the rest of mine. To tell you the truth, it's the *best* holiday I've ever had.'

A year later

'Did you hear about Sophie Irvine? She's engaged to some wealthy Spanish doctor she met when she was working in Majorca. They're getting married next month, Denise was telling me. Flying the whole family out to Majorca for the wedding!' Angie O'Neill told Melissa as they tidied up the salon after a very busy day.

Melissa's fingers curled and her lips tightened with envy. What a bitch that Sophie Irvine had turned out to be. Leaving her alone in that grotty little apartment with a broken leg. She hadn't seen her from that day to this. And now to hear that she was engaged to a rich Spanish doctor. Was there no justice in the world?

'Don't mention that girl's name to me. I thought she was a friend. Little did I know until she stabbed me in the back.'

'She *stabbed* you in the back!' Angie was astonished.

'Not literally, you idiot!' Melissa snapped. 'I invited her to go on holiday and then she met these people and left me in the lurch, on my own, with a broken leg. Can you believe that?'

'*Really?* I'd never have thought it of Sophie. She sounds like a bit of a fairweather friend. Just as well you have me to go on holiday with this year,' Angie soothed. 'I wouldn't do anything like that.'

'I know, sweetie.' Melissa smiled. 'You'll love where we're going to. It has a marina full of yachts and rich people. It will be the best holiday ever.'

'I can't wait!' exclaimed Angie excitedly. 'Thanks for inviting me to come.'

'You're very welcome,' said Melissa graciously. 'Could you be a pet and finish off here? I've a thumping headache.'

'Oh! OK,' Angie murmured. Funny how Melissa always got a thumping headache on Friday evenings when the salon had to be cleaned.

'See you at the airport tomorrow.'

Melissa swanned out of the salon, leaving her new best friend to tidy up. Angie would be an *excellent* holiday companion, she thought with satisfaction. Not like the-soon-to-be-married Judas Irvine.

True Colours

I'd better tell you straight away, before we go any further – I think I murdered my husband. This is the first time I've actually admitted it and said the words aloud.

'*I think I murdered my husband!*' It's quite a relief really to verbalize it. It's been a strain keeping it to myself this last year or so.

I won't tell you my real name, just in case. You never know, I might live in your area. We might be on nodding terms as we walk our dogs in the park, or buy our lotto tickets every Friday.

I'll call myself Melanie. I liked Melanie Hamilton in *Gone With the Wind*. I know she was a bit wishy-washy compared to the magnificent Scarlett O' Hara but she was a softie with a kind heart and I was like that once. And that's what got me into trouble.

I suppose I should start at the beginning, it might make more sense to you then and you won't judge me so harshly.

I lived in a small seaside town with my elderly parents. I have two sisters and a brother. Let's call them Carla, Tina and Larry. I'm sixty-three, on the plump side, and I've stopped dying my hair. It's now an ashy-blonde colour that I rather like. My husband used to nag me when he was alive about eating properly. Our diet was very wholesome. He was a disciplined person. Image was ultra important. Dyeing my hair came with the territory of being a consultant anaesthetist's wife.

I was the eldest. It's tough being the eldest. My parents were strict with me. I was expected to be the responsible one and had to look after the younger ones. I wasn't allowed go to discos or into town to shop with my friends on Saturdays. I had to be in by nine-thirty at night even when I was in sixth year in secondary school. Not for me, sneaky fags and slugs of vodka and furtive gropings down by the boat shed with the rest of the gang. My mother would have gone berserk if she caught the whiff of fags or drink off me and my father would have leathered me with his belt.

He was a bully. My mother was afraid of him and I suppose it was partly for her sake that I didn't rebel. He would have made her life more of a misery than it was. He was a tight, mean, selfish bastard and I hated him. His word was law in our house.

He didn't like me. I always knew that. It was only years later that my mother told me that she'd got pregnant with me and he'd had to marry her. He always felt she'd tricked him into marriage and he never forgave her, or me.

A Gift For You

I suppose I was lucky that the girls I hung around with tolerated me as I lurked enviously on the fringes of their seemingly carefree, unfettered lives. They spoke with smug insouciance about getting pissed, and French kissing or even, in some cases having it off with their fellas. Us more timid, constrained souls could only listen in awe and envy. These conversations left me feeling even more like a pariah than usual. Would *my* chance ever come or would I die a virgin, never knowing carnal pleasure? To die 'wondering' was one of my great preoccupations during my teenage years.

I remembered being at the funeral of an elderly spinster neighbour and hearing an old fella from down the road saying, 'God love her, she died wondering with never a rub of the relic,' and the other old men laughing. I thought they were horrible and disrespectful and the jocular derisive comment made me feel vaguely sad for my elderly neighbour who had been a quiet inoffensive soul. I was twelve at the time, on the cusp of puberty and in love with Paul Newman. I didn't want to die wondering.

I fretted about how was I ever going to escape from the straitjacket of parental control. I longed to be free of my father's strict, oppressive stranglehold.

I was bright enough at school and I loved art. When I was painting I was free, able to express through my use of colours the rage and despair that seethed within me. I knew I was in a catch-22 situation. If I worked really hard and got the points to go to university, I'd be stuck under my father's thumb for another four years. If I went out to work straight after school, I might not earn enough that I could afford to rent a flat in Dublin and get away for good.

I would love to have gone to college and studied art but my father thought this was nonsense. 'You won't get anywhere in life studying arty farty crap and I won't be paying for it,' he told me bluntly, once, when I'd ventured to suggest it.

I wouldn't want to be beholden to him anyway, I fumed in the privacy of the bathroom, mocking myself for even thinking it was an option and cursing myself for opening my big mouth to him about it.

'If I were you I wouldn't waste my time even talking about college to *him*,' my mother said flatly. 'Go and get a job and get a life for yourself out of this place.' When she said that to me, I felt uncharacteristically close to her. We didn't have a warm relationship. She was too worn down by my father's bullying to be able to enjoy a normal relationship with us. My mother had a sad dullness in her eyes that never left her until the week before she died.

It wasn't all gloom and doom though. I loved where we lived in a snug cottage overlooking the beach. I shared a bedroom with my two younger sisters but my bed was beside the window, under the eaves and I could turn away from their giddy chatter and look out to sea and drift off into my fantasy world. The beach was my saviour. The sea and all its glorious moods was my companion. Thundering angry waves against the shore when you couldn't see where its pewter grey ended as it merged with an equally leaden sky, it mirrored my mood. Or on a good day, caressing my toes in feathery little white-wave kisses under balmy blue skies when the sun scattered, glittering diamond prisms across the azure blue, as far as the eye could see.

Our dog, Waggy, and I would tramp along the beach in hail, rain sun or snow, enveloped by salty invigorating sea breezes that couldn't but induce a sense of wellbeing. I was mostly happy on the beach, except on moonlit nights, when I'd watch the blood-orange moon rise slow and majestic on the horizon and wish with all my heart that I had a boyfriend to hold hands with and kiss and cuddle and talk to. There's nowhere lonelier than a moonlit beach when you're alone.

Anyway, to move on. I did a good Leaving Certificate. Six honours, enough to do accountancy, my father's choice of career for me. I couldn't think of anything I'd hate more and, when I told him I wasn't doing it, his face darkened in anger and he told me I was a silly little fool to miss out on an opportunity to make something of myself.

For once, my mother took my side. She had a sister – I'll call her Vera – living in Dublin, and she asked her would she put me up for a couple of months until I got a job and got sorted. Vera agreed and, to my father's fury, I left home the week after our bitter row and I tasted the first fruits of freedom.

Vera was the greatest fun, ten years younger than my mother; she worked in PR and had the most glamorous lifestyle. Parties, launches, lunches, brunches. She'd whizz into her small two-up, two-down in Ranelagh, change an outfit, and whizz out again. She taught me how to apply make-up and how to dress up an outfit with a scarf or a bag or piece of jewellery, and she introduced me to champagne. It was exhilarating. I got a job as an admissions officer in a private hospital, I won't say where, and I couldn't have been happier.

I even dated boys! I will never forget my first kiss, even though, to be very honest with you, I didn't really enjoy it. So much slurping; he had wet lips. Even so, as I was being kissed and as Mr Wet Lip's hands roamed under my jumper, I thought to myself, I don't know what the fuss is all about but at least I've been kissed and fondled – groped might actually have been more appropriate to describe it – I am on the right road to not dying 'wondering'. I'm just like those girls I envied, at last.

The naivety of me. The foolishness of me. I would have been better off I think sometimes if I *had* died wondering!

I met my husband in the hospital I worked in. I met him at the staff Christmas party. He was an anaesthetist, a tall gangly chap with the beginnings of a receding hairline. He was just starting out on his career, and though he wore a smart pinstriped suit, he drove a battered old Ford that hiccupped and farted its way out of the car park, leaving a waft of black smoke in its wake.

I had often seen him walking briskly, confidently, along the Parquet-floored corridors – a faux confidence, I was to learn later. All the consultants seemed to stride purposefully;

as if it was something they had been taught. I always knew by the sound of the firm, decisive footsteps that a consultant was on the floor.

His name was Martin – one of the receptionists introduced us – and he appeared reserved and ill at ease but, after a couple of drinks, he loosened up and I couldn't believe it when he asked me to dance a slow set. There were plenty of gorgeous nurses there. Consultants generally ignored us plebs.

'I've seen you down at reception a few times. Do you like working here?' he slurred as we lurched around the floor. I wasn't exactly drunk, but I wasn't exactly sober, either.

'Yeah, I love it,' I half shouted – the din of music and chat was so loud you had to shout to be heard.

'I suppose you're looking to marry a doctor. I see ye all batting your eyelashes at us when we come in.' He gazed at me, his grey eyes slightly glazed and bloodshot.

Don't flatter yourself, I wanted to say, but I thought it would be rude. After all, doctors and consultants were treated like gods when they were on their rounds. 'I'm having too much fun to want to get married,' I fibbed, pretending to be liberated and sophisticated. The truth was, I *wanted* to be married. I wanted what I had never had: a happy family life. I wanted the security of having my own home, a husband who loved me and children around me. It would be so different to my parents' marriage. It would be a *real* marriage when I got married, I vowed to myself.

'Do you want to split and have some fun with me, then?' Martin murmured into my hair, pressing himself against me.

I could feel that I was turning him on and that gave me an unexpected and gratifying sense of power.

'OK then,' I said recklessly, and we made our way through the swaying throng.

'I know where there's a couple of rooms where on-call staff crash,' Martin said, leading me towards the back of the hospital to a wing I never had any reason to go to. It was my first and last time there. I lost my virginity in a heated rush with my dress in a tangle around me, on an old hospital bed with a wonky wheel that squeaked against the lino floor when Martin took me by surprise and penetrated me almost as soon as he had thrown me on the bed and yanked off my knickers.

It was over in moments, painful moments, and I lay there listening to him panting on top of me and wondered how it could be so different to all I had imagined. All the romantic novels I had devoured from the local library had not prepared me for this crushing sense of disappointment and bewilderment. Nor had they prepared me for the sudden, terrifying panic when I remembered how my mother had got pregnant with me, resulting in a life of misery.

I started to cry and that sobered Martin up quick enough.

'Sorry, sorry, he muttered. 'Are you OK? I didn't know you were a virgin. I thought you were experienced. You seemed so . . . so . . . Don't cry.'

'I'm just afraid I'll get pregnant.' I howled.

'Shush! Shush! You won't!' He looked as panicked as I felt.

'How do *you* know?' I'd bawled, pushing him off me, rolling off the bed and gathering up my knickers, shoes and bag. All I wanted to do was to get out of that moonlit dingy room that smelt faintly of antiseptic.

'Where do you live? Will I bring you home?' He stood up and zipped up his fly.

'No. I'll get a taxi.' I tried to adjust my clothing.

'OK, OK, here's money for the fare.' He fumbled in his wallet and extracted a pound note.

'I don't want your money, I'm not a bloody whore,' I'd sworn at him, trying to regain some semblance of dignity before hastening out the door praying that no one would see me.

I cried myself to sleep that night in my sore, deflowered and possibly pregnant state. No doubt my poor mother had spent a night such as I, had all those years ago.

I didn't see Martin for another ten days. The hospital did not admit patients over the Christmas season and I spent the holidays petrified that I was pregnant.

I got my period the morning I went back to work, and to this day, I remember the utter relief that flooded my body as the for-once welcome, painful cramps signalled that an unwanted pregnancy would not be my fate this time.

That same day, a hesitant knock on the door led me to open it to find Martin standing there, abashed and awkward, swallowing nervously as he ran his hand through his thinning hair. 'Hello, are you all right? I'm sorry about the night of the party,' he said gruffly.

It was then I knew we would end up together.

To make a long story short, we married a year later. I was contented rather than happy, I think, when I look back now, especially when I got pregnant and we had twin girls on our second wedding anniversary.

I had everything I wanted in life, all I ever dreamed of.

But as the years passed, cracks began to appear in my relationship with my husband. The stress of his job seemed to overwhelm him, particularly after a patient died on the table from a heart attack. It wasn't his fault but it unnerved him and affected his confidence. You might ask me, why did my husband not confide in me and talk to me about his worries. That was not his way. We didn't have that loving degree of intimacy that I envied in other couples.

He would take it out on me, though, in cold, vicious, undermining exchanges. 'What would you know about it, you never even went to college!' he said once, in front of his parents, when I proffered an opinion on some political crisis or other that was taking place.

'That's all you're good for,' he flung at me one day when he came home between surgeries to find me painting a still life in our conservatory, and no sign of lunch on the table. I'd been so immersed in my work I'd forgotten the time.

He became more grumpy and bitter as he grew into late middle age, claiming that some colleagues seemed to have more surgeons on their lists than he had. It got worse when our daughters left home to work abroad. He was annoyed neither had followed him into medicine and moaned continuously about how much money he had spent on their education in private school and for what. It was wearing living on my own with him and I withdrew into myself and sought solace in my painting.

And then, one day as he scrubbed up before an operation, my husband had a serious stroke. It affected his left side and his speech and left him hospitalized for many months.

To be very honest, and again I've never said this to anyone, but after the shock of it, once I got used to our changed circumstances, I rather enjoyed my freedom. I visited him every afternoon between two and four even though I could have stayed longer because he was in a private room. I stayed longer in the early months until he was no longer critically ill but as he slowly improved physically, his mental state deteriorated and he became even more dour and bad tempered as he struggled to communicate. Some sense of self-preservation kicked in and gradually I reduced the time I spent with Martin. The day he wrote on his pad that I was to stop talking because he wanted to watch a snooker match, I decided to reclaim my life.

From that day onwards, after my afternoon visit, I was free to do as I pleased without having to worry about cooking or cleaning or doing his laundry. I painted and gardened and met my sisters and friends for brunch or dinner or sometimes just a coffee, and enjoyed the company of my daughters when they came home to visit.

Eventually, Martin was moved to a rehab hospital and when they had rehabilitated him as much as they could, I was told to start making preparations for his return home. Occupational therapists came to assess the house. I needed to turn one of the downstairs rooms into a bedroom, with an adjoining walk-in shower suitable for his needs, as he wouldn't be able to manage a chairlift.

I'm ashamed to say that my heart sank at the thought of him coming home. He was so angry and frustrated at his situation, an invalid to all intents and purposes – shuffling around on a cane – who could no longer communicate except through strangled grunts that we could barely understand. He could still write though. And the notes came fast and furious.

Tell that gobshite night nurse to stop shining her fucking torch in my face.

Tell them to sack the bloody chef, that soup they serve up is watery slop.

Sell the BMW, and get something I can get in and out of the passenger seat easily, and don't spend a fortune, we need to cut back.

That last one threw me. I was going to have to drive him around. He's never rated my driving and I rarely got to drive the Beemer. I loved my little hatchback but I'd have to change it for something with a higher passenger seat that he could swing in and out of easily. I couldn't think of anything worse than having him sitting beside me grunting and gesticulating and clutching the seat because he felt I wasn't braking in time or some such.

I felt like running away.

One wet blustery Sunday, the rehab hospital mini-bus rolled up the drive. Martin was coming home for an afternoon visit. A carer assisted my husband down the ramp and he shuffled into the house for the first time in almost a year. I felt I was welcoming a stranger into my home. He sat sullen and morose in the brand new cream leather riser chair we'd bought for him. The girls fussed around him and I saw the tears in his eyes and nearly cried myself.

It was the only time I felt sorry for him; after that, it was myself I felt sorry for, and honestly, I'm not a nasty person, I do my best, but he would try the patience of a saint. It seemed as though he blamed me for everything that had gone wrong and when I mentioned this to a friend in my book club, she said, wearily, 'They always want to blame someone and it's usually the wife that gets it.' Her husband had MS and his mood-swings frequently had her in tears.

One Sunday afternoon in March, squalls of sleety rain battered the windows while we sat and watched TV. Martin had been dropped off after lunch at the hospital and the driver said he would be back for him at four-thirty. A film came on and I settled back on the sofa, glad to have something to take my mind off our circumstances. *Death at a Funeral*: not the most appropriate subject, I reflected, but I said nothing and we sat in silence watching it. The film was hilarious and I was laughing heartily at the antics of a character that had taken LSD thinking it was Valium when Martin glared at me and flicked the remote.

'I was watching that and enjoying it, Martin!' I exclaimed indignantly, as an old episode of *Murder She Wrote* filled the screen.

He gave a guttural grunt and scrawled <u>*Bloody rubbish!*</u> on his writing pad.

Oh, Divine Mother, this will be my life when he comes home, I thought with dread as Herr Flick surfed the channels until he found a football match.

He picked up his pad and scribbled furiously and handed it to me.

By the way, I want to be cremated when the time comes, just so you know. And scatter my ashes in the back garden.

'I'll cremate you myself on a bonfire out in the back garden, if you're not careful, or throw you on the compost heap,' I snapped, handing him back the pad.

He glared at me and his eyes narrowed.

<u>*I mean it*</u> he wrote in big black letters, underlined.

You make sure you follow my wishes to the letter. No hymns, eulogy or flowers.

'Fine!' I retorted. He had mentioned some years previously that he was thinking of being cremated rather than buried. The idea of his body mouldering in a grave gave him the heebie-jeebies.

He scowled and bent his head to write again.

I want a mug of tea and a ginger nut biscuit, and go upstairs and get me some fresh handkerchiefs.

If he had written, please, and said, *may* I have, instead of I *want*, I might not have flipped but it was like a red mist exploded behind my eyes and I shot to my feet and roared. 'If you don't have some manners and treat me with a bit of respect, you won't be cremated, you'll be buried. And the worms can feast on you, you rude ignoramus. Because get used to this, mister, I'm in charge here now, not you.'

His eyes bulged and I saw temper and something else . . . fear.

It seemed to trigger something in me, a viciousness I didn't know I possessed. Something of my late father, perhaps.

'Yes, Martin,' I said nastily, giving full rein to my feelings. 'I'll put you in a coffin and you'll be buried underground and then,' I glared at him and bent my face close to his and recited in a sing-song voice:

'*The worms crawl in and the worms crawl out.*

'*The ones that go in are lean and thin.*

'*The ones that come out are fat and stout.*

'*Your eyes fall in and your teeth fall out—*

Martin gave a gasp and turned a grey-green ashen colour.

His pad fell out of his hand and I could see the panic in his eyes as he struggled for breath.

I stared at him, stunned. He was trying to say something, pointing to his mobile phone, which was on the coffee table in front of us. I picked it up, about to tap in 999 for an ambulance.

I felt strangely calm, disconnected almost.

'I'll put the kettle on for your tea,' I heard myself say and walked out to the kitchen.

I sat for twenty minutes at the kitchen table before calling the paramedics.

Martin was dead when they wheeled him into the ambulance.

I had him cremated, just as he wanted. No hymns, eulogy or flowers. I drew the line at scattering his ashes in the back garden. The girls and myself surreptitiously scattered them in the Rose Garden in the Botanic Gardens in Glasnevin.

I have nightmares sometimes but I don't dwell on the way of Martin's passing. The way I see it, it was him or me. He would have seen me under if he had come home to live with me.

My life is back to its calm, peaceful rhythm. I'm enjoying my widowhood, apart from the nightmares and the occasional pang of guilt when I wonder, Am I, or am I not a murderer.

Ripples

'The McHughs were a bit frosty tonight,' Mike Stuart said.

'That's an understatement if ever I heard one,' his wife, Kathy murmured out of the side of her mouth. 'They'd have been at home in the Arctic.'

'What's new?' Mike asked glumly. They stood at the front door, waving goodbye to their guests.

They were caught in the wide beam of the car's head-lights as Garry McHugh reversed down the drive. He gave a toot on his horn. Beside him, his wife Alison looked utterly pissed off. Kathy knew that the tight smile she gave them would be gone in seconds as soon as the car headed towards the main road.

Kathy gave a sigh of relief as the Audi's rear lights disappeared into the night. Tonight had been a disaster. Alison had sniped at Garry constantly. At times he'd ignored her completely. This had been like a red rag to a bull. As her rage and antipathy, fuelled by several large G&Ts,

overflowed, she'd turned to her friends and said angrily, 'I'm married to the biggest bastard you could meet.'

'Either take your go now, Alison, or forfeit it. You've been holding up the game for the last five minutes,' Garry said coldly. His eyes were like flints behind his glasses as he glowered at her.

'Get lost. I'll go when I'm ready. Just because you think you're *Mister Intelligence*. Well, you're not. You're just a cheat. I mean, who else would try and get away with putting Monaco down and say it was a font? It's not in the dictionary. It shouldn't be allowed. And you shouldn't get a triple word score.'

'Well, if you weren't so *thick*, you'd know that it *was* a font. I'll show it to you on the computer when we get home.'

'Oh, stick your bloody computer. You should have married one, you spend so much time on that one in the office,' Alison snapped. She slapped down her letters.

'Is that the best you can do? *Rat!* Pathetic!' Garry's brown eyes flashed with scorn.

'Well, I'm married to one, aren't I?' Alison riposted coldly. 'Don't forget it's a double word score.'

'The first one you've managed so far,' Garry jeered, as he wrote down the score.

They'd all been playing their usual Saturday-night game of Scrabble, a tradition that went back to the carefree giddy days of their early twenties. They'd all been newly-weds then with not a lot of money to spend. The future had looked rosy. Now, fourteen years later Garry and Alison weren't getting on too well, much to Mike and Kathy's dismay.

Over the last few months, things had got so bad that the weekly game of Scrabble that they'd always looked forward to, after a few drinks and a Chinese takeaway, was becoming a bit of an ordeal.

'I've never seen them as bad as they were tonight,' Kathy reflected, as she collected the dirty glasses and emptied the cold, congealed remains of the meal into the bin.

'Why they ever married each other, I'll never know. They're like chalk and cheese. They always were. I mean, Alison is always gadding about and Garry hates going anywhere.' Mike picked the bones of a cold spare rib.

'Put that in the bin, you glutton.' Kathy grimaced. 'They say opposites attract. Maybe it worked at the start but it's not working now.'

'Yeah, well, Alison made the big mistake of thinking that she was going to change Garry. He'll never change. He's not even making the effort now. I don't think he wants to come over to us on Saturday night any more. All he wants to do is go to his football matches. Or bury himself in his work. He lives in that office.'

'Would you say that Garry's got another woman?' Kathy asked her husband. 'He can't be spending all those nights at work.'

'Garry! Garry McHugh! Don't be daft, woman,' Mike scoffed as he licked his fingers. 'He'd run a mile if a woman came near him. Imagine Garry sitting down and having a conversation with a woman. It's hard enough for him to have a conversation with us. And he's known us for years.'

'Maybe you're right.' Kathy poured Fairy Liquid into a basin of hot water. 'He's great fun, though, when he's in form. He's got a real dry sense of humour. I feel sorry for him sometimes. Alison is always nagging him.'

'Garry likes being nagged. He likes being told what to do. He never makes decisions. Alison makes them all. Did you hear her telling him he was to get his hair cut next week? And telling him that she'd told Brenda Johnston that he'd tile her bathroom. Without even *asking* him! What is he, a man or a mouse?' Mike picked up the towel and started to dry the dishes. 'It's like he's the child and she's the mother. It's always been like that with them. That would drive me nuts. If I came home and found out that you'd told Brenda Johnston that I'd tile her crappy bathroom, you know what your answer would be.' He grinned.

'Well, Alison always was a bossy boots. And I wouldn't inflict Poison Dwarf Johnston on you. I'd know better.' Kathy giggled. Brenda Johnston was Alison McHugh's best friend. Kathy didn't like her. She thought she was sly. She was always flirting with other women's husbands. Brenda who was unmarried and in her early forties, had recently bought a house that needed a lot of renovation. Brenda was an expert at the Poor-Little-Me-I'm-A-Helpless-Female act. Every man she knew was being roped in to help decorate. Garry was doing the lion's share.

'*Poison Dwarf!* . . . Miaow! Brenda's not in the good books. What's she done now?'

'She had the nerve to say that I didn't know what stress was. She said that I had you to provide for me. She said that I could come and go as I pleased because I'm a *housewife*. She thinks that I have very little to do.'

'Well I *do* provide for you. You *can* come and go as you please,' Mike said innocently.

'You know what I mean.' Kathy flicked frothy suds at her husband. He flicked back and drenched her.

'Stop it,' she squealed.

'Shush, you'll wake the kids,' Mike warned.

'Well, if the baby wakes up *you* won't be getting any nooky tonight because it's your turn to get up to her. And *I* intend to sleep my brains out . . . in the spare room if necessary,' Kathy said smugly.

'Well, see about that.' Mike dropped the towel, grabbed his wife and gave her a long smoochy kiss.

'Let's leave the rest of the washing-up and the *two* of us can sleep in the spare room.' He nuzzled her ear.

Kathy giggled. Even after ten years of marriage and three children, Mike still turned her on and she loved him passionately. Hand in hand, they crept upstairs into the spare bedroom and thoroughly enjoyed themselves for the next hour.

Later, nestled in the curve of Mike's arm, Kathy said sleepily, 'Would you say that Garry and Brenda are having a fling?'

'Who in their right mind would want to have an affair with Bug-eyes Johnston? Are you mad? She wouldn't shut up long enough to let someone kiss her. She loves the sound of her own voice too much. She's such a bloody know-all. Who'd want to listen to that one yakin' in that squeaky voice of hers and watch her flicking that lank greasy brown hair of hers over her shoulders the way she does?' Mike snorted.

'Well, Garry didn't say he wouldn't tile her bathroom for her. He's always doing bits and pieces for her. Maybe *he* likes her.'

'She's bossy enough for him, anyway. She's even more of a dictator than Alison.'

'Ah, Alison's not that bad,' Kathy defended her friend. 'If she didn't nag Garry he'd never do anything except watch soccer and play with his computers.'

'If I lived in their house that's all I'd want to do. It's like a pigsty. Alison is not good at housekeeping. You don't know how lucky you are. I never watch soccer. I don't have a computer,' Mike murmured into her hair.

'And I don't have a job, like Alison. I'm always here to cook your dinner. I have your shirts ironed every morning. *You* don't know how lucky *you* are, buster!'

'I know how lucky I am,' Mike whispered. His arms tightened around her.

'Poor Garry and Alison, it's horrible, isn't it? Kathy said sadly.

'I couldn't stick a marriage like that. All that bitterness

and anger and resentment. It's almost as if they hate each other now. Maybe they'd be better off divorced.'

'Oh, don't say that, Mike!' Kathy exclaimed.

'Well, it's true. What kind of a life have they got now? No life. The trouble with Alison and Garry, and I don't say this lightly, they're very dear to me, we've been friends a long time, but the two of them in their own way are very selfish people. There's very little give and take there. Garry should never have got married. He should never have had a child either. He's not prepared to make the effort. Poor Ciara's a nuisance to him. He thinks once he provides financially for her, that's his responsibility over. He's not prepared to give any more. It's like our friendship. If we didn't have them over and keep in touch he wouldn't bother. It's too much effort. He's a strange chap.'

'I wonder, does our friendship mean anything to him? Or is it just habit with him?' Kathy mused.

'You never know with Garry. You never know what's really in his mind. Garry's very . . . how would I describe it . . .? Sort of calculating, I suppose. He always was. Says nothing much, but takes it all in.'

'He's very good-natured, though. He'd never see you stuck. Maybe it's just a bad patch. Maybe they'll work things out.'

'I hope so, because if they don't, I don't really want to go away for a long weekend with them. I don't want to have to sit listening to that for three days.'

'Me neither,' Kathy agreed glumly. 'But I always looked

forward to that weekend away without the kids. It wouldn't be the same going on our own. Remember the time we went to West Cork and we found out that the hotel was an-out-and-out kip and Garry told the mad one behind the desk that he was from Bord Failte and there was no way he and his party were going to spend one minute there, let alone a night and she'd better hand over his deposit fast. And he waved his Union card under her nose and she believed him and gave him back the money. God, we legged it out of there so fast.'

'Remember the time we were camping and Alison set the tent on fire?'

'Yeah, and remember the time we went on the Shannon cruiser and Garry caught a pike and chased you along the quay wall at Dromod with it and you tripped over a rope.'

'I nearly broke my neck.' Kathy grinned in the dark at the memory. 'We did have fun, though, didn't we?'

'Ah, maybe they'll get over it. Maybe a weekend away would do them all the good in the world,' Mike, ever the optimist, declared.

'Maybe,' Kathy agreed but she wondered if they'd all ever have such good times again. The way things were going, it didn't look like it. Alison had told her in the kitchen that she'd got off with a fella she'd met at a dance and she'd enjoyed a mighty good snog with him too for good measure. If she met someone, she was off, and Garry could like it or lump it.

A Gift For You

That didn't sound like someone who was prepared to try and make a go of things. Poor little Ciara. Kathy's motherly heart went out to her goddaughter. She felt very angry as she lay in the dark listening to Mike's volcanic snores beside her. Couldn't either of them see what they were doing to the child? Couldn't they see how insecure she was? Always fighting in front of her. Ciara had told Hannah, Kathy's eldest, that Garry had told Ciara that her mother was an imbecile. Imagine saying that to a child? Mike was right, they were bloody selfish and neither of them was taking any responsibility for what they were doing to their daughter. Kathy didn't like the crowd Ciara hung out with. Imagine letting a twelve-year-old go to a mixed slumber party? Hannah had been asked and was in a monumental huff with her parents at the moment because she wasn't allowed to go. She could stay in her huffs, because no way was she going to any mixed slumber parties. It was very awkward, though; Ciara was allowed to do so much. She was on Facebook and Twitter, she was allowed to watch films Kathy considered totally unsuitable for her age and she wore way too much make-up. In Hannah's eyes, Mike and Kathy were very strict and it was starting to cause terrible hassle.

Her eldest daughter did have the Olly Murs concert to look forward to, Kathy reminded herself. Bringing up kids was no joke. Where did you draw the line between being over-protective and letting them grow up safely? At least she and Mike were trying. Garry and Alison didn't seem to have any such concerns. But then Ciara was very 'responsible' for her age, according to Alison, when Kathy had asked her how in the name of God had she agreed to let her go to this goddamned slumber party. Of course, it suited Alison to think that. It let her off the hook when hard decisions had to be made. 'Responsible' was not the way Kathy would describe Garry and Alison right now, she thought crossly as she gave Mike a dig in the ribs to stop him snoring before drifting off to sleep herself.

I think I'll have a lazy day today, Imelda McHugh decided, as she snuggled under the duvet and pulled it up over her ears. The bed was lovely and warm and she could hear hailstones clattering against the window. Imelda smiled. What bliss! She could stay in bed *all* day if she wanted to. At seventy years of age, she was a liberated woman! 'Thank you, God, for making me a widow.' It was a heartfelt prayer. Since her husband Ben had died two years ago, her life had changed completely. She'd discovered a whole new lease of life. She didn't have to get up at the crack of dawn any more to cook a breakfast for a cantankerous, mean-spirited old man that she hated. And she hated Ben McHugh to whom she'd been married for forty years. He'd made her life a misery with his moods and his meanness and his vicious temper. Ben had been a most thoroughly selfish man. He'd courted her for three years, married her and she like a fool had believed that life would be happy ever after. The relief of having a ring on her finger, saving her from spinsterhood, and the excitement of having a home of her own, helped her overlook her disenchantment with her husband. Once the honeymoon was over and they'd started living in the small terraced house they'd bought in Fairview, her dreams of happy ever after had quickly turned to ashes. Ben wasn't the slightest bit interested in doing anything other than going to work, reading his sports news, watching TV and going to his football matches. He expected his breakfast on the table at 7.30 a.m. Sharp. His dinner had to be on the table when he came home from work in the evening. They had sex every Friday night and that was over almost before it started. After a few grunts and groans and rough fumblings, Ben would roll over and fall asleep.

That had been the pattern throughout their marriage. They'd had one child, Garry. A quiet, introverted, lonely boy who'd left home as soon as he'd done his Leaving Cert. He'd gone to live in a flat in Drumcondra when he'd got a job in the Civil Service. He'd married a girl from Phibsboro, Alison, and they had one child. Imelda didn't see much of them. They'd rarely come to visit when Ben was alive: Christmas, Easter that was it. And Imelda couldn't blame them. Who'd want to come and try and make conversation with the old grump sitting by the fire?

Well, Ben was dead and she was glad of it. She was in the ICA Ladies' Club now. She went bowling, and flower arranging and they were always going on little trips to places of interest. She was having the time of her life and she was going to make the most of it as long as she could. But today it was miserable, the weather had changed and she was staying in bed. Imelda sipped the coffee she'd brought back to bed and nibbled on her toast and marmalade and settled herself against the pillows to read the latest copy of *Hello!* that had some lovely pictures of the Queen and Kate and the Royal Family.

'You're a stupid cow, that's what you are!'

'And you're a scummy bastard. I wish you'd get the hell out of here and never come back.'

'Yeah, well, maybe I will, ya bigmouth bitch . . .'

Ciara McHugh pressed her thumbs into her ears. They were at it again, shouting and roaring and ranting and raving. She hated them. Why couldn't they be like other parents? Why did they have to be fighting all the time?

Why couldn't her mother leave her dad alone? She was always nagging him. Nag, nag, nag. He'd just ignore her and that would make Alison worse and then she'd say something that would get him going and then they'd be yelling and shouting at each other and her dad's face would go dark with fury and Ciara was afraid he'd hit her mother. It frightened her. Sometimes when they fought she'd run up to her bedroom and lie on her bed and her heart would be pounding so loudly she'd think it was going to burst out of her chest.

Ciara heard the door slam so hard that it seemed to shake the whole house. She heard the engine of the car rev. That would be her dad. He'd drive off and not come home for hours after a row. There was a dull silence in the house.

Soon her mother would come upstairs to Ciara's room and start giving out about Garry. She'd tell Ciara that Garry was selfish and cruel and that he'd never given her any support in their marriage, not like their best friend, Mike, gave to Kathy. Alison thought Mike was a great husband and father. 'See how Mike helps around the house, and cooks dinners at the weekend instead of sitting with his nose stuck into a football match on TV.'

'See how Mike helps his kids with their homework.'

'See how Mike takes them out at weekends and gives them . . . *quality* . . . time.'

Alison always paused before she said 'quality' time and made it sound like something holy and reverent. She was always reading books about relationships and quality time and communication.

'Mike . . . *communicates* . . . with his kids. Your father can't *communicate*, Ciara. I've spent years, *years*, trying to get him to talk to me, to share the way Mike and Alison share and it's like banging my head against a stone wall. I tell you, Ciara, if I can make a go of it with someone else, I bloody well will. I'm not wasting any more time on that thick, squinty-eyed shit. Life's not a rehearsal, Ciara. We only get one go on the merry-go-round. Always remember that. And if you've any sense . . . *never* get married. You don't want to end up like me, stuck with a selfish, cruel callous bastard.' She'd usually burst into tears at that point.

When her mother said she was going to go off with some-one else it always frightened Ciara. She didn't want Alison to go off with someone else. What would happen if her parents split up? Where would her daddy go? She didn't think her dad was *that* bad. He didn't drink. That was good. Liz Kelly's father was always drunk. Once, he even puked up his dinner in front of a gang of them who were staying over for a slumber party. Poor Liz was so mortified she just burst into tears.

Ciara's dad was good for giving lifts, even though he moaned about it. When his team won and he was in a good humour, he sometimes gave her five euros. His team was doing very badly this season, so financially, it had been a bit of a disaster for her, Ciara thought glumly as she doodled on the brown paper cover of her copybook. She could do with some extra money. She'd been invited to another slumber party in a friend's house and it was going to be mixed. Alison said it was OK, but she told her not to say anything to Garry. Alison maintained that Garry was far too strict. She wanted Ciara to be independent and stand on her own two feet.

It was going to be a camping slumber party. They were going to buy some alcopops and get langers. Ciara had tasted them at Sharon Ryan's barbecue in August and they had made her feel nice and woozy. She'd smoked three fags as well. She didn't really like smoking, but it was a cool thing to do and she wanted to hang out with the rest of the gang. She was the youngest – twelve – the only one not in secondary school. Ciara sighed. She was starting secondary school next year. She'd have to do her assessment next February and she was extremely worried about it. Her maths was a disaster. She hated it. Hannah Stuart was dead lucky. Her dad was a wizard at maths and he was great for helping her. Mike Stuart was a real nice dad even if he was a bit strict, Ciara thought enviously. Hannah wasn't allowed go to the slumber party and she was freaking out about it. Actually, secretly, deep down, Ciara didn't really *want* to go to the slumber party. Terry Owens was going to be at it, and Ciara didn't like him any more. Once she'd thought she fancied him, but he'd given her a French kiss and stuck his tongue down her throat and she'd thought it was *disgusting!!!* He'd touched her boobs once too, and that made her feel dirty. She wished she hadn't got boobs. She didn't like having them. She hated wearing a bra but Alison had insisted. 'You're a young woman now,' her mother said. 'Enjoy it.'

What was so enjoyable about having fellas sticking their tongues into your mouth and touching you up? Yuck! Ciara shuddered. Another horrible thought struck her. What if she got her first period the night of the slumber party? They could come any time now. Some girls in her class had them already. It was scary. What would she do? Imagine if some of the blood dripped down her leg and the fellas saw it. She wished that she could stay at home but her dad was going to a match and her mother had arranged to go dancing in Tamango's when she knew Ciara was going on a sleepover.

Why, why why couldn't she have normal parents like the Stuarts? Kathy Stuart wouldn't be caught dead in Tamango's. She was a *real* mother. She cooked bread and tarts and she made proper dinners, not burgers and chips, Alison's idea of a dinner, Ciara thought angrily as she heard her mother coming upstairs. She didn't want to get an ear bashing about the row she'd overheard between her parents. She jumped up, switched off the light and dived under the duvet still in her clothes. She heard Alison open the door and peer in cautiously.

'Are you awake, lovie?'

Leave me alone. Leave me alone. Leave me alone. Ciara screamed silently as she lay perfectly still, eyes scrunched tightly shut.

'Ciara?' Alison tried again, hopefully. Ciara knew she needed a shoulder to cry on. She always did after a row. It wasn't fair. It was very confusing. She felt guilty. Maybe she should comfort her mother. She was just about to sit up when Alison closed the door with a little sigh. Ciara lay in the dark and felt tears brim from her eyes in a hot waterfall down her cheeks. Her stomach felt tied up in knots and she felt sick and very scared. She couldn't do her maths, she didn't want to go to the slumber party and her parents were fighting. What would happen to her if her parents got a divorce? She didn't want them to get divorced. She just wanted them to be normal.

Brenda Johnston smiled happily as she lay back in her lover's arms. She hadn't been expecting Garry to call tonight but he'd arrived unexpectedly just after nine. She and Garry had been having an affair for the past three years and she didn't feel one bit guilty. How many times had her best friend, Alison, said, 'I'm sick of him'?

The trouble with Alison was that she didn't *appreciate* Garry. She'd never looked after him. Not the way Brenda did. The trouble between Garry and Alison had started when Ciara was born, according to Alison. She claimed Garry resented not being the centre of attention.

Maybe it was true, Brenda conceded privately. She'd known Garry as long as Alison had and Garry *did* like being the centre of attention. Not in a flamboyant in-your-face way. His way was much more subtle. He'd sit, shoulders hunched up, staring out from behind his glasses with his Poor-Sad-Misunderstood-Me-With-The-Weight-Of-The-World-On-My-Shoulders look that you'd have to feel sorry for him and ask him what was wrong. He'd say 'nothing'. Then you'd have to keep at him. Wrinkling it out bit by bit.

Then you'd get a litany about the pressure he was under at work. Or about Alison and the state she'd left the house in. Once he'd said to her, 'Look, Brenda, I'm a loner, I always have been and always will be, so don't even try and understand me.' He'd been feeling very sorry for himself that night.

But of course she understood him. She understood him more than anyone and she loved him very much. And if he'd let her, she'd make him happy. Much happier than Alison made him. It was just, she was never quite sure where she stood with him. He swore he loved her and he wanted to be with her. His marriage to Alison was over; they were just staying together for Ciara's sake. He promised that when

Ciara had finished college in another ten years he and Brenda would be together for good. He had his responsibilities as a parent and he knew she understood.

It was very decent of him to be so concerned for his daughter, Brenda thought stoutly. He was a good, sound, honest, hard-working man and she couldn't fault him for taking his responsibilities so seriously. That was a good trait, surely? But ten years seemed like such a long time away. She'd be over *fifty*.

Crikey! What a horrific thought. Brenda hastily banished it to the recesses of her mind as she stroked Garry's back. He had pale, pasty, spotty skin. Garry wasn't God's gift in the looks department or even in the sex department, come to think of it. But beggars couldn't be choosers. He was her last chance to have a man of her own.

Her bubble of happiness at his unexpected arrival was getting a little flat. Imagine even thinking like that. Was that how pathetic she was now? Why couldn't she have been like all the rest of her friends and acquaintances? Why couldn't she have met a nice man who would have courted her properly and bought her flowers and chocolates and held car doors open for her and then proposed and given her a day to remember with a beautiful white dress and veil and all the trimmings? Had it been so much to ask for? Had she just grasped at Garry because the years had been slipping by? Because she'd been so panicky and lonely that she was afraid of ending up a spinster on the shelf with no man to show for a lifetime of Friday and Saturday nights of dolling herself up, to go out on the hunt to find a mate? Year after year, dance after dance, disco after disco, nightclub after nightclub.

Was she crazy to believe that Garry would divorce Alison and marry her? When she'd casually mentioned marriage to him one night when they'd had sex, he'd just grunted and said, 'One marriage was enough.' They could just live together, it was much less complicated, he'd muttered.

Of course she'd agreed, but deep, deep down, she was scared. She wanted him to *want* to marry her. That was how it should be. What if he dumped her for some babe in the office? If he could cheat on Alison, he could cheat on her. The thought came unbidden. She buried it. Don't think about that now. He was here, in her arms. That was all that mattered.

He wouldn't have been here if there hadn't been a row. Another sneaky horrible little thought escaped and she shoved it back in the Pandora's box she'd opened this evening. What was wrong with her, for crying out loud? Another even more hideous thought erupted. Maybe she was starting the meno-pause early. Hell! That was all she needed. To become a dried-up old prune as well.

She thought of Eileen O 'Neil at work. Eileen had been having an affair with a married man for years. He spent Friday to Mondays with Eileen and the other three days at home. Eileen was nuts about him. She was so cracked about him she'd even got in Sky Sports for him so that he and his pals could watch live football. He'd assured Eileen many times in the past that he'd marry her if he could . . . safe in the knowledge that divorce wasn't legal in Ireland at the time. Well, it was now and there was no sign of him leaving his wife to marry her. He was an-out-and-out shit, though. He couldn't be satisfied with one mistress; he had several strings to his bow. He didn't think being faithful to Eileen was a priority, and still she took him back and listened to his lies and believed him when he told her his flings were over. Twice, he'd deceived her with another woman and she had just closed her eyes to it.

Brenda snorted. What a foolish woman she was. There he was, living with his wife, living with his mistress, seeing other women, having his cake and eating it. And Eileen was so desperate to keep the lying, cheating, two-faced creep she'd got Sky Sports for him!

Never! Never in a million years would Brenda sink to such levels. She had her pride. Besides, Garry wasn't *anything* like that two-faced slug of Eileen's. Garry had *integrity*.

Brenda felt a little happier. He'd change his mind about the divorce. She was sure of it. If only Alison would find a new man. That would solve everything, Brenda thought with renewed hope. Maybe it might happen next Friday night. She was going to Tamango's with some friends. Ciara was going to a party and Brenda was going to have Garry all to herself for a few hours. She was going to go to a football match with him. She wanted to share every part of his life. 'I suppose I'd better go,' she heard her lover say. How she longed for the time when he could stay all night. That would be the most wonderful thing in the world.

★　★　★

Ciara felt sick, One of the fellas had brought vodka in a Seven-Up bottle to the party and she'd drank some and it made her feel very odd. Then she'd smoked a cigarette and it made her feel dizzy. The music was very loud. She didn't really like Baauer. She much preferred Adele. Her friend's parents had gone off to the pub and two fellas that hadn't been invited had gatecrashed and they were causing trouble. Ciara wanted to go home. Terry Owens grabbed her.

'Let's snog.' He smirked, shoving his pimply face close to hers.

'In your dreams,' Ciara said, in what she hoped was a sufficiently cold and sophisticated rebuff. Terry ignored her and kissed her anyway. She thought she was going to puke.

'Can't wait to see you in your nightie. Whose tent are you sleeping in?' he asked hopefully.

'Not yours, for sure. Besides you know it's one tent for the boys and one for the girls,' Ciara retorted. Terry winked.

'We're coming visiting.'

'Get lost,' Ciara slurred irritably. She didn't want to sleep in a tent. She wanted to be safe and snug in her own bed knowing that Terry Owens couldn't get near her. She felt most peculiar. Her fingers closed around her house key in her jeans pocket. She always carried a key. She got home from school at three, every day, and her mother was never home from work until after six and often later. She was used to being on her own in the house. She wouldn't mind being alone until her dad came home from his match tonight.

Ciara slipped out of the side gate and hurried along the footpath, glancing around every now and then to see if anyone had seen her. She felt very sick and dizzy. Her knees started to shake. She felt scared as she hunkered down, trying to take deep breaths.

'Ciara, Ciara,' are you all right?' She heard Mike Stuart's anxious enquiry.

'I drank some stuff. I feel funny.'

'Come on. Come home with me.' Mike sounded very kind as he helped her up and she leaned against him. His house was just across the street and it was a huge relief to sink down onto his sofa and close her eyes while Kathy covered her with a blanket.

'It's a bloody disgrace. Those kids are all half pissed down in Hennessy's. I rang some of the parents. How could Garry and Alison let Ciara go to something like that? They should be shot.' Mike was furious.

'They don't care about that poor child. Do you know they left her on her own in the house after school with two men who were fitting a new alarm system. Maybe they were perfectly nice men, but who's to know these days? Have they no cop-on? Don't they worry about things the way we do? I wouldn't leave Hannah on her own with two strangers for three minutes, let alone three hours. It's just not safe any more. Have those two lost their marbles, or have they any sense of responsibility? By God, I'm going to give Garry and Alison an earful when I bring Ciara home,' Kathy fumed.

'She's out gadding. He's out at his match, and that poor child is wandering the streets pissed out of her skull. Haven't they a great life all the same, the pair of them?'

'Let her stay the night,' Mike suggested.

'No, Mike. I want Garry to see Ciara's little white face, God love her. I'll bring her home in an hour or so; besides she wants to go home to her own bed.'

'OK, maybe you're right.' Mike agreed as he handed his wife a mug of coffee.

An hour later, Kathy drove her weary goddaughter home. She'd tried to phone to check that Garry was there, but the phone was engaged. So one of them must be there. She felt very sorry for Ciara but it was time that pair accepted some responsibility for their child, she thought grimly, as she swung into the McHughs' drive. Garry's Audi was there and there was a light on in the hall.

'I've my key, the bell's not working properly. You can't hear it if the TV's on,' Ciara said miserably. 'Dad's going to kill me.'

'No, he won't. I'll explain. I know you won't drink again after this,' Kathy assured her.

'I promise I won't, honest,' Ciara said fervently as she slid the key into the lock.

Kathy followed her into the sitting room and heard Ciara's gasp of horror as she halted in her tracks at the scene in front of her. Wailing loudly, she ran from the room as Garry cursed vehemently and Brenda squeaked, 'Ohmigod, ohmigod' from her prone position underneath him on the sofa.

Kathy was so shocked she could only think, *What a hairy arse he has!*

'I . . . I . . .' she stuttered. 'I'll bring Ciara home with me.' She had to get out of here. This was a nightmare. 'You prat, Garry, could you not have gone to *her* house?' Kathy exploded. She raced upstairs after Ciara. 'Come on, love. Come and stay the night with us.'

'I hate him. I hate him. I hate all of them.'

'I know, sweetheart. We'll talk about it at home. Come on, you need a good night's sleep.' Kathy's heart bled for her. Ciara, only five weeks older than her own Hannah, had just had her innocence and security snatched from her in the cruellest way imaginable.

Kathy had lost all respect for Garry. Having an affair was his business, but couldn't he have the decency to conduct it somewhere other than his own home. And Brenda was supposed to be Alison's best friend . . . some friend. The McHughs' marriage was well and truly over, that was for sure, Kathy thought sadly as she ushered the distraught young girl out of the front door. Hard as it was on Garry and Alison, it was a thousand times worse for Ciara.

A year later

Thank God he was staying with his fancy woman tonight, Imelda thought with a sigh of relief, as she plonked herself in front of the TV with a cheese and pickle sandwich. He wasn't coming home for lunch, so she could watch *Home and Away* in peace without having to worry about cooking a meal. What had she done to deserve this trial in her life? Imelda wondered angrily. It was almost eight months since Garry had arrived on her doorstep, muttering that there was a bit of trouble at home and could he stay with her for a while. Imelda had been dumbstruck, but what could she say? She couldn't turn her own son away, even if he was the last person in the world she wanted living with her.

He was so like his father, surly and bad-tempered. He'd moved in, bag and baggage and the days turned into weeks, then months and slowly but surely her precious hard-won freedom was eroded away. She had to wash and iron his clothes, and cook his meals for him. She couldn't even watch the programmes she liked on TV any more if there was sport on.

He had another girlfriend, he'd told her that, and he usually spent a night or two and the weekends with her. But if they had a row, which they did frequently, he ended up staying with Imelda. She bitterly resented the situation but couldn't bring herself to ask him to leave. She'd never been good at standing up for herself; a lifetime married to Ben McHugh had seen to that. Now it was if he'd come back to haunt her. She woke up angry in the mornings and went to bed angry at night.

A little flicker of hope glimmered. Maybe Garry would get a divorce and go and marry that Brenda one. Imelda had never met her nor did she want to meet her, but if she took Garry off her hands, Imelda would be eternally grateful. She wondered, could she pray that Garry would get divorced and remarried? Hardly. It didn't seem right. Maybe she'd just pray that Garry would move out and get a flat of his own. He surely didn't want to spend the rest of his life living with her?

It was all so distressing. Imelda pushed away her sandwich. She wasn't hungry. Her life was a hard old grind again. Just like before. And she didn't have the guts to do anything about it. That was the hardest thing of all to live with.

Kathy glazed the top of the chicken and mushroom pie and popped it in the oven. It would be cooked by the time the kids came in from school. She'd made it especially for Ciara. It was her goddaughter's favourite. Ciara was spending the weekend with them . . . yet again.

Kathy's mouth tightened into a thin line as she remembered how Alison had phoned with her one of her rigmaroles about how she needed Ciara looked after as she'd just got a lovely offer of a weekend away with her new boyfriend and she couldn't ask Garry and Brenda to take her because it wasn't their weekend to have her and they weren't at all flexible in that regard. 'And she just loves being with you and Mike. And Hannah's her very best friend,' Alison gushed, as usual.

Poor old Ciara – she was just a nuisance to her parents, who were far too concerned with having a good time to worry about the effect it was all having on their daughter. Kathy was so angry she really wanted to tell Garry and Alison what she thought of them. She hadn't seen Garry since that dreadful night when she'd walked in on him and Brenda. He hadn't had the manners to contact her or Mike once. It was as if they didn't exist in his life. Some friend he'd turned out to be. He didn't have the backbone to face them. Or maybe he just didn't want to. He'd dropped them like hot potatoes when he didn't need them, and all their happy times together meant nothing.

Kathy could understand why Garry couldn't face her, but she couldn't forgive him for the way he was treating Ciara. She'd never forget Hannah telling her last summer that Ciara had got a postcard from her daddy and his girlfriend on holiday and she hoped they'd buy her a nice present.

He'd only seen her three times that summer. At least Alison had taken her away for a week. But Garry had taken his two weeks holiday and spent them driving around the country with his mistress. The best he could do was to send Ciara a postcard. Kathy had been incensed.

'It's neglect, Mike, that's what it is, and I'm going to have it out with him. And with Alison. The two of them are off having the life of Reilly and it's you and me that are here worrying about Ciara.'

'And if you cause a row, who's going to suffer? Ciara. Say nothing. It's not our place to interfere. All we can do is be here for Ciara as long as she needs us. If there's an argument, they might stop her from seeing us. That poor kid has enough traumas in her life without that. Say nothing,' Mike had advised.

Kathy knew he was right and she'd held her tongue, but she sizzled with resentment. She'd liked Garry and Alison as friends. They'd had a lot of good times in the past. Never in a million years had she expected this of them. It was quite obvious Garry didn't give a hoot about her and Mike and that hurt.

Alison was using them at every possible opportunity, emotionally blackmailing them by saying how much Ciara loved staying with them. Kathy was sick of it, heartily sick of it. Users, that's what they were. If it wasn't for the fact that she loved Ciara like one of her own she'd tell them to get lost, and never wish to see them again, she thought angrily as she set the table for the dinner.

Brenda sat in the staff canteen drinking coffee. The chatter and buzz and the rattle of china and cutlery was giving her a headache. Being involved with Garry left her feeling as if she was walking on a tightrope. One false move and that was it. Why didn't he want to marry her the way she wanted to marry him? Why wouldn't he commit to her? Why did he keep using Ciara as an excuse? It wasn't as if he was exactly *Father of the Year Award* material. Actually, he wasn't as good a father as she had once given him credit for, that couldn't be denied. He admitted it, but he was too selfish to do anything about it. It was a side of him that Brenda didn't like, but she tried not to think about it.

If he was living with her permanently, Ciara could spend more time with them. The trouble was, Brenda knew he was happy enough living with his mother. He was well looked after. Better than when he'd lived with Alison. He had all the home comforts. And then he had her for sex when he needed it.

How could she compete with Ma McHugh? Garry had told her that his mother liked him living with her. It made her feel more 'secure,' he said. He wouldn't like to 'desert' her.

That had chilled Brenda to the bone. Something drastic had to be done. She needed to make living with her a more attractive proposition for him.

Brenda got up from the table and marched upstairs. She Googled for a couple of minutes on her iPhone, found the number she was looking for and dialled it.

'Hello,' she said to the person at the other end, 'I'd like to make an enquiry about getting Sky Sports. How do I go about it?'

Ciara sat in class listening to her teacher explain about the assessment test for deciding the maths groups. It was like a huge big weight on her shoulders. It made her feel sick to think about it. She was *such* a dunce at maths. She was going to stay with Hannah this weekend. She'd ask Mike to explain Simple Interest to her. He was very good at explaining things.

She was glad she was staying with the Stuarts. She didn't want to go to Kilkenny for the weekend with Alison and her new boyfriend. She hated seeing her mother in bed with another man, just as she hated seeing her Dad in bed with Brenda of the knitting needle legs. She'd never forget the sight of those skinny legs wrapped around her father's white arse. Ciara bit her nails. They were down to the stubs. They looked awful but no matter how hard she tried to, she couldn't stop.

Biting her nails made her think of food. She hoped Kathy would cook chicken and mushroom pie for the dinner. It always tasted scrumptious. Everyone thought she was dead lucky to have a mother like Alison. A mother who let her wear make-up and minis and who brought her into pubs and gave her sips of wine and who allowed her have a TV in her room. Her friends thought Alison, who went to night-clubs, and knew all the words of the latest pop songs, was dead cool. Ciara just wished she'd stay at home and cook real dinners and help her with her homework. Like Kathy. Kathy was a *proper* mother, Ciara thought enviously. Hannah was very lucky.

'Are your Ma and Da going to get a divorce, like mine?' Sadie Flynn had whispered to her in class earlier.

'No, they're just separated for a while; they're going to get back together,' Ciara whispered back. She always said that, hoping against hope that it would come true.

'Oh!' said Sadie . . . disappointed.

The knots tightened in Ciara's stomach. She'd pushed the D word to the back of her mind over the last while. Now it loomed large and threatening again. Another great worry to add to the ones she already had.

★   ★   ★

A Gift For You

Alison McHugh sang to herself as she packed her toilet bag for the weekend. She was looking forward to the trip to Kilkenny immensely. She felt young and carefree, so different from the past few years. It was a joy to be free and almost single again. Not that she wanted a divorce, she decided as she folded her white lacy negligee. She'd given the matter a lot of thought.

No, she was happy as she was. She wasn't going to disgrace the family name with a divorce. Brenda could have Garry, but she wasn't getting her mitts on a half share of the house and whatever money would be divided between her and Garry if they divorced.

Alison didn't want Brenda to become Mrs McHugh. That would alter the status between them too much. She'd had always enjoyed being the object of Brenda's envy and, as long as she stayed married to Garry, Brenda would be the poor little spinster who couldn't *quite* get a man of her own and had to settle for used goods, while Alison would have the security of her wedding ring and still have men attracted to her like moths to the flame. It was almost like being a teenager again.

I'm quite the *femme fatale*, she thought giddily as she packed her sexy black suspender belt.

Garry switched off the news and switched over to Lyric as he drove home along the M50 after work. He hoped his mother had cooked a roast dinner. He was hungry. He'd have his dinner with his Ma before going over to watch the match on Sky in Brenda's. He'd heard on the grapevine at work that the Carrolls, a couple he and Brenda knew, had divorced. No doubt she would give him another ear-bashing tonight. Well, she was barking up the wrong tree there. He had no intention of ever getting married again. Once was enough. Besides, he was dammed if that cow, Alison, was going to get her hot sweaty little paws on one penny of his money. He'd worked hard for that house. It was his investment. He wasn't going to split the profits for it down the middle so she could go and set up with her new toy-boy lover. Let *him* buy his own house and set her up in the style to which she was accustomed. Not that he'd let on to Alison that he didn't want a divorce. He'd keep her dangling. It was the best way to keep women. On their toes. Anyway, he had Ciara to think about, he thought self-righteously. He wouldn't inflict divorce on her. He had to be a responsible parent. And besides, if Brenda got tired of him, and his mother kicked him out, he'd need to have a roof over his head.

No, Garry scowled, divorce was not an option and if people didn't like it, they could bloody well lump it. His life suited him just fine the way it was.

A Dish Best Served Cold

George Hume paced the Italian marble floor in the lounge of his Kensington apartment and let fly a stream of profanity as he flung the paper he'd been reading onto the leather sofa and glowered at his wife. 'It's not looking good for me declaring bankruptcy here; they've turned down another pair from home now. They're appealing but I have my doubts. I should have gone to the States like that Anglo fucker, and "The Baron". Those cute hoors will get away with it.'

'Don't curse,' his wife Cora said wearily.

'I'll curse if I bloody want to,' George snarled. The phone rang and he stiffened. 'Answer that,' he ordered brusquely. 'I don't want to talk to anyone. Tell them I'm out.'

Cora picked up the receiver. 'Hello,' she said, trying to keep her voice composed.

'Cora, it's Brian Dolan from Brook and McConnell. I had an enquiry about houses in your area – a Chinese businessman wants to buy. Discretely. I said I'd let George know. Not a bad offer, considering prices have dropped fifty per cent. He's willing to go two and a half.'

'Oh, dear, Brian, that's a big drop. I'll tell George you rang,' Cora said dispiritedly.

'I might get another 20K at push; unfortunately, it's a buyer's market.' Brian said glumly.

'Indeed. Thank you, Brian. I'll get back to you before the weekend.'

'What was that all about?' George glowered at her. Middle age had not been kind to her husband, Cora reflected, studying George dispassionately. He was florid, balding, and two jowls on either side of his mean little mouth gave him the look of a particularly aggressive bull-dog. His eyes were sunken beneath puffy eyelids, like two little grey marbles.

Cora took a deep breath; he was going to flip when he heard what Brian had to say. 'Some Chinese businessman is interested in buying in our area. Brian thinks he could get two and a half million for the house, or perhaps two seventy at a push,' she said calmly.

George's eyes bulged and he turned purple. 'Is he for real?' he spat. 'That house cost me five and I had an offer of ten for it in 2006. Tell him to go fuck himself if that's the best he can do for a detached seven bedroom house in Ballsbridge.'

'At least we'd have money at our back if we sold it; they can't come after it because it's in my name,' Cora pointed out. 'And we'd get at least another million for the paintings and furniture.'

'I couldn't live on two and a half million; are you mad?' George looked at her as if she'd lost her mind.

'Well George, bankruptcy is our only route and you're spending a fortune here trying to declare it in the UK. And we can't afford the mortgage on this place any more and—'

'Enough, Cora, why can't you say something positive instead of spouting out negative crap,' he raged. 'Do something to help me for a change.'

'Like what?' she asked exasperatedly, thoroughly fed up of him and their precarious financial situation.

'Go over to Dublin and make sure the house is OK and make sure that fella you hired to maintain the gardens is doing a proper job. I don't want the place going to rack and ruin, and then go and put the place in Spain on the market. That's in your name too. Open a separate account out there; we can use that to pay some of these bloody legal fees. We're going to take a hit out there but it's costing too much to maintain. I'll get Valentina to book your tickets. I'm going to the club.' He marched out of the room and a few minutes later she heard the front door slam.

Goodbye and good riddance, Cora thought jadedly, walking over to the window to look out over the elegant square with its small private park in the centre. Their three-bedroom, three-bathroom, two-reception, high-ceiling apartment in a smart mansion block, ten minutes' walk from Kensington High Street, had been their home for the last year, as George tried to persuade the courts and his creditors that London and not Dublin was the base of his business operations so that he could avail of the UK's far more lenient bankruptcy terms. Nothing Cora could say would dissuade him from his quest, despite the fact that every Tom, Dick and Harry at home knew he had worked out of a swanky office in Merrion Square. George couldn't accept that his greedy, acquisitive career as a developer was well and truly over and he owed the banks millions.

Cora couldn't care less about the banks. They had behaved so appallingly and given loans that were clearly unsustainable, where no checks had been carried out regarding ability to pay. Those immoral bankers had gambled just as much as the clients they had actively encouraged to borrow massive amounts. They had all wooed George in the boom and now were determined to get their money back.

George and his fellow gamblers were all squealing like stuck pigs, maintaining they had been taking for a ride. Well, she was no genius, or financial expert, but she understood what a 'personal guarantee meant', and had insisted years ago that her husband pay off the mortgage on their home and that it was never to be used as a guarantee for *any* loan he applied for. He had pooh-poohed her but she'd stuck to her guns and eventually he'd paid off the house in Ballsbridge, with a loan from Anglo. Now they were suing him, but the mortgage had been with another bank, it was paid off, she had the deeds and they couldn't touch the house. When the first signs of the bust became apparent, he transferred the house to her name as well as the villa in Spain.

Cora watched her husband rev the engine of the Merc and scorch out of the square, and exhaled. He wouldn't be home until late. She was free of him for the rest of the day.

It was a warm May afternoon and she suddenly felt claustrophobic, wanting to get out of the whitewashed elegant square to see trees and blue sky and a vista that didn't include buildings, no matter how elegant. She missed Dublin and the ease and speed she could get from Ballsbridge to the sea or the countryside.

She walked down the hall to her bedroom and took a pale pink pashmina from a drawer in the tallboy. She was wearing cream linen trousers and a black long sleeved V-necked cotton top. She wrapped the pashmina around her and took off her nude L.K.Bennett slingbacks and slid into a pair of espadrilles. She took her bag, library book and keys and hurried down the hall, anxious to get out in the fresh air.

The sound of birdsong lifted her heart as she emerged onto the square. The trees were leafy and fresh, still spring-like, and a balmy breeze lifted her ash-blonde hair from her forehead, refreshing her as she walked briskly along the tree lined streets towards the High Street. She normally liked to dawdle along and window shop, or poke around the antique shops, but today she wanted to be away from traffic and people and she kept up her pace. She'd call into the whole food market on the way back and get some corn-fed chicken breasts, and salads for supper. She would be eating alone.

George wouldn't thank her for corn-fed chicken and salads. She'd pop into M&S and get him some lamb and steak dishes and plenty of their creamy mash for while she was away.

She crossed at the lights just before the Royal Garden and thought wistfully that it would be nice to have a massage and facial in their sumptuous spa. But George was scrutinising all her bills now and it wasn't worth the hassle. How times had changed, she reflected wryly, as she saw the hotel's doorman whistle for a taxi. She'd even cut down on the amount of taxies she took and sometimes took the tube, although she tried to avoid it in the rush hour.

She made a left turn down Palace Avenue and strode through the gates into Kensington Gardens and felt herself relax. It was her favourite place in London and the sight of the palace reminded her of a lovely day she had spent with her sister who had flown over to spend the weekend with her in March. They had explored the palace from top to bottom, thoroughly enjoying the tour of Queen Victoria's rooms, and the exhibition of Diana's dress, before poking around the well-stocked gift shop. They'd had a delicious lunch in the Orangery, where she was now headed. She sat at a table outside and ordered coffee and a smoked salmon salad. She tried not to feel guilty spending money on lunch out but she felt she deserved it. George was giving her a dog's life. He was taking it all out on her and she was at the end of her tether. Tears welled in her eyes and she swallowed hard and strove to regain control before the waiter came back with her order.

It was the unfairness of it all. She had stood at his side for all these years, the perfect wife and mother, ignoring his little flings in the boom years when little blonde gold-diggers made a play for him and his oversized wallet. She had entertained for him, spent hours making polite chit-chat to people she neither knew or cared to know, she had kept his houses in perfect running order and seen to their impeccable decor and all the thanks she got from him was tirades of abuse as each new unwelcome development unfolded.

Well, she'd had enough of him and his appalling moods; she was going to go home and do what she had to do in Dublin and try and avoid the prying eyes of the press, and then go to Spain and stay for at least a month chilling out, she thought crossly, composing her features into a smile when the waiter placed her food in front of her.

She ate her meal and drank another glass of wine and, after leaving her waiter a generous tip, she made her way across the Broad Walk to the Round Pond, and took a deckchair. Another expense for George to worry about, she thought with grim humour as she paid the collector. It was peaceful to sit and watch the tourists feeding the swans and ducks, and children floating little boats over the water, as the breeze caressed her and the azure blue sky delighted her. She took her library book, a Catherine Dunne novel, out of her bag and settled herself to read. Deeply engrossed, she jumped when her mobile rang, and impatiently rooted for it in her bag. She scowled when she saw the name flash up. 'Hello,' she said coolly.

'Mrs Hume, Valentina here. Mr Hume has asked me to book your flights to Dublin and then from there to Malaga. Shall I leave the return flight from Malaga open? And how long do you want to spend in Dublin?' George's secretary said in her snooty, clipped voice.

'Four days in Dublin will do fine, and get me the early-morning flight to Malaga please, Valentina,' Cora said crisply.

'Certainly, Mrs Hume. Anything else you require?' Valentina enquired with her customary condescending air.

'That will be all, thank you. Goodbye.' Cora hung up and made a face. Valentina was a supercilious little madam whose attitude left a lot to be desired.

Twenty minutes later, her phone rang. It was George. 'Why are you not at home?' he asked irritably.

'Because I'm going shopping in M&S to get the meals you like for when I'm away,' she retorted.

'Oh! Well, I've sacked my legal team and taken on a new one. They're taking a different tack entirely and I think we've a real chance of winning. I want—'

'George, are you out of your tree? How much is that going to cost you? They'll promise you the moon. They don't care whether you win or lose, all they want is your—'

'I'm sick of you and your negativity, Cora. Get off my back, for crying out loud. It's my money. I worked my ass off to make it I'll decide how to spend it.'

'Fine, George, that's fine. I'm going now.' Cora clicked off and flung her phone into her bag. Her husband wouldn't be happy until they were penniless and in the gutter. She felt a headache begin to throb in her temple and a knot of anxiety twist her insides. This was crazy stuff. George was unable and unwilling to face their financial predicament. He would not accept responsibility for his part in their situation. She had had enough. She'd given him thirty-five years of her life. She would be sixty next year. She wanted a life without turmoil. She placed her book in her bag and reluctantly stood up to return home. She was too agitated to try and relax again. What was the point? It was like this every day now. One thing after another. No one wrote articles in the papers back home about the ulcer-inducing stress many of the wives of the once high-flying businessmen were under. She had tried her best to rein her husband in, to no avail. She should have left him years ago, but she had been too loyal. This was where her loyalty had got her. A nervous wreck, who had nothing to look forward to.

What the hell was wrong with Cora? She was driving him around the bend. George scowled. It was a different kettle of fish when money had been no object and she was the queen of the castle, throwing parties here and there. Decorating houses with the most expensive art and furniture. And he hadn't said a word. He'd *encouraged* her. She'd been the envy of women up and down the country. Now all she could do was nag! Some wife she was.

He was glad she was going home and then on to Spain. He could do with a break from her. He had a nice little filly who still thought he was a player. A little Russian blonde a friend of his had introduced him to. Olga! She'd be more than impressed when she saw the apartment, George mused, cheering up at the thought. The sooner Cora was out of his hair for a while, the better.

'And so, Brian, I want you to go ahead with the sale to your Chinese client. I want you to get your fine arts people to sell the paintings and the furniture, discretely. I want it all to be done very quickly, and you are to deal with me and me alone. George is under so much stress I'm afraid he'll have a heart attack,' she instructed authoritatively.

'No problem, Mrs Hume. That's fine. Any problems and I'll come to you.'

'There shouldn't be any; it's a straightforward sale,' Cora said calmly. These are my new solicitors; they'll be looking after the conveyancing. She slid a typed sheet over the desk to him and stood up. 'I'm going to Spain the day after tomorrow, but you have my mobile number.' She shook hands with the estate agent and walked out of his office, feeling an enormous boulder had lifted from her shoulders.

She dialled her husband's mobile on her Bluetooth as she drove along the Grand Canal, sparkling and undulating under the dappled light of the trees. It was lovely to be back in her native city even for a few days. 'The house is fine, I'll forward on the post. The gardens look good, but I got papped,' she fibbed, driving towards Baggott St

Bridge. 'You better stay well away; I'll deal with things here. I'll fly back from Malaga to Dublin and check the place out again.'

'Right,' George said grumpily. He had no desire to set foot in that benighted isle that had ruined him. His son and daughter were working in Australia; there was nothing for him in Ireland, only begrudgery and hassle.

'Stay in Spain for a while, don't rush back here on my account; there's no point in the two of us having a miserable summer, and I'll be very busy,' he added magnanimously, remembering his plans for an entertaining evening with Olga.

'I might do that. We'll see. Bye,' Cora said non-committally, and hung up.

'Bye yourself,' George muttered, scrolling down his mobile for the Russian's number.

Some new little tart on the scene, Cora guessed, swinging the car into the circular drive of the big redbrick mansion that she no longer considered home. Let him have his fun while he could, it just made it all the easier for her to do what she was doing.

That little cow Valentina had only booked economy for her, Cora saw in disgust while sitting in the taxi to Dublin airport. Well, the day was coming when she'd have nothing to do with her and that couldn't come soon enough. Cora upgraded to first class and relaxed in the Gold Circle Lounge until it was time to board. She sat back in the leather first-class seat, yawning. She'd been up at four and she was tired but exhilarated. For the first time in years she felt in control of her life and her future. All she had to do was get the villa sold and then she could sit back and decide what her next step was. The Air Lingus airbus soared high out over Dublin Bay, and she caught a glimpse of the iconic twin ESB chimneys and knew the next time she landed in Dublin she would be mistress of her own fate.

'What do you mean, you're not coming back to London?' George roared. 'You've been away the whole summer.'

'Stop shouting, George, or I'll hang up,' Cora said coldly. 'I'm not coming back to live with you in London or anywhere else for that matter. I've paid my dues; I've done my best for you; now it's time for me. I've sold the house; I've a sale agreed on the villa. They're both in my name. It's all legal and above board. No one can come after me. Your debts are your own from now on—'

'You can't do that!' George exploded.

'I can and I have. And this is the last time I'll be phoning you. You can tell Valentina I'm changing my mobile number so there's no point in trying to contact me. I've put all your personal possessions' in storage in Dublin. I'll send you the details; you can take over the payment next month if you want to. I'll make sure the kids have a home if they want to come back to Ireland, although I doubt they would—'

'Cora! Now Cora listen to me.' There was a note of panic in his voice. 'There's no need to overreact. You've sold the house, fine, we'll get somewhere else, it was too big for us any—'

'George, there *is* no "we" any more. I'm only taking what I put into the marriage. You're getting away lightly, believe me,' Cora said grimly. 'Good luck with that new legal team.'

'Cor—' But it was too late; she'd hung up and turned off her phone.

Cora stretched out on the lounger on her hotel balcony and raised her face to the sun. The yachts in Puerto Banus across the harbour gleamed in the silver-hued water. George could fly out to Spain if he wanted. The locks on the villa were changed, the estate agent had the keys. She was flying back to Ireland tomorrow to view a detached house near the seafront in Clontarf. It looked bright and airy on the internet photos, and had three large ensuite bedrooms, perfect if the children ever wanted to stay. She wanted to live near the sea. She would still have a very healthy nest egg when she had bought it. She had secured her future and that of her children. When she died, her estate would go to them alone.

George could tilt at windmills as long as he wanted. He could have as many little foreign tartlets as he wanted. She didn't care. He had used her to try and fiddle the banks and the taxman, never thinking that she would take advantage of the situation to secure her future. Big mistake, George, Cora thought coldly. The banks couldn't come after her, the taxman couldn't come after her; unlike her husband she was tax compliant. She was free.

Cora sipped her gin and tonic and looked forward to the back massage and facial she had booked for later. It was time to start afresh. She would captain her own ship from now on.

Sitting in the sweltering heat in his office in London, George Hume put his head in his hands and wept; while in the outer office, Valentina tried repeatedly to ring her boss's wife with every phone number she had on file for her . . . to no avail.

'I bought a magnificent new house for us at a bargain price,' the Chinese businessman told his delighted wife on the phone as he stood in the leafy-green garden of the red-bricked double-fronted mansion in Dublin 4 – a most sought-after address – that he could now call home.

The Judge

He sits, tombstone straight. His back does not touch the chair. His feet, surprisingly neat and dainty for such a portly man, are positioned at twelve o' clock precisely. This is the way he has sat in his court for the last thirty years.

How he wishes he were sitting in his court now, with his wig on his head. His black gown immaculate and uncreased, enhancing his girth. An imposing figure. A judge that engenders respect, apprehension, dismay – even fear – among the myriad flocks of legal and criminal fraternities alike that are his subjects.

His maroon silk dressing gown will not stay closed over the Buddha dome of his stomach. It is a constant, niggling irritation and he tuts while tightening the belt for the umpteenth time. His new carpet slippers are too tight. Swollen, gouty fluid-filled flesh strains again their cruel restraint. His feet are the colour of bruised plums.

A preemptory knock alerts him to the arrival of the

mid-morning tea and biscuits, which were signalled ten minutes earlier by the cacophony of the clatters of trollies arriving from the kitchen at the end of the corridor.

'Mornin', luv, here ya go, enjoy it!' A thin, careworn woman in a yellow uniform and matching yellow hat plonks his tea tray on the grey trolley that stretches across his bed.

'Thank you,' he clips coldly, affronted at her casual, disrespectful salutation. '*I am not your "luv". I am "Your Lordship", one of the most senior judges in the country*,' is what he would have said if anyone in his court had ever had the temerity to address him thus.

'Yer welcome,' she reciprocates over her shoulder and then she is gone, the door closed none too gently behind her, shutting out the never-ending sounds of the hospital, in which he feels incarcerated.

The Judge eases himself up out of his chair. Sharp, pointed needles of pain pierce his joints. His arthritis is giving him hell. He pours the tea from the small aluminum teapot into the thick white cup. The amber liquid leaks from the spout, soaking into the white doily dressing the plate, on which three ginger biscuits lie.

Ginger biscuits are his favourite. He milks and sugars his tea and reaches for a biscuit. Unthinkingly, he eats it in two mouthfuls, takes a gulp of the tea and swallows. He takes another biscuit. Halfway between plate and mouth, he pauses. His surgeon has told him he must lose weight for his bladder surgery to be successful. He has also told him to cut back on his caffeine intake.

Just this last one, the Judge promises himself, as he greedily devours the sweet tidbit. He pours himself another cup of tea. In his latter years on the bench, mid-morning tea has not been a luxury he has allowed himself. Interrupting a case he is hearing to void his bladder is not conducive to the smooth running of his court. He sets the bar high, he tells his wife, amused at his clever legal pun. 'You're still entitled to go to the restroom,' she sniffs, unimpressed at his 'martyrdom' as she calls it.

He finishes the last biscuit. He has always loved his food and drink. It is the only weakness the Judge permits himself. That, and staying at expensive hostelries when he is on the circuit. He has no qualms at all about ordering chateaubriand and the finest wines to entertain whomever he choses to dine with. He is Judge Harney, after all. One of the best, if not *the* best, known judges in the country. He dispenses justice on behalf of the citizens. It is only right and proper that they, in return, pay out of their many taxes for the lifestyle to which he has become accustomed over thirty years in his position. No cheap inns and B&B's for him. Standards have to be maintained, recessions or no, he believes, despite his wife's dire warnings that taxpayers will take umbrage at his sense of entitlement and unwarranted expense account. She is afraid it will cause a scandal.

'No one will question me. I am a member of the judiciary, a man of the highest integrity. I have nothing to answer for,' is his response. But she worries that some troublemaking journalist will draw attention to what she perceives as a lack of moral rectitude. Her attitude annoys him. He feels he is being judged and he does not like it.

The door swings open, and a young redheaded nurse pushing a machine breezes in. 'Time for your TPR, Frederick,' she says cheerily, 'And I'll take your blood pressure too.'

Frederick! His lips thin. 'You may call me "Judge", or "Mister Harney",' he snaps.

'Oh! No problem, Mr Harney,' the nurse responds, clearly taken aback at his stern rebuke. She sticks a thermometer in his ear and waits for it to ping. He sits, fuming, while she checks his pulse before uncoiling the black blood pressure cuff to wrap around his upper arm.

The urge to urinate becomes overwhelming. He should never have had that damn second cup of tea. He sits, clenching, legs crossed tightly as the cuff puffs and expands, tightening around his arm. The numbers on the monitor rise inexorably, taunting him.

'Are you all right there, Mr Harney?' The nurse notices his agitation.

'I have to go to the toilet,' he says abruptly, struggling to get out of his seat.

'Fine, fine.' The nurse says, calmly taking the cuff off his arm.

'Out of my way, out of my way.' He pushes past, bumping into the machine in his haste to get to the bathroom. It hits the side of the bed and almost topples over but he manages to straighten it up. 'Sorry!' he mutters. He has just rounded the corner of the bed, and has a clear run to the bathroom when the tea lady arrives to collect her tray.

'Out of the way,' he says frantically, trying to brush her aside as she inadvertently blocks his path.

'All right, luv, keep yer hair on,' she responds good humouredly, stepping aside. He steps in the same direction and they do an awkward shuffle.

'For God's sake!' he exclaims irritably, circling around her. But it is too late. He feels the hot, wet trickle of urine down his leg, darkening his pajama bottoms. He is mortified as the now familiar smell of incontinence assails his nostrils before he finally reaches the sanctuary of the small, tiled ensuite bathroom.

This has been his nightmare for the past year. This is why he has only allowed himself a small cup of tea with his breakfast every morning before work. His bladder is a weak spot over which he is losing control. A metaphor for his life, the Judge thinks grimly, positioning himself at the toilet bowl.

A cold sweat breaks over him as he relieves himself, his sodden pajama trousers damply clinging to his purple-veined legs. A memory that he has buried deep in the dark recesses of his mind resurfaces.

No, no, I will not think of that. He forces himself to concentrate on his predicament. He will have to shower. Change his pajamas. But first he will have to face those two females outside who have witnessed his shame.

'Everything OK in there, Mr Harney?' The nurse calls through the bathroom door. Waves of humiliation wash over him as he bends to wipe the urine spattered floor with wads of toilet paper.

'Yes! Yes! I, eh . . . I . . . could you give me a couple of moments privacy please? I'll ring you when I'm ready for you,' he says with as much authority as he can muster.

'Certainly, no rush,' she says evenly. 'I'll do the other patients first.'

'Thank you,' he manages, utterly relieved when he hears the monitor being trundled away.

He is rooting in his locker for clean pajamas when the door opens again and the tea lady appears with a mop and bucket. The strong harsh smell of disinfectant scents the air as she sets the bucket down. He cannot meet her gaze.

'The cleaners are on lunch break so I'll just give this a little swizz around,' she says matter-of-factly, dipping and mopping in wide circular motions. 'I know it's not me job, but it won't take a minute, luv. Don't tell the union though. Ye know what they're like!' She laughs at her little joke.

'I . . . I apologise, er . . . for . . . em—'

'Nothing worse than leaky waterworks. Don't worry about it, luv, I'll just do the bathroom floor. Kate's gone to get you a plastic bag for your pj's.'

'Kate?' he says distractedly, trying to keep his dressing gown from touching his damp pajamas.

'Yer nurse, luv,' she calls from the bathroom.

He hears the sound of running water. 'I turned on the shower for ye; sure you'll be as fresh as a daisy before ya know it. Is there anything else I can do for ye, luv?' She emerges from the bathroom and fixes him with a kindly stare. In it he sees something that infuriates him. Pity.

'Nothing more, thank you,' he says curtly, and turns his back on her. How *dare* she pity him! How dare someone of her ilk feel sorry for the likes of him, he rages, wishing she would be gone.

He marches into the bathroom with his clean pajamas and slams the door.

'Jayziz, he's a grumpy ould fuck, Kate,' he hears her say to the nurse, who laughs.

The nerve of them laughing at him. He seethes, stepping into the shower. The absolute nerve!

The slow bubble of resentment simmers for the rest of the day. When the tea lady comes with his lunch, he keeps his head in his paper and merely grunts when she lays down his tray. He has no difficulty maintaining an air of *froideur* when the nurse comes to take his blood pressure again several hours later. He remains mute, staring out the window onto the spring-adorned grounds below. An apple tree, voluptuous with pink and white buds bursting into bloom, soothes his troubled spirit. When the nurse has gone, taking all her accouterments with her, the Judge exhales and lets some of the tension release from his body.

'A grumpy ould fuck,' the tea lady had called him. And she had pitied him because she had seen his dignity in tatters. To her, he was just an old man, with all the problems that come with aging. Not a judge in his wig and gown, feared and respected in equal measure. Those symbols, that he has taken such pride in, were merely props that he has hidden behind for many, many years. And now here in this alien place, they have been stripped away and he is revealed in all his frailty. Another elderly patient that has to be attended to in this small, pleasant, airy room where status is of no importance.

'Will you be having a cup of tea tonight? You don't need to fast until midnight,' the tea lady asks, when she collects his tea tray. The rays of the evening sun shine harshly on her face causing her to squint. He sees each line etched into the pale, thin visage. She has known hardship, he can see that. She reminds him of some of the mothers who have stood stoically in his court with their sons and daughters, weary to their bones at the hardship their offspring's criminality brings.

'You may bring me one,' he says coldly, remembering what she had called him earlier.

'Grand,' she says and then is gone with the tray. He hears her calling to one of her colleagues that Number 224 is due up from theatre and will be wanting tea and toast in a while.

He is in room 222. No doubt she calls him Number 222 when she is not calling him derogatory names, the Judge thinks, sulkily flicking his TV channels to get the news.

He has a busy evening. His consultant calls and explains yet again about the bladder-sling procedure he will preform the following morning. The anesthetist comes to listen to his chest. His wife and brother call to visit and he is fatigued by the time the tea lady comes to collect his supper tray.

It is after eight p.m. She has been on duty since early that morning. Tiredness seeps through her bones; he can see it in the gray pallor of her face. No doubt, he muses, she has to go home and catch up on chores, but still she is determinedly cheerful.

'Sleep well, see ya tamarra.' She wipes his trolley, gathers his tray and bestows a smile on him, before hastening out the door to take her load of dirty crockery to the ward kitchen.

They work long hours, those hospital staff, he admits, after the night nurse has bought him his theatre gown and switched off the main light. He slumps against his pillows wishing he was at home in his own bed, in his maroon and brown bedroom surrounded by his books and toby jugs that he has collected since childhood. His bedroom is his haven. He and his wife have their own rooms, at her suggestion. His snoring is not conducive to a goodnight sleep for her and she has abandoned him for the sanctuary of a duck-egg-blue bedroom with frills and female fripperies.

He feels nervous at the thought of what is to come. Tomorrow will be even worse than today. After his surgery, he will have a catheter. He will have nurses fiddling with his privates. He can think of no greater indignity. Well, perhaps one. He grimaces, remembering his earlier shame when he lost control of his bladder. It is a long, long time since he has felt such mortification. And then, unwelcome and repugnant, that memory from his school days roars like a tsunami into his consciousness.

'No!' he moans, shaking his head as recollections he would prefer to erase surge back with unwelcome clarity.

'Spekkie Four Eyes. Spekkie Four Eyes, Mama's Little Pet,' the older boys taunt, waving a dead crow at him. They advance towards him and he is terrified of those hideous, staring black beady eyes, the pointy fearsome beak and clenched talons. He screams and they laugh and come closer, backing him against the grey stone wall that wraps around the school playground.

Shaking, he feels the wet stream flowing down his leg and his tormentors shout in delight. 'Pissy Pants! Pissy Pants! Frederick is a Pissy Pants!' Shame and fear and helpless fury engulf him and he weeps uncontrollably, sobbing and peeing simultaneously until his persecutors spot his older sister coming and run away, their bellows of derisive laughter deafening his ears.

'You have to learn to stand up for yourself, Freddy,' Alexandra says angrily. 'Or they will never leave you alone. Stop being a cissy and learn to fight.'

Lying in his hospital bed, the Judge remembers as though it were yesterday. Silent tears slide down his cheeks, as years of suppressed grief and hurt finally have their say.

It seems as though he has only closed his eyes to sleep when the rattling of the breakfast trollies awaken him. The night nurse, a middle-aged woman called Fran, hurries into the room with an air of distraction. 'Frederick, they've just rang down from theatre, Number 234's op has been cancelled so you're first on the list. Quick now, into your gown,' she says authoritatively, pulling up the blinds and flooding the room with the pale lemon rays of the rising sun.

He is too flustered at this unexpected turn of events to chide her for calling him by his first name. He fiddles with his pajama buttons, all fingers and thumbs and as soon as his top is opened, she is assisting him out of it and shoving his arms into the laundered faded hospital gown.

'Into your slippers now,' she urges, checking his wristband and making a note on her file.

'My slippers?' He is bemused. 'Shall I wear them on the trolley?'

'There's no trolley, Frederick,' she says, briskly tying his gown behind his back. 'Cutbacks. Patients walk to theatre now or go in a wheelchair. You'll be wheeled back to your ward, of course, after your surgery. Wrap your dressing gown around you like a good man, and let's be on our way.'

He is genuinely shocked as he follows her meekly out the door. This is a private hospital; at the very least, he would have expected to be wheeled to his operation by a hospital porter. When he had his hip replaced some years back, a big burly Kerry chap had whisked him at speed down the corridor, like a rally driver in the grand prix. Perhaps his wife has a point about his expenses. He feels a brief moment of shame that his social conscience has been dampened down over the years. He knows there are much bigger cutbacks than porters and trollies that will never impact on *him*.

The tea lady is pushing her carriage of trays along in the opposite direction and he is, thankfully, distracted. 'Are ya off!' she exclaims as though she has known him all his life. 'I'll have the tay for you when you get back. Good luck, luv,' she throws over her shoulder, hurrying past them to start delivering the morning meals.

'Thank you,' he murmurs, strangely touched at her good wishes.

He is welcomed kindly to the anteroom adjoining the theatre. Fran helps him divest himself of his dressing gown and pajama bottoms. He feels unusually vulnerable in his gown with the wide gaps that let in the breeze and display his bare posterior to all and sundry.

'Up on to the bed here now,' the theatre nurse instructs, helpfully catching him at his elbow to steady him. Briskly, efficiently, he is eased back against the pillows, swaddled in a blue blanket, and a cannula is inserted into the back of his hand with a minimum of fuss. All the while, the theatre nurse is doing her checklist, asking him the questions Fran has already posed.

'Ready for the off?' The gowned anesthetist appears through the swinging doors that lead to the theatre. The Judge gets a glimpse of the big arc lights shining down on the operating table that awaits him and feels a sudden, unanticipated dart of fear.

'Umm,' he grunts, swallowing hard.

'Nothing to worry about. It will be over in no time,' the anesthetist asserts with faux chumminess.

A hand gently touches his shoulder. It is Fran, looking down at him. 'You'll be fine, Frederick,' she says comfortingly, as the anesthetist inserts a large needle into the cannula and slowly depresses the plunger.

'You won't even count to three,' she says, smiling. Then blackness envelops him and he slides away.

'Wake up, Frederick. Wake up now. You're in the recovery room.' A voice commands as he struggles to surface through the dark miasma that swirls around his brain.

'Am I done?' he mutters, dry mouthed.

'You are. It all went fine,' he hears, before he drifts off again with an uncharacteristic sense of well-being, knowing he is in safe hands.

The next time he awakes he is back in his room. The red-haired nurse is smiling down at him, unwrapping the blood pressure cuff from his arm. He has no memory of his journey from the recovery room.

'You're back with us again down on the ward, Mr Harney. You're doing great,' she assures him, 'and your blood pressure is perfect. Your wife rang. She'll be in later.'

His eyelids droop again and he surrenders to this rare and pleasurable feeling of being nurtured and taken care of, free from all his responsibilities and the expectations of others.

He is lying against his pillows looking at the apple tree when the tea lady arrives. 'Ah are ya back in the land of the livin'? She stands at the foot of the bed, studying him.

'I am, thank God!' he says, utterly relieved the ordeal is over.

'And are ya ready for the tay and toast?'

'I am indeed,' he assures her. He is hungry and thirsty.

'It will be like the nectar of the gods,' she promises.

'Now luv, get tha' inta ya,' she orders ten minutes later, placing a tray of tea and hot buttered toast in front of him. 'An' if ya fancy another slice, I'll bring it to ya.'

'That's very kind of you . . . er . . .' he peers at her name badge.

'Janet,' she supplies, helpfully, pouring his tea for him. 'In case ya have the collywobbles after the anesthetic and yer hands shake,' she explains patiently as though to a child.

'Thank you, Janet.' He inclines his head graciously.

'Yer welcome, luv, enjoy it. I'll be back for the tray and, if ya want more, I'll bring it to ya,' she assures him and then she is gone and he is alone once more. The tea is indeed the nectar of the gods and he savours it. The toast, oozing butter is as tasty to him at that moment as the finest most succulent red-juiced steak has ever been.

The uncommon sense of wellbeing the Judge experiences lasts until he reluctantly dons his suit and overcoat the following day, to return home to recuperate. Trailing his wife down the hospital corridor, he is disappointed that neither Kate, his nurse, nor Janet, his tea lady, are on the floor so that he can say his farewells and thank them for their care.

He spends his two weeks of recuperation quietly resting, contemplating how his life will change when he retires. Sometimes his thoughts turn to his brief hospital stay and the events therein. For the most part, it was a surprisingly enjoyable experience, he admits. Even his episode of shame no longer seems so darkly dire.

On the day of his post-operative check-up, the Judge sits at his desk, writing in his neat, elegant cursive on expensive, embossed stationery. He slips the three notes he has written into cream watermarked envelopes and drops each into a small gift bag. Humming to himself, he picks up his car keys and strides to the front door. His wife has offered to drive him to his appointment but he wishes to make his own way. He has a small chore to do after he has seen his consultant.

'All healing well. Watch the weight, no tea or coffee after six p.m., and take regular exercise,' his urologist instructs matter-of-factly, having conducted the dreaded examination. The Judge is so relieved the ordeal is over he almost skips down the steps of the clinic and makes his way to the private hospital adjoining it. Cognizant of the advice he has recently been given, he takes the stairs rather than the lift, to the second floor. Panting somewhat, he turns right.

He hears her before he sees her. 'Number 222 is givin' out yards about been put on a reduced diet. He's *demanding* a cooked breakfast for tamarra, Kate. Will ya deal wid him?'

'No prob, Janet,' he hears his nurse say, as he rounds the corner and sees them standing by the ward kitchen. A sudden shyness overcomes him. He clears his throat. They turn to look at him. It is Janet who recognizes him first.

'Ah, tiz yourself. Howarya getting' on, luv?'

Kate takes a moment longer. If he were in his pajamas, she'd probably remember him, the Judge thinks with a flash of humour.

'Room 222, the judge fella,' Janet prompts, glancing over her specs at him.

'Oh, yes, Judge Harney. How are you keeping?' The young nurse asks politely.

'Very well, thank you. Very well indeed. I just wanted to er . . . drop these in to you both, to thank you for your kindness during my stay here.' He knows he sounds pompous and searches for something to add. 'I was extremely well looked after, especially by both of you and I very much appreciate your care. And if you would be so kind as to give this to Fran I would be obliged.' He thrusts the gift bags at them.

'There was no need for that, but thank you very much,' Kate demurs.

'Ahhh, Jayziz, now, isn't tha' very kind of ya to remember me too!' Janet exclaims, delighted, peering at the box of chocolates nestled in the pink tissue paper that lines the gift bag.

'Well, now, Janet, how could I forget that tea – the nectar of the gods – and toast you made for me after my operation? I know I was somewhat grumpy but I hope you'll forgive me,' he adds slyly, a rare twinkle lighting his hazel eyes.

'You men, yer all the same when yer sick, but ye can't resist me tea an' toast in the end.' Janet laughs and pats his arm.

'Thank you again, ladies.' He nods before turning on his heel to march away towards the stairs.

'Well, I wasn't expecting tha'. Sickness an' old age are great levelers, luv, aren't they, even for judges?' Janet remarks sagely, taking out the box of chocolates. 'Oh, look, Kate, they're posh an' all. Handmade.'

'*Chez Emily, very* posh!' agrees the nurse, opening the envelope. 'Ah, Janet, look at the way he signed it, after all his giving out. 'I bet yours is the same.' She laughs, studying the embossed, headed notepaper of Mr Justice Frederick Harney, and the signature that ends the Judge's note.

Thank you so much for your kindness and care. It was much appreciated. If I was at all grumpy, I apologise and ask your forgiveness.

Best regards,
Frederick (No. 222)

BIRTHDAY

Life Begins At Forty!

'So you're absolutely sure that you don't want a surprise party for your fortieth?' Liz, my older sister, asks, as we sit sipping vanilla coffee in the trendy new café on the seafront.

'I'm positive.' I grimace. 'It's bad enough being forty without having to make a song and dance about it in public.'

'Life begins at forty, honey,' she says airily, as our tuna wraps and salads arrive 'Look at me, a half a stone heavier, eyesight failing, grey hair multiplying at a rate of knots, everything going south and do I care?'

'That's because you've given up. You've gone all Zen-like with all that yoga and meditation stuff you do. Well, I intend to fight ageing tooth and nail.'

'You do that, Amy,' Liz soothes, munching on a slice of cucumber.

I'm dreading forty.

I'm thirty-nine years, eleven months, two days and

forty-five minutes old. I've a husband, Steve, eight-year-old twin daughters, Molly and Daisy, all much loved. My work as a medical secretary in a busy consultant's clinic is varied and satisfying. Life is good.

'Well, we have to have some sort of a celebration now that you're joining the club. I told Steve I'd try and find out what you'd *really* like to do. Will we have a girl's night in Wicklow?' Liz asks.

'Don't you mean "ladies" or "women's" night?' I say dryly. 'Girl's we ain't.'

'Oh, get over it. We all had to go through it; wait until you're my age. If you think forty is bad, try forty-five.' My sister is unsympathetic to my trauma. Still, she's treating me to lunch and trying to help my darling husband, who knows my feelings about turning forty, organize some sort of birthday treat. I shouldn't be so ungracious.

We finish our wraps and order more coffee and a selection of cream cakes. It's my last fling, I promise myself. I've got to stop this comfort eating. I bite into a creamy éclair, pushing away the thoughts of calories and cellulite and all those other horrible, guilt-inducing words that are starting to become part of my vocabulary.

'We could go to The Tap for a slap-up and stay the night in the cottage quaffing champers in front of the fire. No children and no husbands,' my sister suggests enthusiastically.

'Sounds blissful,' I agree. 'I'd love to get down to Wicklow for a few days. But do you think it would be a bit mean leaving Steve and the twins out of it?'

'Leave it to me. We'll have our girls' day and night on the Friday and Steve and the girls and Declan and my lot can come down on Saturday. We can have a barbecue if the weather is dry.'

I laugh. Only Liz could suggest a barbie at the end of February.

'The kids would love that. We can wrap up and drink hot ports on the deck. Jennie's all on for it,' Liz continues. Jennie is Liz's sister-in-law and she's a dote. She owns the holiday cottage next door to Liz, who has the one beside ours. We're like a little tribe in the small development of holiday cottages where we all decamp for weekends and holidays.

'You're on,' I say, enjoying the frisson of anticipation my sister's plan generates. What could be nicer than a long, brisk walk on the beach and then to sit on the deck of our small beachside haven listening to the roar of the surf with family and dear friends, easing myself into my new decade?

'Great. That's that organized. I'd say Mum and Dad will be happy enough not to have to travel from Cork, especially if the weather's bad. We can have them to stay at Easter and have an excuse for another cake. It's so helpful of you to make organizing your birthday so simple.' Liz is clearly relieved that I've taken the hassle-free birthday route.

'Barbara won't be too happy that I'm not having a big bash.' I lick the last bit of cream off my fingers. Barbara is my sister-in-law. She's married to Steve's brother, Tom. She's a selfish, lazy cow, to put it mildly.

'And how *are* the Scroungers?' Liz queries, as she pays the bill and shrugs into her coat.

I giggle. Liz shoots from the hip and always has. She's constantly telling me that I let Barbara walk all over me and that I should draw my boundaries. I know she's right. I'm just not good at that sort of thing. But it's getting beyond a joke at this stage. Scroungers are not far wrong when describing my in-laws. You know the type . . . the ones that arrive with one arm as long as the other, eat and drink you out of house and home and, half the time, buzz off without even doing the washing-up. My in-laws, Barbara, Tom, and brats Roger, Barry and Vanessa could give master classes in freeloading.

When Steve and I bought our small holiday cottage in Brittas Bay six years ago, we certainly didn't envisage an invasion for two weeks every summer of the in-laws from hell. But that's what's happened. Barbara, Tom and Co. have come to see it as *their* cottage too.

They started arriving for weekends, unannounced, the first year. In the beginning it was fun. We all had young children. It was nice for the cousins to play together but it started becoming a habit. And Steve and I were doing all the shopping, cooking and housework.

Then Barbara started bringing the kids down for a couple of days during the summer holidays, and that was when I should have stepped in and nipped it in the bud. But I'm no good at being assertive. It's a huge personality flaw and I hate myself for my wimpishness.

Of course, I plan all the things I'm going to say, like:

'*Barbara, I don't mind you coming the odd weekend with the kids but my holidays are the only decent time I have with the girls and I want to be able to concentrate on them.*'

Or, '*Barbara, we really don't have the space, especially as the children are getting older.*' This is not just an excuse. We only have two bedrooms in the cottage and when the Keegans arrive, my pair end up on camp beds in the sitting room.

I keep saying I'm going to do something about it, but all I end up doing is moaning to Liz. I know she's sick of me. She'd have no problem putting the skids under Barbara.

Steve is ambivalent about it. He feels we're lucky to have a holiday home and should share our good fortune. I wouldn't mind so much if she pulled her weight, but honestly, Barbara is so lazy that I end up doing everything while she chills out on the deck reading and drinking wine and I just feel *so* resentful because it's my holiday too. Her kids are allowed to run riot and the poor twins invariably end up getting into trouble when it's Vanessa and the boys I should be shouting at.

It's all right for Steve, to be so magnanimous. It's not his holiday that's ruined. We split our hols so that the girls can have the maximum time at the beach. Barbara invariably arrives for my two weeks. I feel my husband should back me up and speak to his brother about it, but he doesn't want to cause bad feeling.

'What about *my* bad feelings?' I ask resentfully, every summer as I prepare to go back to work after another ruined holiday. It's the one issue that causes conflict between us and I'm weary of it.

This year, *definitely*, I'm putting and end to it, I decide, as I emerge from the café into a howling gale that whips my hair from around my face and assaults my cheeks with its icy, stinging fingers. We don't linger. Liz has to pick up my twins and her youngest boy from school and I've to get back to work. I'm so lucky to have her. If it weren't for Liz I'd have had second thoughts about staying at work once the girls were too old for the crèche. She's like a second mother to them. Barbara would never offer to help out if you were in a fix. She's one of life's great Me, Me, Me people and that's probably why I feel so resentful.

The Keegans go on a foreign holiday every year. Barbara and her girlfriends jet off to Boston or New York for pre-Christmas shopping weekends. She's never once asked me to join them. She always had some excuse on the rare occasions when I asked her to mind the twins when they were younger. I stopped asking but it took me a long time to realize that Steve and I were being used.

I know it's childish and silly but part of me is glad that I'm not having a big party just so that I don't have to invite them. What is it about the Keegans? They press all my buttons and bring out the worst in me.

Fortunately, I'm so busy when I get back to work, I forget all about my in-laws and they are far from my mind until I get a call from Barbara a few days before my birthday.

'Hi, Amy,' she trills. My heart sinks to my boots. The only time Barbara rings is when she wants to moan or has something to boast about.

'So!' she demands. 'What are you doing for the big 4-0? Is Steve bringing you away? Tom took me to Prague for mine.'

We're sick of hearing about the trip to Prague. 'No, it's going to be very low-key,' I say offhandedly. If she gets wind of the weekend in Wicklow I wouldn't put it past her to muscle in, so I say nothing.

'Oh, come on, no party, or even a meal out?' Barbara is incredulous.

'Just a cake with the kids. It's all I want, honestly. You know me, I hate fuss.'

'But it's your fortieth,' she protests. 'Steve should push the boat out.'

'I didn't say he wasn't, Barbara!' I can't keep the edge of exasperation out of my voice. 'Look I'm up to my eyes here today. I'll catch you again,' I fib.

'Oh . . . oh! OK, I'll pop a card in the post for you, then.' She's clearly disappointed.

'Lovely,' I say, insincerely. 'Bye, thanks for ringing.'

Phew! I think, as I hang up. Then I start to worry. What if she hears of my night out with the girls in Wicklow? I resolve to warn them not to mention it to her if they see her in the summer. Bad humour wraps itself around me like a dark murky cloud. So what if I'm having a girls' night. It's none of her business. Why can't I just deal with it and say it to her straight out? Why am I such a wuss? Or am I just a thoroughly horrible person?

I try to forget about it, but it niggles and I bring up the subject with Liz that evening. 'Am I being a wagon. Should I invite her?' I grumble.

'Absolutely *not!*' Liz is emphatic. 'We are not spending our precious night listening to her wittering on about her new conservatory or her trip to New York and all the rest of it. Forget it.'

'Fine,' I capitulate happily, glad of my sister's authoritative stance. I don't feel such a heel after all.

My birthday dawns, dark and windy. I'm smothered with hugs and kisses from the girls, and Steve's gift of a sapphire and diamond pendant brings gasps of appreciation from his three women.

'I thought it would match your eyes,' he says, a tad bashfully. 'You can change it if you don't like it.'

'It's gorgeous, Steve, I love it.' I'm thrilled with his thoughtful gift and kiss him soundly, much to the girl's delight.

'Oohhh . . . kissy kissy!' squeals Daisy. Steve laughs but I can tell he's pleased that I love it.

'We helped Dad pick it,' Molly assures me, slipping an arm around my neck.

'I couldn't have got a nicer present, I tell her, basking in the joy of being so loved and cherished.

'Auntie Liz has a surprise for you, so you have to be dressed by eight o' clock,' Daisy informs me gleefully. I know Liz has something up her sleeve. She's told me to be ready to leave early.

This is great, I think happily as I stand under the bracing spray of the shower while my darlings make pancakes for breakfast. Forty's not so bad after all.

'Where are we going?' I ask an hour later as Liz heads for Wicklow via the East Link.

'You'll see,' Liz replies smugly.

'You never took our exit,' I exclaim half an hour later, as Liz continues to speed along the N11.

'Just a while longer,' she soothes and I laugh. Whatever my sister is up to, it's going to be fun. When we whizz onto the Arklow Bypass and she revs up to one hundred and twenty, comprehension dawns.

'Are we going to Amber Springs?'

'You bet we are. Happy birthday, little sis. I hope you're all prepared for a day of blissful pampering. I sure am. Jennie's meeting us there.'

A day at a luxurious health spa with the girls. What more could I want? Forty is getting better by the second.

It is the most perfect day. I'm massaged, manicured, pedicured and pampered to within an inch of my life and then as the sun begins to turn the Wicklow Hills pink and gold, chauffeured to dinner at a candle-lit restaurant and *forced* to drink gallons of champagne. Later, snuggled in warm dressing gowns in front of a blazing fire, listening to the roar of the sea, we watch a DVD of the second *Sex and the City* film, which I haven't seen, and guffaw at

Samantha's menopausal rant in the souk. It's the best birthday I've ever had.

It's lovely to see the girls tumbling out of the car and galloping across the dunes the next day. A brisk walk in the bracing, salty air, the waves pounding against the shore, diminishes our hangovers. We adults laugh and joke as the kids investigate the treasure troves to be found among the rocks. I feel really happy and contented and look forward to our barbecue later on.

'Oh, no! It's *that* gang!' Daisy scowls, as recognition dawns when we see figures approaching along the beach.

I don't believe it. It was too good to last. Barbara is waving gaily and I hear Liz curse under her breath. A knot twists my gut, not today, not them. Can't I have *one* day free of their unwelcome, intrusive presence? They're like ivy, smothering me, their grip getting tighter and tighter each year.

'Hey, you guys, better late than never,' Tom declares expansively.

I look at Steve. He not best pleased; I can see by the way the muscle gives a little jerk in his jaw and his eyes narrow.

'Steve told me you'd all gone to Amber Springs when I rang to wish you Happy Birthday. You had your mobile turned off. You never let on,' Barbara accuses with false gaiety, eyes beady flints behind the smile as she falls into place beside Jennie, Liz and myself.

'I didn't know,' I manage weakly. I want to smack her.

'It was a birthday surprise for Amy, Barbara. My treat,' Liz informs her curtly.

'Oh! I could have joined you last night then,' she persists.

This is *too* much; since when do I have to start telling Madam Barbara my every move.

'We were having a girls' night,' I hear myself say. 'I guess we didn't get to New York, like you and your friends. But Wicklow suits us fine. I just wanted to be with my two best friends really.'

She inhales sharply and Liz flashes me an approving glance. 'Oohh, I see,' she says snootily. 'Um . . . right. Well, Steve mentioned he was coming down for the weekend. We thought we'd come and give you your present.'

'That's very kind, Barbara. It's a bit of a trek up and down in the one day just to give me a present. It could have waited.' I'm feeling reckless now. She's not getting away with it this time.

'*Oh!*' She says again. She stares at me, not sure how to react. 'We brought the sleeping bags; we can doss on the floor,' she ventures.

I don't care any more. I've had enough. I'm forty and it's time to draw a line in the sand. Literally. I draw a breath. I can sense Liz and Jennie waiting for my response. Bill is collecting periwinkles with the kids while Tom and Steve skim stones along the waves. Gulls circle and squeal. My lovely day is not going to be ruined.

Do it, do it, a voice urges.

I swallow, hard. And then I think, to hell with her. She's not my friend and never had been. She's just someone I have to put up with.

'Actually, Barbara.' I come to a stop and eyeball her. 'I've been meaning to say this for a while. The cottage really is too small for all of us and I don't like putting the girls out of their beds. It's not fair. And while we're on the subject, if you don't mind, this year and from now on, I'd like to spend my holidays alone with the girls. Our time is precious and that two weeks I have off in the summer is the only decent chunk of time I get to spend with them. There are nice, reasonably priced hotels and B&Bs in the area. I'm sure you can find somewhere cheap 'n' cheerful to stay. And to be honest, I'd prefer if you would give me advance notice if you are coming down, to see if it suits. It would makes life easier for me in case we've made plans and so on.' I'm on a roll. It's actually exhilarating.

Barbara lowers her gaze first. Two ruby spots stain her cheeks. 'I see,' she says tightly, thin-lipped. 'Fair enough.' She can't hide her shock.

'Great, that's sorted. Let's go and put the kettle on,' I suggest brightly. I'm elated. I've done it. I've said my piece. I can't believe it. 'Let's head back to the cottage, I'm sure you'd like a cuppa before you head back home,' I say lightly but pointedly.

'Very kind,' Barbara says sarcastically, nostrils flaring but I'm beyond caring and I raise my face to the sun's pale yellow light and feel the merest hint of heat that reminds me that winter is over, the days are getting longer and we have much to look forward to.

'Well done, Amy,' Liz murmurs as we pour steaming tea into mugs ten minutes later. 'You should have done that years ago.'

'I know.' I sigh. 'I wish I had, but better late than never.'

Barbara is chatting to Jennie on the deck; her brittle tones carry in on the breeze. 'She's raging, look at the face on her, it would stop a clock.' Liz chuckles as my sister-in-law flashes a daggers look in our direction.

I start laughing too. 'I don't care. She's a snooty little wagon and she's used me for the last time.'

'*Loved* the dig about New York. There was no answer to that. Forty suits you, keep it up.' My sister grins.

'When the Keegans get up to go, let them go,' I whisper to Steve in the kitchen a while later. 'I've had a word with Barbara. It's been a long time coming.'

'Fine,' he agrees. 'If that's what you want.'

'It is. My present to myself.' I smile at him. He hugs me.

They leave half an hour later. Barbara can't bring herself to give me her usual air kiss as her kids protest loudly. 'But we want to stay! You *said* we were staying.'

'Sorry, not this time,' Steve says firmly, seeing them to the door.

A weight lifts off my shoulders. I'm free. Roll on summer.

The Best Birthday Ever

How do you know when a friendship is over . . . kaputt . . . past its sell-by date?

I'm sitting in a coffee shop, waiting to meet my oldest 'friend' to tell her that her daughter will not be invited to my daughter's forthcoming birthday party and that, in fact, she will no longer be part of my daughter's circle of friends.

I take a sip of creamy latte. My stomach feels slightly fluttery as apprehension grips me. Yet I know this moment has been coming for a long time. It was something I should have done many months ago but I'd stubbornly held onto the notion that Victoria Cassidy and I had a long, enduring friendship. Who was I kidding? And what did it say about me and my ostrich-like behaviour that I still thought like that?

We were a strange pair, Victoria and I. Even as kids, the contrast between us was striking. We both lived on the same street, Victoria three doors down from me. She bird-like, gangly, driven to succeed, me short, plumpish, easy-going. Chalk and cheese. As a child I didn't realize that Victoria felt superior to me. That came later as I grew up and gained a modicum of self-knowledge and self-awareness.

I certainly didn't feel superior to Victoria then, but I felt *sorry* for her. There *is* a difference. Victoria's parents were divorced. Her father left Victoria's mam and moved in with a toned, tanned estate agent he'd met at the gym, when Victoria was seven, just a little younger than our daughters are now. It must have been horrific, I think, still able to feel sorry for Victoria for all the pain, grief and anxiety she'd endured as a child.

I can remember her little, pinched, worried face as she knuckled down to her studies, even then, so that she could get a good job and become very rich so her mam wouldn't have to worry about bills. She was never going to get married, she told me.

Victoria was very possessive of our friendship and hated it if I played with the other kids. I was outgoing and friendly and railed against her sulks and tantrums and 'Do you like so-and-so better than me?' interrogations. Now, of course, I can see how completely insecure she was, and how the fear of rejection informed all of her behaviour, right into adult life.

'You have to be kind to Victoria,' my mam would insist when I'd moan that I was sick of her and didn't want to play with her any more. 'See how lucky you are. Our family has fun; we have Dad to take care of us and have good times with.'

'Yeah, but she says things about us. She says we're silly 'cos we believe in Santa and go to pantos and that's only for kids.'

'She's only jealous, Claire, take no notice,' my mother said kindly ignoring my fierce, bubbling resentment and making me feel mean for moaning.

How old patterns repeat themselves. I'd been saying the same sort of thing to my eight-year-old daughter, Joanna, about Victoria's daughter, Kristen.

Joanna and Kristen had been 'friends' since they were born with only six weeks between them. And it was like watching a re-run of my relationship with Victoria: Kristen pushy, driven, combative, competitive; Joanna open, laid back, cheerful, and very soft-hearted.

My heart melted as I thought of my beloved daughter. She was such a good kid and a loyal friend and Kristen had never valued her, had only nagged and niggled at her, comparing and contrasting her own edgy, unsatisfactory existence with Joanna's happy-go-lucky, and very secure environment.

Don't get me wrong. Kristen has a very affluent lifestyle. Victoria and her husband Stuart are both well off, successful lawyers with a flourishing practice. They'd met at college and Victoria had found a soulmate, someone as ambitious and driven and hungry for success as she. They married when they qualified and set up practice together. Now theirs is the biggest legal practice in town. They have three foreign holidays every year, a villa on a golf club near

Puerto Banus, flashy cars, a big house and private schooling for Kristen.

Kristen has her own TV and DVD in her bedroom, a computer, Wii, iPod, iPhone, everything her little heart desires, while my Joanna shares a bedroom with her younger sister Rosie, is allowed computer time and TV time, and goes to the country for six weeks in the summer, to a mobile home.

'I'm so lucky I have my own room and all my own stuff, I can watch what I want and do what I want, that's much better than your stupid "family time"', Kristen had boasted recently. Joanna had been fire-engine red with rage.

'Mam, Kristen said our family time is stupid. She's really rude. I'm sick of her saying things about us all the time.'

'And what do *you* think? Do you think our family time is stupid?' I enquired, used to their squabbling.

'No, I think it's fun,' Joanna declared, little freckled nose flaring in indignation.

We have a rule in our house that everyone sits down to the family meal together. The TV is turned off, computers put to sleep, and for an hour or two my husband, Sean and I sit and natter with our kids about their day at school and our day at work.

Kristen had stayed for dinner once and had been aghast that the TV had been turned off in the middle of *Drake and Josh*.

'I'll eat my dinner on a tray,' she insisted.

'No, you won't. You can sit at the table with us. This is our family time,' I'd explained.

'But I always eat my dinner in front of the TV. My child-minder lets me,' she whined.

'Nope, come on, sit with us and eat up,' I'd instructed firmly, watching her cross little face and thinking how like her mother she was at that age. She'd sat sulkily, while the girls and I began to talk about the events of our day as Sean ladled spoonfuls of tasty chicken casserole onto her plate.

In spite of herself, she began to eat. She always cleared her plate in our house. Her childminder fed her pizzas and processed meals that could be heated up in a microwave so a home-cooked meal was a rare treat.

Kristen hadn't made her 'family time is stupid' announcement in my hearing. She knew better. I always took her to task if she stepped over a boundary, much to her annoyance, but I could imagine her superior little face, with her blonde hair tossed back, as she made her cutting remark to Joanna. She knew how to push my daughter's buttons, and as they got older their relationship was becoming more fractured and factitious.

'She's only jealous because she doesn't have family time,' I pointed out to Joanna. 'Her mam and dad are too busy. They don't get home from work until late.'

'Yeah, well, she says her mam says you don't have a proper job, you only work for peanuts,' Joanna said crossly.

Smug bitch, I thought, feeling an uncharacteristic flash of fury, and a frisson of hurt. OK, so my mornings-only job-share as an office administrator in a busy primary school might not pay the huge salary Victoria was accustomed to but it was certainly more than peanuts and, more importantly for me, it meant I was at home in the afternoon when my daughters were finished school and I cooked their dinner and did their homework with them, and not some poorly paid childminder who didn't give a toss.

I *know* Victoria had made the remark. Kristen wouldn't have come up with it herself and it was that dismissive observation I suppose that made me take a good long hard look at our 'friendship'.

I take another sip of latte and glance at my watch. Twelve fifteen. Victoria was supposed to be here at twelve. Typical. She's always late when we arrange to meet. She is firmly of the opinion that her time is far more precious than mine. She is, after all, a lawyer. They now live in an exclusive gated estate just outside of town. They go to all the posh dinner parties and hold even posher ones themselves. Needless to say, Sean and I never get invited to them. I get invites to meet in coffee shops.

I'd been invited to lunch every so often, in the Taj Mahal, as Sean had christened it, when they'd first moved into it, but the invites had dwindled over the past few years. I can't even remember when I was there last.

No, a coffee shop was deemed suitable for me, not even the chic new wine bar on Abbey Lane that was doing a roaring trade, where Victoria might see colleagues or clients and would have to introduce me to them.

It was now twelve twenty-five. I had taken a precious day's leave to visit the dentist and buy Joanna's birthday present and order her cake. I could be having a manicure or even a mini-facial, or a tapas lunch, in my favourite haunt, Domingo's Tapas Bar down in the Square. Instead, I was twiddling my thumbs, sipping a now cold latte, waiting for someone who didn't value my friendship or my time.

It helped that by the time Victoria arrived, I was steaming.

'Sorry I'm late,' she said airily, as she dropped her Louis Vuitton briefcase by her skyscraper heels and sat down opposite me. She was wearing a sharply cut black trouser suit with a cream silk cami. Her hair, in a short feathery style, was perfectly highlighted. I felt almost dowdy beside her, although I had dressed with care in a long straight black skirt, and a short, nipped in at the waist burgundy jacket that gave me a good shape and drew the eyes away from my ass, which was starting to head south.

'I won't be able to stay too long, seeing as I'm running late,' Victoria announces, waving imperiously at a young waitress. I *seethe* with resentment. *She* delays *me* by almost half an hour and she has the cheek to tell me *she's* running late.

'That suits me. I'm short on time myself. I didn't think I'd be twiddling my thumbs here for twenty-five minutes,' I say curtly.

'*Oh!*' She looks at me in surprise. I don't think she's ever heard me use *that* tone before.

'Sorry. Our conference call ran over. It's a very important case. Very hush-hush but there are planning implications for the town,' she confides.

Her cases were always 'very important', I thought, unimpressed, as the waitress stands poised to take our order.

'Green tea for me and no chocolate on the side,' Victoria declares briskly, eschewing the big round chocolate sweet that always accompanied the teas and coffees, my favourite part. I love the taste of melting chocolate and hot coffee.

'Regular coffee for me please,' I smile. I'm certainly not ordering another latte in front of Victoria.

'So, great to see you, Claire, what's new? What's hip and happening?' Victoria sits back in her chair and studies me, eyes moving up and down, noting the empty latte glass the waitress is removing. 'You've lost weight,' she says in an almost accusatory tone. She had always hated if I lost weight. As I've said before, Victoria's friendship is based on her sense of superiority; in her eyes I'll never be thinner, more successful, or more affluent than she is so I'm no threat.

'So what are you doing swanning around Abingdon mid-week?' She grins, showing perfectly even, laser-whitened teeth.

'Dentist appointment,' I murmur, knowing the time has finally come to do what I should have done a long time ago. 'And I was buying Joanna's birthday present.' That brings up the subject of the birthday, the whole reason I'm here.

'Ah, yes, the famous birthday party. Kristen's been pestering me about her outfit; she wants a pair of Uggs. I've told the childminder to take her shopping. Honestly, they're so fashion-conscious at that age. What should I get for Joanna? Could you make life easy for me and give me some pointers?'

'Well . . . er . . . actually, that's what I wanted to talk to you about, Victoria .' I sit up straight and take a deep breath. I think about the look on Joanna's face when she said to me, 'Mam, I really don't want to invite Kristen to my birthday this year. She always ruins thing and starts fights with Lisa. She's very mean to Lisa.'

I love Lisa Delaney, Joanna's best friend. Wide-eyed, breathless, full of enthusiasm, there isn't a malicious bone in her body and Kristen is supremely jealous of her. I remember a couple of weeks ago Victoria had asked me would I pick Kristen up from school, as the childminder was sick. I was regularly asked to pick Kristen up from school and Victoria took it for granted that I'd do it.

I listened to the three of them in the back of the car discussing Britney Spears. 'She has implants, you know, not as big as Jordan's though. I saw it in one of my childminder's magazines,' Kristen declared. She's so precocious, I thought, reading those sorts of magazines. Joanna and Lisa read comics.

I saw Lisa turn wide-eyed to Joanna and declare breathlessly. 'I know a celebrity that flew to America and her implants *exploded* and the heart came out with it. There was blood *everywhere.*'

'OMG!' exclaimed Joanna, agog, eyes like saucers. 'I'm never getting them.'

'That is *so* stupid, Lisa. You're very, very silly.' Kristen dripped contempt and sarcasm. 'That's not true, sure it's not, Claire?' Kristen tries to get me onside.

I ignored the question. 'Kristen, it's rude to call someone silly. Apologize to Lisa please.'

'But—'

'Apologize, please.'

'Sorry,' she muttered. 'But she *is* silly,' she said under her breath.

'Mam, I really, really don't want Kristen at my birthday 'cos she's very rude and she fights with my friends and please, Mam I know that you always tell me too be kind to her but she's not a very kind girl and I just don't like her any more.'

Out of the mouths of babes. I knew exactly what Joanna meant as I sat looking at Victoria. Victoria and Kristen are users, pure and simple. What is the point of holding on to the friendship when neither of us had anything in common and when Victoria clearly looks down her nose at me, just as Kristen does with Joanna?

Why should I allow my daughter's birthday to be ruined by forcing a relationship that is not good for her? Why do I let Victoria walk all over me and treat me with such disrespect? She has never appreciated any of the 'kindness' shown to her. Even my mother has gone off her. 'Got above herself, the little madam,' she said to me one day when we met Victoria in town with a client and she barely said hello to us.

My voice is surprisingly firm as I say calmly, 'Actually, Victoria, Joanna's birthday party is one of the things I want to have a little chat with you about.'

'Oh, yes, planning something special? I'm going to have a marquee with a selection of entertainers for Kristen's next one,' Victoria boasts, when the waitress places our hot drinks in front of us.

'Nope, Joanna just wants to go to the pictures and come home and order pizza and "hang out with the gang", as she says herself,' I explain.

'Oh . . . lucky you. Kristen wouldn't put up with that.'

'I know, she'd think it's boring,' I agree. 'That's what I want to talk to you about. You must have noticed over the past year and more, that they haven't been getting on very well.'

Victoria looks startled. 'Er . . . no . . . they squabble, but all kids do that.'

'It's more than that, Victoria.' I didn't want to say bluntly that Kristen is a spiteful little bitch. I couldn't be that hurtful.

'What do you mean?' She straightens up in her chair, brows drawn together in a frown.

'They have nothing in common any more. You've hit the nail on the head when you said Kristen would find the kind of party Joanna's having boring and yet Joanna, Lisa and her friends are looking forward to "hanging out eating pizza" immensely.'

'Oh, it's just that the parties she's invited to are always catered and there's always some sort of entertainment provided; it's what the parents in our circle do. It's a pain in the ass actually, trying to come up with even bigger and better parties.' Victoria throws her eyes up to heaven and I realize that success and affluence brings its own problems. Still, that's not my worry, so I plough on.

'Well, that's what I'm saying, Kristen moves in different circles and has higher expectations and she can be quite dismissive of Joanna and her friends and it leads to a lot of arguments,' I point out.

'Oh, for God's sake, Claire, cop on, you're not letting childish bickering become a big issue!' Victoria snaps, beginning to see where the conversation is headed.

'It's a lot more than childish bickering, Victoria,' I say, eyeballing her, annoyed by her dismissive attitude. 'And it's constant. For example, when a child tells another child that their "family time" is stupid, that's dismissive, rude and superior. When a child constantly tells a child that her best friend is a "silly twit", that's undermining, nasty behaviour. When a child taunts another child by saying that her mother earns "peanuts", that's a lot more than childish bickering, in my view,' I say quietly.

Victoria blushes to the roots of her dyed-blonde hair. 'Oh, you know the things kids say. I'm surprised at you for listening to them,' she mutters, taking a sip of green tea.

'Kids often repeat things their parents say, Victoria.' I'm not letting her get away with that one and think how mean of her it is to let Kristen take the blame for her spiteful remark.

'Kristen didn't come up with the "peanuts" remark herself. I know you think my job pales in comparison to yours. I know you think Sean and I wouldn't fit in at your dinner parties. I know you didn't even give it a thought that you were twenty-five minutes late meeting me today, but my time is as precious as yours, Victoria, believe it or not.

'Now I think it's time to do the mature thing and admit that we have very, very little in common any more. Our daughters have even less, so what's the point? What's the point of hanging onto a relationship that can't by any stretch of the imagination be called a friendship any more? You won't miss me and I won't miss you. Be honest.'

'Don't say that!' Virginia protested hotly. 'I—'

'What's my telephone number?' I interject.

'Oh, don't be ridiculous!' she snaps, flustered.

'You don't know it because the only time you ever use it is when you need me to pick Kristen up. When was the last time you rang me for a chat?'

'I'm very busy, Claire, I don't have time to be ringing people for chats.' She scowls.

'I'm very busy too, Victoria, believe it or not, but I always have time for my friends. I like talking to them. I need them and I'm glad to have them.'

'Oh, Miss Bloody Perfect, aren't you? You always were. You with your "perfect" family growing up, and your dozens of friends and your family time and your home cooking that I never hear the end of when Kristen comes home from your place.

' "Claire makes lovely dinners why don't you?"

' "Why can't we stay in a mobile home for the whole summer?"

' "Joanna has family time in her house; why don't we?"

'"Why can't I be Joanna's best friend?" On and on and on . . . it does my head in!' she explodes.

'Well, then, it will be as much a relief for you as it will be for me if the girls don't mix any more,' I say calmly, taking a slug of much-needed coffee.

'Just because you're jealous of me is no reason to ruin our kids' friendship,' Victoria counters snootily.

'Excuse me?' I almost choke on my coffee.

'Well, that's what this is all about, isn't it, if you're honest? Now that we're down to the nitty gritties. It galls you that I've made it; I'm successful and wealthy. You can't deal with it, clearly, but I think it's extremely childish of you to let it affect Kristen and Joanna's relationship.'

'You think I'm *jealous* of you?' I repeat, not sure if I'm hearing correctly.

'Aren't you . . . even a little bit?' she challenges.

Am I? Is that what this is all about . . . jealousy? Now she's made me question my motives and myself. For a moment, I'm unsure and then I recognize her usual modus operandi: to challenge and undermine.

'Not even the tiniest bit, Victoria. Well done on everything you've achieved. You've worked hard and you deserve it, but I love what I have and I wouldn't swap it for the world. Now, you must excuse me, I'm pushed for time,' I say standing up. 'Don't rush your tea. I'll pay for it on the way out. See you around.'

Victoria's jaw drops. And that's the way I leave her. I don't give her time to answer. I pay the bill at the cash desk and emerge into the street, breathing in the clement breeze scented with spring and the promises of long, hot days to come.

I feel light-hearted, unburdened. I've done something that will affect my daughter in the most positive way and I feel really good about that. I won't miss Victoria. And that's the sad thing, I suppose. I've known her for thirty-five years and I'm walking away from our relationship with not an ounce of regret. We didn't have a friendship in the true sense of the word we were just . . . a habit.

I walk briskly towards the bakery and order an extra-large chocolate buttons cake, Joanna's favourite.

'Mam, this is "*The Best Birthday Ever*",' she whispers to me a week later, as she and the gang 'hang out', chomping on pizza and wedges and discussing the pros and cons of choir and singing class versus speech and drama, and the various teachers involved.

'And you know something, it's great Kristen couldn't come, 'cos there's no fighting, and Lisa was *so* relieved,' my daughter confides.

'You know, Kristen's not going to be around much any more. There's not much point; you don't really get on, do you?' I say to Joanna. Relief washes over her.

'Not really, Mam. Is that OK?'

'Of course it's OK.' I hug her. 'You don't have to like everyone,' I explain.

'Phew, that's a relief, 'cos even though I tried to, I just couldn't like that girl any more!' Joanna exclaims.

'I know, love. You did your best and that's all that matters. So forget about everything except having fun. Let's go light the candles.'

I watch my daughter's shining face as her sister and friends bellow, '*Happy Birthday!*' and I'm overwhelmed with love for her. She did try hard with Kristen. She has a good spirit and I'm proud of her, and a little proud of myself too. I also did my best with Victoria over the years, but as I explained to my daughter, you don't have to like everyone and that's true for me too.

I cut the cake of 'The Best Party Ever' and watch, contented, as my daughter, surrounded by friends who truly love her, hands around the plates. She gives the one with the biggest slice to Lisa Delaney.

A Low Threshold of Pain

'Thank you, that was a superb massage.' The scrawny, bird-like blonde woman tightened the belt of her towelling robe around her waist and nodded at Emma.

'Thank you, Mrs Staunton,' Emma said politely, handing her a small bottle of Perrier. 'Don't forget to drink plenty of water.'

'Yes, of course.' The woman slid her hand into the pocket of her robe, took out a folded five-euro note and held it out to Emma. 'My partner is booked in for waxing with you this afternoon. We're going on a cruise down the east coast of the States, including the Hamptons and Nantucket. He's only agreed to get his back and neck done. If you could persuade him to get his chest hair waxed as well it would be *wonderful*! If not I'll have to dye it for him.' She rolled her huge chocolate-brown eyes. 'Grey chest hair is so *ageing* on a man. So *do* try and convince him to have it done won't you?' She gave a brittle smile and ran her fingers through her expertly highlighted hair.

'I'll do my best, Mrs Staunton.' Emma held open the door for her, wishing Ms Pipe-cleaner Legs would buzz off so that Emma could have a few minutes' peace to prepare her treatment room before the next client came.

'Excellent.' Adrienne Staunton gave one last flick of her tousled mane, sweeping past Emma with a waft of bergamot and aloe vera.

Emma exhaled deeply, closing the door before crossing the tiled floor to open the shuttered blinds. She stood for a moment, gazing out at the vista of luxuriant emerald lawns, and the chocolate-brown loamy shrubbery bursting with voluptuous red and pink rhododendrons and purple and white heather. Beyond, the midday sun adorned the molten sapphire sea with a tiara of glittering diamond rays that cascaded to the far horizon. She might have her lunch outside on the small private patio that led off the staff dining room of the luxurious, cliff-top health spa she worked in. It would be nice to breath the salty sea air and feel the heat of the sun on her face. Today was her birthday and when she had finished work her husband was taking her away for the weekend to a small boutique hotel in Seville, for a long weekend. The salon manager had told her she could leave at three. Her bag was all packed and she was ready to go straight to the airport.

Humming to herself, Emma prepared the plinth for her next client, placing fresh soft towels on top of the exotic patterned silk covering with its amber, honey-gold and burnt amber shades that matched the colour palate of the room. Jasmine-scented candles flickered in their shadowed niches in the walls and the soothing tones of New Age piano music played in the background.

She cleaned the small sink area and washed her hands before setting the temperature on the warmer oven for her next client's hot stone massage. She closed the blinds so that the room was once again a womblike cocoon in the flickering candlelight, and went to fetch her client from the spacious airy lounge that looked out to sea.

Unlike Adrienne Staunton who had chattered her way through the treatment, her new client, a weary middle-aged woman with elderly parents, a stressful job, and three teenage children, was happy to lie silently on the plinth and let Emma and the stones work their magic. As she gently massaged the woman's shoulders, feeling the knots of tension begin to soften, she felt a surge of satisfaction as her client let out a little snore. Job well done, Emma congratulated herself, pouring more oil onto her palms as her client sank deeper into relaxation.

'I see you had Adrienne Staunton; you won't go too far on the tips you get from her,' Rita Moran, another therapist, said sourly as they ate lunch together an hour later at a small round table on the patio. 'She's beginning to look a tad overdone, isn't she? Those plump lips and cheek fillers are *so* obvious. Nothing subtle about them. She's got a new fella too, I hear.' Rita took a bite out of her chicken-tikka wrap and followed it with a gulp of tea.

'Well, whoever he is, he's coming to me for a back and shoulders wax and she wants me to persuade him to get his chest done too. They're going on a cruise, it seems.' Emma finished her baked ham and chutney sandwich and raised her face to the sun, loving the beneficent heat that radiated through her.

'Some hotshot consultant, apparently. The wife found out he was having an affair with Widda Staunton and threw him out. Adrienne's giving him a make-over apparently. She's got him dyeing his hair and eyebrows and pounding the treadmill. I give it six months,' Rita said sagely. 'And then he'll be begging the wife to take him back. Adrienne's hard going by all accounts.'

'Yeah, she's totally self-absorbed. She never shut up when I was massaging her. She's trying to organize a charity gala, apparently, and is having terrible trouble getting her set to take tables after Angela Kerins and Rehab and the CRC debacles.' Emma stretched, catlike.

'I wouldn't bloody well take a table even if I *had* the money, paying those fat cats massive salaries and pensions, instead of it going to the charity. What a rip off! My mother supported those charities out of her *pension*. I'd love to sue the shaggers and get her money back.' Rita glowered. 'Good luck to Adrienne and her charity gala – those days are gone.' She stood up. 'Better go, I've got Antonia Kavanagh-Keogh, no less, for a full body.'

'See if she has any racing tips,' Emma grinned, gathering up her plate and mug. AKK, as she was known, was married to one of the biggest horse breeders in the country and was never out of the society pages and glossy lifestyle magazines.

Ten minutes later, she headed for the lounge to collect Mr Barnes, of the hairy back and shoulders. Emma was interested to see Adrienne's new 'fella', as Rita had called him.

There were two men in white robes, strangely incongruous, among the small clusters of women. One a broad-shouldered, tanned rugby type in his thirties, the other tall and thin with dyed chestnut hair, his skinny calves white, hairy, matchstick thin, his bony bunion hammer toes sticking out of the top of his spa slippers.

'Mr Barnes?' Emma called politely, knowing immediately which of them was her client. The older man put down his paper and uncoiled himself from the lounging chair.

'Hello!' he said stiffly, clearly uncomfortable. Some men took to the spa experience like ducks to water; others hated it. Emma was fairly sure her new client was one of the latter.

'This way please.' She led the way down the opulently carpeted hallway towards the treatment rooms. There was something vaguely familiar about the man flip-flopping awkwardly down the corridor beside her. Had she seen him in the society pages? Emma wondered, opening the door to let him precede her into her candlelit domain.

'I haven't had this procedure done before,' he said curtly, folding his arms and pursing his thin lips. He had a pointy aquiline nose, and deep-set hazel eyes. His face was crumpled, saggy, and lugubrious, and she suddenly remembered where she had met him and his gloomy bulldog visage before.

Feck my ass, it's John Paul Barnes! Emma barely managed to keep her jaw from dropping as recognition slowly dawned and she recognized her former gynaecologist. She swallowed hard and struggled to hide her dismay. He clearly didn't recognize her. So JP Barnes had hooked up with Widow Staunton. What a pair. They were welcome to each other!

'It won't take long,' she managed, proud of her fake poise. 'It's very simple and straightforward. Mrs Staunton mentioned something about having your chest waxed as well?' Emma arched an eyebrow at him, utterly relieved that he still didn't appear to realize that she was a former patient.

'Oh, did she now?' JP snorted grumpily. 'Our agreement was back and shoulders. That's women for you, never satisfied.'

'It will be over in a flash. Lots of men get it done. It makes sense to get it all done at the one go,' Emma assured him matter-of-factly, folding over a triangle of the cover sheet on the plinth. 'I'll leave you for a few moments to get out of your robe and, if you decide to get your chest waxed, I'll do that first, so lie on your back. If not, lie face down, with the sheet over you from the waist down. Make yourself comfortable, Mr Barnes,' she said politely, before closing the door behind her.

Emma walked slowly to the water cooler and poured herself a drink. She couldn't believe that a man who had been so dismissive of her, so arrogant and patronizing towards her when she was at her lowest and most vulnerable was lying on her plinth, at her mercy. A waxing virgin, so to speak.

Flashes of their last encounter five years ago came to the surface.

'I'd like to have a hysterectomy,' she'd told him after telling him the sorry saga of her gynecological history. 'I have endometriosis; it's made my life a misery. I have to come off the Pill because of my age. I don't want all that pain and sickness to get worse. I want it gone.'

He'd held up his hand impatiently. 'There are other avenues to explore. I feel you are being too hasty. I think we should consider treating you with the Mirena—'

'No, I don't want it. I don't want a synthetic hormone inside me; and besides, there's a history of cancer in my family.'

'Studies have proved the Mirena is quite safe in that regard,' he interrupted dismissively.

'It's not my periods that cause me the most pain – it's ovulating,' she argued in desperation, seeing that he wasn't listening to her. He already had a treatment plan formed in his head, no matter what she said.

'How do you know you're ovulating?' He gazed at her patronizingly over the top of his bifocals. 'You probably have a low threshold of pain,' he added briskly, standing up. 'Try the Mirena for a year. I'll do an endometrial ablation and insert the coil on the same day. You won't need to stay overnight. My secretary will make the hospital booking and attend to the details.'

'But I don't want—' Emma protested.

'Here's a leaflet; it will explain everything.' He wouldn't let her finish, clearly not interested in what she might or might not want. 'It works for thousands of women.' He thrust a leaflet into her hand, opened the door and practically shooed her into his secretary's office before striding out to the waiting room to bring in his next patient.

Emma shook her head, remembering her dismay, frustration, rage and indignation. She had left John Paul Barnes's rooms two hundred euros lighter in her bank account, with a glossy leaflet telling her stuff she already knew, and feeling like the powerless young teen she had once been, who had been sent from Billy to Jack and back again because of her 'painful periods'.

She'd wanted to barge through his door and roar at him. 'I'm a fifty-year-old woman who has endured more pain than you ever will and I damn well know when I'm ovulating, you patronizing prick.'

Even now, five years later, she could still remember her helpless fury.

'I have the very man for you; he's extremely in tune with women, and he's a friend. Let me get you an appointment,' one of her well-connected, long-standing clients had offered, when they had been discussing gynecologists while Emma was giving her a pedicure.

'Oh, I don't want to go to another male gynae *ever*!' Emma demurred.

'Listen, sweetie, some of the women are worse than the men, believe me,' Jill St Clare said grimly. 'I've been to so many of the species. This guy will sort you. He sorted me. Trust me.'

Emma smiled. Jill had got on the phone there and then, and within the space of eight weeks Emma was wombless and almost pain-free. *And* she'd had the satisfaction of knowing that JPB knew she'd ditched him for someone else. That was the icing on the cake. As she'd lain against her pillows in languorous post-op lethargy, dosed with morphine, enjoying the much longed for tea and toast, her mobile had tinkled. It was JP's secretary, Anthea, reminding her that she was booked to have her procedure the following Monday.

'Oh, you may cancel that,' Emma said sweetly. 'I've just *had* a hysterectomy.'

'Good Lord!' exclaimed the secretary, and Emma grinned, imagining the immaculately coiffured Anthea's dismay. No doubt, she was even clutching her pearls. 'Who did it?' the other woman demanded.

'Well, that's neither here nor there. He's renowned for his work and knows how to treat his patients. You may tell Mr Barnes, I not only had endometriosis but I had adeno-myosis, also. That sends pain levels soaring ever higher, even for someone who has learned to tolerate pain like I did, not that he'd ever understand that. Bye-bye.' Anthea's sharp intake of breath at this unheard of lack of respect for the godlike Mr John Paul Barnes had been music to Emma's ears and she'd sipped her tea and eaten her toast and felt a million dollars.

Please, God, if you have any sense of fair play, let him have his chest waxed, please, Emma prayed, knowing that the back and shoulders were much more painful than the chest but that he wouldn't be able to chicken out of having them done, not with the cruise coming up.

She took a deep breath and threw her plastic cup in the bin. Giving a firm knock on the door, she entered the room to see her client lying on his back with his eyes closed. *There is a God!* she thought exuberantly, testing the temperature of the wax. She cut the strips smaller than usual. Not for JP the mercy of a quick tug of a large strip. *Ooohh, nooo!* Emma thought gleefully. Slow and painful, that's how it would be.

'I'm just going to spread some wax on you now, Mr Barnes,' she advised. The prone man gave a grunt.

'Just get on with it, please.'

Oh, indeed I will! Emma bent her head to her task, smoothing the first strip over the molten wax.

'Deep breath,' she instructed briskly, before slowly pulling the strip back, enjoying the tearing sound of body hair being pulled from the roots.

'Oowwww! Aaahhh!' John Paul Barnes's eyes shot open and he yelped. 'That bloody hurt!' he exclaimed indignantly, glaring at her.

'*Really?*' Emma pretended surprise, applying another strip. 'Most *men* find it bearable,' *you big sissy*, she added silently, slowly pulling on the next strip as the gynecologist let out another howl. 'Oh dear,' she commiserated with a saccharine smile, applying more wax. 'You must have a low threshold of pain! *Very* low indeed,' she murmured. *And I'm not finished with you by a long shot, Mister John Paul Barnes. The worst is yet to come!* She gave another tug and her client's eyes watered as he emitted another stunned gasp, while Emma pulled the strips with measured, deliberate movements, inflicting as much pain as she possibly could.

Happy Birthday to me, Happy Birthday to me, Happy Birthday, dear Emma, Happy birthday to me! she sang silently, thinking her new year couldn't possibly have got off to a better start.

Read on for an extract from Patricia Scanlan's latest
heart–warming bestseller . . .

Patricia SCANLAN

A Time for Friends

**SIMON &
SCHUSTER**

London · New York · Sydney · Toronto · New Delhi

A CBS COMPANY

PROLOGUE

The sun is shining through the window on the landing. Rays of diffused light streaming onto the red-gold-patterned carpet that covers the stairs. This will be one of the many things to remember on this life-changing day that will be buried deep in the recesses of the mind in the years that follow.

The sounds will never be forgotten either. The groaning and grunting getting louder at the top of the stairs. The absolute terror of feeling something is wrong. That a loved one is ill.

The bedroom door is open. The sickening tableau is revealed. A gasp of shock escapes as innocence is lost, and life alters its course forever in that instant.

The man and woman turn at the sound. Horror crosses the man's face as the woman untangles her legs from him. Both of them are naked. The woman's hair is mussed, cascading like a blonde waterfall over her rounded creamy breasts. The man grabs his trousers to hide his pale-skinned, hairy nudity.

'Wait!' he calls frantically. 'Wait!'

But it's too late.

A burden is added to the hurt and sadness already borne.

July 1965

'Do I *have* to ask her to my party, Mammy? She just is so mean to my friends. She says horrible things and she tells Aileen that she's *fat!*' Hilary Kinsella gives a sigh of exasperation as she studies her mother's face to try and gauge what Sally's response will be. Surreptitiously she crosses the fingers of both hands behind her back as she gazes expectantly at her mother who is rubbing the collar of her elderly father's white shirt with Sunlight soap, before putting it in the washing machine.

'Colette shouldn't say things like that, but I think she's a little bit jealous of you and Aileen being friends. She doesn't really mean it,' Sally says kindly. 'And it would be a bit cruel not to invite her to your birthday party. Wouldn't it now?'

Hilary's heart sinks. She has been hoping against hope that just this once she can have fun with her friends and not have to listen to Colette O'Mahony boasting and bragging about her huge birthday party which will be two weeks after Hilary's own.

'But, Mammy, she says that we can't afford to go on holidays to Paris on a plane like she does, an' she says her mammy and daddy have more money than we do,' Hilary exclaims indignantly, seeing that she is getting nowhere.

'Well we can't afford to go abroad and the O'Mahonys *do* have more money than we do,' Sally says equably, twisting another shirt to get rid of the excess water before dropping it into the twin tub. 'But do you not think you have much more fun in our caravan, going to the beach every day and playing with your cousins on our holidays, than walking around a hot, stuffy city, visiting art galleries and museums with adults, and having no children to play with? Do you not think it must be very lonely not to have any brothers and sisters?' Sally remarks, a smile crinkling her eyes.

'I suppose so,' sighs Hilary, knowing what is coming next.

'Poor Colette with no sisters or brothers, and not many friends either. And no mammy to have her dinner ready after school like I do for you, pet. You're so lucky with the family and friends you have. You always have someone to play with when you come home from school, so wouldn't it be a *kindness* to invite Colette to your party? Because I know that you are a *very* kind little girl. Now go and play with her and I'll bring some lemonade and banana sandwiches out into the garden for the two of you, and you can have a picnic for tea,' her mother says briskly.

But I don't *want* to be a very kind little girl, Hilary wants to shout at her mother. But she knows she can't. Sally has high expectations of her children. Kindness to others is mandatory in the Kinsella household. Whether she likes it or not, Hilary has to be kind to Colette O'Mahony and, yet again, endure her unwanted presence at her much anticipated birthday party.

Tears smart Colette O'Mahony's eyes as she scurries away from the door where she has been listening to Hilary and Mrs Kinsella discussing whether or not she should be invited to Hilary's crummy birthday party. Colette's heart feels as though a thousand, no a *million* nettles have stung it. Mrs Kinsella has said 'poor Colette' in a pitying sort of voice. She is *not* poor. She has her own bedroom and doesn't have to share with an older sister. She has loads of good dresses and other clothes. Hilary Kinsella only has *one* good dress for Sundays. *And* most important of all, Colette has a *servant* at home to make her dinner when she comes home from school.

Mummy calls her 'the housekeeper', but Colette tells all the girls in her class that Mrs Boyle is her 'servant'.

Mrs Boyle will make jelly and ice cream and many delicious fairy cakes and chocolate Rice Krispie buns and a *huge* chocolate birthday cake for her birthday. Hilary will only have a cream sponge and Toytown biscuits and lemonade and crisps. This thought comforts Colette. It is only through her supreme sense of superiority that she is able to process the enormous envy she has for all that Hilary has. She hates that her mother works four days a week and Mrs Boyle – who is quite strict for a servant – looks after her three days, and Mrs Kinsella minds her on Thursdays.

How she longs to spend a summer in a caravan and play on the beach all day. How she longs to join the Secret Six Gang that Hilary and her sister and cousins are part of every summer in Bettystown. It sounds even more exciting than the Five Find-Outers stories that Mrs Boyle sometimes reads to her. Well she is going to start her own secret gang and Hilary is not going to be allowed to be part of it, Colette vows.

The nettle stings in her heart are soothed somewhat at this promise to herself as she observes Hilary marching out of the kitchen with a cross look on her face. 'We have to go and play outside and then we're having our tea in the garden,' she announces with a deep sigh.

'*My* servant gives me a push on *my* swing before *my* picnic in *my* garden,' Colette declares, eyeballing her best friend. 'It's a pity *you* don't have a servant or a swing,' she adds haughtily before sashaying out into Hilary's back garden.

'Get me twenty Player's, and ten Carrolls for your ma and get yourself a few sweets.' Gus Higgins hands Jonathan a pound note and pats him on the shoulder. 'Don't be long, now,' says Gus. 'I'm gaspin' for a fag!'

'OK, Mr Higgins,' Jonathan says, looking forward to the Trigger Bar he's going to buy as his treat. The fastest way to the shop is through the lane, halfway down his road, but he decides against it. The lane is a gathering place for some of the boys in his class to play marbles or football. It is no place for him. 'Nancy boy' and 'poofter' they call him, and while he does not know what 'poofter' means, he knows it's a nasty and spiteful taunt. He takes the longer route, and crosses the small village green to Nolan's Supermarket. 'Hi, Jon,' he hears Alice Walsh call, and smiles as his best friend catches up with him.

'Guess what? My daddy gave me six empty shoeboxes from his shop so we can make a three-storey doll's house with them. Can you come over tomorrow?'

'Deadly.' Jonathan feels a great buzz of excitement. 'Mam has some material from curtains she is making for Mrs Doyle; we can use it for our windows. And we'll make some ice-pop-stick chairs and tables. But I have to clean out the fire and set it and do some other jobs for Mam first and then I'll come over. See ya.'

'See ya!' she echoes cheerfully before he opens the door to the shop and hears the bell give its distinctive ping. Mr

Nolan is stacking shelves and he takes his time before serving Jonathan. 'Don't smoke all those at the one go,' he says, giving him a wink as he hands over the change. All the big boys buy Woodbines after school. Jonathan tried smoking once and it made him sick and dizzy, so Mr Higgins's and his mam's cigarettes are quite safe.

'Did you buy something for yourself?' Mr Higgins asks when Jonathan hands his neighbour his change and the brown paper bag with the cigarettes in it.

'I bought a bar,' he says when Mr Higgins takes the Carrolls out of the bag and hands them to him.

'Gude wee laddie. Nie here's the cigarettes for your mother. It can't be easy for her being a poor widda woman. I have three daughters of ma own to support but at least I bring home a good wage. Tell her it's a wee gift.' His neighbour is not from around Rosslara. He and his family moved into the house next door to Jonathan's two years ago when Mrs Foley died and sometimes Jonathan finds it hard to understand him if he talks fast. He says 'nie' instead of 'now' and 'wee' instead of 'small'. The first time Jonathan heard him say 'wee' he was shocked because he thought he was talking about wee wees. Until his mammy explained it to him, saying that people from different parts of the country had different accents.

Jonathan's mammy has to work very hard doing sewing and alterations, as well as working every morning in the doctor's surgery answering the phone and making appointments for patients. Jonathan's daddy died when he was three and his mammy has to pay a lot of bills and take care of him and his two older sisters.

Mr Higgins says his mammy is a grand wee woman. He's kind to her and buys her cigarettes, because she can't afford them herself. Jonathan thinks this is a great thing to do and so he never minds running errands for his neighbour.

'Tell your wee mammy, ma missus will be wanting her to make a communion dress for ma wee girlie. She's away into town to get new shoes for them all and I'm having a grand bit of peace.' Mr Higgins gives a little laugh and pulls the sitting-room curtains closed.

'I'll tell her, Mr Higgins,' Jonathan says politely, wondering why his neighbour is opening the button at the top of his dirty blue faded jeans. Perhaps he's going to lie on the sofa and have a nap, he thinks.

'Before ye go, I want you to do me another wee favour. It's just between you and me now. Our little secret. And there'll be another packet of ciggies for your ma and a treat for yourself next week if ye do as I ask,' Mr Higgins says. His breathing is raspy and his face is very red and Jonathan is suddenly apprehensive. Something isn't right. Something has changed but he's not sure what. And then it's as though everything is happening in slow motion, even the very particles of dust that dance along a stray sunbeam that has slipped through a gap in the closed curtains, and even the pounding of his heart thudding against his ribcage, as Mr Higgins advances towards him.

PART ONE

1990

Upwardly Mobile

CHAPTER ONE

'See you tonight,' Niall Hammond said, planting a kiss on his drowsy wife's cheek.

'What time is it?' Hilary groaned, pulling the duvet over her shoulders and burying her head in the pillow.

'6.35,' he murmured and then he was gone, his footsteps fading on the stairs. She heard the sound of the alarm being turned off, heard the front door open, then close, and the sound of the car reversing out of the drive.

Hilary yawned and stretched and her eyes closed. I'll just snooze for ten minutes, she promised herself, before drifting back to sleep.

'Mam, wake up, we're going to be late for school.' Hilary opened her eyes to see Sophie, her youngest daughter, standing beside the bed poking her in the ribs.

'Oh crikey, what time is it?' She struggled into a sitting position.

'8.12,' her daughter intoned solemnly, reading the digital clock.

'Holy Divinity, why didn't you call me earlier? Where's Millie? Is she up?' she asked, flinging back the duvet and scrambling out of bed.

'She's not up yet.'

'Oh for God's sake! Millie, Millie, get up.' Hilary raced into her eldest daughter's bedroom and hauled the duvet off her sleeping form.

'Awww, Mam!' Millie yelled indignantly, curling up like a little hedgehog, spiky hair sticking up from her head.

'Get up, we're late. Go and wash your face.' Hilary was like a whirling dervish, pulling open the blinds, before racing into the shower, jamming a shower cap onto her head so her hair wouldn't get wet. Ten minutes later, wrapped in a towel, she was slathering butter onto wholegrain bread slices onto which she laid cuts of breast from the remains of the chicken she'd cooked for the previous day's dinner. An apple and a clementine in each lunch box and the school lunches were done. Hilary eyed the full wash-load in the machine and wished she'd got up twenty minutes earlier so she could have hung it out on the line seeing as Niall hadn't bothered.

She felt a flash of irritation at her husband. It wouldn't dawn on him to hang out the clothes unless she had them in the wash basket on the kitchen table where he could see them. Sometimes she felt she was living with *three* children, she thought in exasperation. Typical that it was a fine day with a good breeze blowing and her clothes were stuck in the machine and would have to stay there until she got home.

Millie was shovelling Shreddies into her mouth while Sophie calmly sprinkled raisins into her porridge. Sophie was dressed in her school uniform, blonde hair neatly plaited, and yet again Hilary marvelled at the dissimilarity of her children. Millie, hair unbrushed, tie askew, lost in a world of her own, oblivious to Hilary's hassled demeanour. At least they'd had showers, and hair washed after swimming yesterday, she thought, taking a brush from the drawer to put manners on her oldest daughter's tresses.

Twenty minutes later Hilary watched the lollipop lady escort them across the road, and smiled as Sophie turned to give her a wave and a kiss. It was hard to believe she had two children of school-going age. Where had the years gone? she wondered as she crawled along in the school-run traffic.

It shocked her sometimes that she was a wife and mother to two little girls and settled into the routine of family life that didn't seem to vary much when the girls were at school. At least she'd spent a year au pairing in France after leaving school, and she'd spent six weeks on the Greek Islands with Colette O'Mahony, her oldest friend, having an absolute blast the following summer! That had been fun. Hilary grinned at the memory, turning onto the Malahide Road, and groaning at the traffic stuck on the Artane roundabout.

Colette would never in a million years be stuck in school-run traffic, she thought ruefully. Colette had a nanny to bring Jasmine to school in London. No doubt her friend was sipping Earl Grey tea in bed, perusing the papers before going to have her nails manicured or going shopping in Knightsbridge. Their lives couldn't be more different. But then, even from a very young age, they always had been.

Colette, the only daughter of two successful barristers, had had a privileged, affluent childhood. Her parents fulfilling her every wish, but handing her over to the care of a succession of housekeepers, as they devoted themselves to careers and a hectic social life, before packing Colette off to a posh and extremely expensive boarding school.

In contrast, Hilary's mother Sally had been a stay-at-home mother, although she did work a few hours on Saturdays in the family lighting business. Hilary's dad, Mick, owned a lighting store and electrical business and Hilary had worked there every summer holiday, either in the large showrooms, that stocked lights and lamps and shades of every description, or in the office working on invoices and orders and deliveries.

Her parents, unlike Colette's, were extremely family orientated. Hilary and her older sister Dee had grown up secure in the knowledge that they were much loved. Sally and Mick enjoyed their two girls and had bought a second-hand caravan so they could all spend weekends and holidays together. Hilary's abiding memory of her childhood was of her mother making scrumptious picnics in the little caravan kitchen, and her dad lugging chairs and windbreaks and cooler bags down to the beach and setting up their 'spot'. And then the games of rounders, or O'Grady Says, with their parents and aunts, uncles and cousins joining in, a whole tribe of Kinsellas, screeching and laughing. And then the sand-gritted picnic with tea out of flasks, or home-made lemonade, and more often than not, a gale whipping the sand outside their windbreak as clouds rolled in over the Irish Sea, the threat of rain somehow adding to the excitement. And when it did fall, all hands would gallop back up the bank to the caravans, and Mick would laugh and say, 'That was a close one,' when they'd make it inside before the heavens opened.

Sally enjoyed the company of her girls and, when time and work permitted, they would head over to Thomas Street, and ramble around the Liberty Market, browsing the stalls, especially the jewellery ones, oohing and aahing over rings and bracelets. Kind-hearted as ever, Sally would fork out a few quid for a gift for Hilary and Dee. Their mother had steered them through the ups and downs of their teen years and had urged her daughters to spread their wings and see the world and follow their dreams. She had been fully behind Hilary's decision to go to France after her Leaving Cert and be an au pair and become fluent in French.

After her year of au pairing and her six weeks roaming the Greek Islands with Colette, Hilary had planned to do an arts degree with a view to teaching languages but Mick had suffered a heart attack the August before she was to start university, and she had felt it incumbent on her to put aside her own plans for her future, especially as she'd been abroad for more than a year, enjoying the freedom to be carefree and unfettered. She had stepped up to the plate to help her parents in their hour of need. Her older sister Dee was in the middle of a science degree and there was no question of her dropping out of university.

Hilary was desperately disappointed at having to postpone her degree course; she had been so looking forward to going to university and enjoying the social side of life. Dee might study hard, but she partied hard too and lived on campus, free of all parental constraints.

Hilary had been looking forward to moving out of the family home. Having spread her wings in France, she was keen to have the freedom to live her own life but her father's illness put paid to that. She buried her regrets deep and put her shoulder to the wheel to keep the showrooms ticking over, while Bill O'Callaghan, Mick's senior electrician, looked after that side of the business.

Hilary had taken a bookkeeping and accounts course at night school soon after, and it was at a trad session one sweltering bank holiday weekend, in the college grounds, that she had met brown-eyed, bodhrán-playing Niall Hammond. She had tripped over someone's handbag and tipped her Black Velvet Guinness drink down his back.

He'd given a yelp of dismay and jumped to his feet and then started to laugh when he'd turned round and seen her standing, hand to her mouth in horror, her glass almost empty.

'I ... I'm terribly sorry,' she stuttered; dabbing ineffectually at his shirt with a tissue, while his friends guffawed.

'Don't worry about it,' he said easily. 'I was getting too hot anyway.' He pulled the soaking shirt over his head, exposing a tanned torso with just the right amount of dark chest hair to make her think: *Sexy!*

Students were in various states of undress because of the sultry heat, so being shirtless wasn't a big deal, she thought with relief, trying not to gaze at her victim's impressive pecs while he wrung out his shirt and slung it over his shoulder.

'You are such a *clutterbuck*, Hilary.' Colette materialized behind her and gave a light-hearted giggle. She rolled her eyes heavenwards and held out her dainty hand to the hunk in front of them. 'Hi, I'm Colette O'Mahony, and this' – she made a little moue – 'is Hilary Kinsella who has two left feet as you've just found out.'

'Well, hi there, ladies. Niall Hammond is my moniker and I guess we should have a round of fresh drinks to get us back on track.' He waved politely at a waitress and she nodded and headed in their direction. 'Guinness for you, Hilary? Did you have anything in it?'

'Um . . . it was a Black Velvet,' Hilary managed, mortified, and raging with Colette for saying she had two left feet. Her friend could be so artless sometimes.

'Brandy and ginger,' Colette purred gaily, fluttering her eyelashes at him.

Hilary saw Niall's eyes widen slightly. Typical of Colette to go for an expensive short when someone else was paying.

'Er . . . mine's with cider, not champagne,' she added hastily in case he thought they were way OTT.

Niall winked at her and gave the order and added, 'A pint of Harp for me, please. So, ladies, are you students here?' he asked, smiling down at Colette. Hilary's heart sank. It was always the way. Once men saw blonde, petite, dainty, effervescent Colette, she was forgotten about.

'Hilary is. She's doing a boring bookkeeping course; I'm just here for the craic! I'm studying Fine Arts in London. I'm home for the weekend.'

'Interesting! Fine Arts. How did that come about?' Niall leaned against a pillar, thumbs hooking into his jeans, and Hilary thought how typical of her luck to encounter a hunky guy when Colette was home from London on one of her rare jaunts across the Irish Sea. Since she had moved to London to live with her father's widowed sister, her friend rarely came home, and wasn't great at keeping in touch either. She was

301

having a ball going to polo matches, and weekend parties in the country, and drinking in glamorous pubs in Kensington and Knightsbridge and shopping in Harvey Nicks and Harrods.

'My parents wanted me to study law. They're both barristers,' Colette added, always keen to slip that bit of information into any conversation. 'I couldn't bear the idea,' she trilled, throwing back her head so that her blonde hair fell in a tumbling mane over her shoulders, and giving a gay laugh. 'My dad's sister has a big flat in Holland Park, and her husband died and they have no children so I went to stay with her for a while and she knew someone in Dickon and Austen's Fine Art and I worked there and did my degree and that's where I've fetched up.'

Fetched up, thought Hilary irritably. Colette was becoming more English than the English themselves.

'And yourself?' Niall's heavy-lidded brown eyes were focused on Hilary. But there was a twinkle in them that she liked and she found herself responding with an answering smile.

'I work in my dad's lighting and electrical business—'

'She's a shop manager,' interjected Colette brightly. 'Oh look, here's our drinks.'

'Let me pay,' Hilary urged. 'After all I've ruined your shirt.'

'Another time,' Niall said firmly, taking his wallet out of the back pocket of his jeans and extracting a twenty.

'And what do *you* do apart from playing the bodhrán fabulously?' Colette arched a perfectly manicured, wing-tipped eyebrow at him, before taking a ladylike sip of her brandy and ginger.

'I work in Aer Rianta International, in travel retail. And in my spare time I play gigs with these hoodlums.' He indicated his three band buddies in the background.

'Really? An interesting job, I'd say?' Colette was impressed. 'Do you travel much?'

'I do indeed.'

'I *love* to travel,' Colette commented gaily.

'What's your band called?' Hilary interjected, knowing that unless she steered her off track, Colette would launch into a description of her travels and Hilary would end up feeling like a real gooseberry. She was beginning to feel like one already!

'We're called Solas, which I'm sure you know is the Gaelic for "light". Somewhat of a synchronicity, Hilary, wouldn't you think? Both of us work with light!'

'Umm.' Hilary was caught mid-gulp of her Black Velvet and was afraid she had a creamy moustache. 'I guess so.'

'Well, I should get back and play another set, or Solas won't get paid tonight. It was nice meeting you both.'

'Are you playing anywhere else over the weekend?' Colette asked casually.

'We are. Are you into trad? I wouldn't have thought that would be your scene,' Niall remarked.

'Oh I *LOVE* it,' Colette fibbed. 'I adore The Dubliners and ... er ... um ... eh ...The Clancy Brothers.'

'And yourself, Hilary?' Niall turned to look at her.

'I like trad.' She nodded. 'I like the liveliness of it, the buzz of a good session.'

'And who do you like?' he probed.

'I like The Bothy Band, Planxty, De Dannan, and The Chieftains are amazing.' She shrugged.

'A woman after my own heart. They're all unbelievable musicians, aren't they?' he said enthusiastically.

'The best,' Hilary agreed.

'So where are you playing tomorrow?' Colette persisted, annoyed that she hadn't thought of naming any of those bands, although she only vaguely knew of them. She was more into The Rolling Stones and The Eagles.

'O'Donohue's. Why, are you going to come?'

'Well, who knows?' Colette flashed her baby blues at him. 'But if you don't see me there you can always ring Dickon and Austen's and catch me there. Thanks for the drink,' she drawled before sauntering back to where they had been sitting.

'Do you think they would take a collect call?' Niall grinned and Hilary laughed.

'Not sure about that.'

'So will you both be coming to O'Donohue's tomorrow night?' he queried.

'Not sure about that either. We're doing a big stock take in the shop, and I have to be there. And it's much easier to get it done after closing time.'

'Sure, if I see you I see you,' he said easily. 'Enjoy the rest of the evening.'

'You too and sorry about your shirt and thanks for the drink,' she murmured, heart sinking when she saw him glance over to where Colette was now chatting animatedly to a tall bearded guy, looking like a dainty little doll beside him.

'Another brandy and ginger coming up soon, I'd say,'

Niall said wryly, amusement causing his eyes to crinkle in a most attractive way.

'What?' She was caught off guard.

'Your little friend has expensive tastes.'

'Er ... she doesn't like beer, or Guinness,' Hilary said loyally, taken aback by his directness.

'She's lucky to have you for a friend; you have a very steadfast quality, Hilary. Would you come out for a drink with me sometime, when your stock taking is over?'

'*Me!* ... Oh! ... I thought it would be Colette you would ask out if you were asking either of us,' Hilary blurted.

'Did you now? Well, ladies who pour their Black Velvets all over me to get my attention are much more interesting than flirty brandy and ginger drinkers.'

'I didn't pour my drink over you to get your attention. It was an *accident*. I *tripped!*' Hilary protested indignantly.

'Well, it worked, didn't it? I'm asking you out for a drink,' he pointed out.

'Is that right?' Hilary said hotly. 'How very arrogant that you would think I'd *want* to go for a drink with you. I'm not *that* desperate to get a man that I'd waste a Black Velvet on him.'

Niall guffawed. 'Sorry, Hilary, I couldn't resist it. Just wanted to see if you'd rise to the bait. I was only teasing, honest. I know you tripped. Come on, give me your number and let me make amends,' he smiled.

'You'll get me at Kinsella Illuminations, Kirwan's Industrial Estate; it's in the phone book. Don't call collect,' Hilary retorted, but she was smiling as she made her way back to the table.

Colette and Beardy were at the bar, Colette making sure she was posed just where Niall could see her as he rapped out a toe-tapping tattoo on his bodhrán. She could pose all she liked, Hilary smiled to herself. For once in her life, her friend had come in second. Niall Hammond had asked Hilary out for a drink, and out for a drink she would go.

'He asked you *out*?' Colette couldn't believe her ears later that night as they tucked into a kebab on the way home. Colette was staying the night at Hilary's, before heading back to her parents' detached, palatial pad in Sutton the following morning.

'Yeah, I told him we were stock taking tomorrow and I wouldn't be in O'Donohue's, so he's asked me out. He's going to ring me.' Hilary licked the creamy sauce off her fingers and took a slug of Coke to wash it down.

'Ah ha! It will be interesting to see *if* he rings. You know what they're like,' Colette said dismissively. 'How many times have you sat waiting for a phone call from some bloke? Don't hold your breath, now,' she advised, nibbling neatly on a portion of their shared kebab. She never dribbled sauce or got it on her fingers. Hilary would have had no problem polishing off a whole kebab and she was always irritated that Colette would refuse to have one, and then tuck into hers.

'You make it sound as though I'm permanently sitting by the phone waiting for a fella to ring,' Hilary said crossly, coming down from her high. Perhaps Colette was right: Niall might not bother to ring her. She had waited on a few occasions for a guy to ring after he had taken her number, and had waited in vain. Colette rarely had such problems. Men were drawn to her like bees to honey. And just this once, Hilary had thought *she* might be the one to get the boy! Now she was beginning to have serious doubts.

'I'm just not wanting you to get hurt, that's all,' Colette said kindly. 'Men can be the pits. Remember what I went through with Rod Killeen?' Her pretty face darkened into a thunderous scowl at the memory of the rat Killeen who had dumped her for a tubby little tart with a raucous laugh and a penchant for sci-fi that Rod was into as well. 'That guy broke my heart in smithereens,' Colette reminded Hilary. 'Used and abused me! And behind my back was having it off with lardy Lynda. Little fat slut!'

Hilary sighed as Colette went into her usual rant about her ex-boyfriend. Colette had fallen hard for the good-looking, laid-back rugby player who was in his fourth year of medical school. Hilary had been dragged to rugby matches, in howling gales and on rain-spattered afternoons, for the duration of the short-lived romance. Rod had initially been very taken with his 'little blonde bombshell' as he'd nick-named a delighted Colette and they had enjoyed a lusty couple of months in the early stages of their romance. But Colette's demanding ways had proved too much for the muscular medic and he had wilted under her need for con- stant emotional reassurance, and the tantrums and traumas that ensued when he had had to knuckle down to study for his exams. Rod had taken comfort in the arms of a cuddly, good-humoured student nurse from Cavan who couldn't have been more different from Colette in personality and appearance. The fact that Lynda was a stone overweight seemed to incense Colette more than anything. How could Rod find that *fatso* more attractive than her? she raged to Hilary, completely oblivious to the fact that because Hilary herself carried a few extra pounds she too could be considered a fatso, in Colette's eyes.

Personally Hilary could see why Rod would like Lynda's curves, as well as the rest of her. Hilary had bumped into them one night in O'Donohue's after Colette had taken flight to London, and Rod had introduced her to Lynda. She was a down to earth, warm, friendly type with sparkling green eyes, and a mop of auburn curls that cascaded onto smooth creamy shoulders, and a full and ripe bosom, and was far from the 'carrot-haired, fat bogger' Colette had so disparagingly described. Natural and voluptuous, Lynda certainly did not share Colette's clothes hanger sophistication.

Rod's rejection of Colette had been too devastating to bear and, when her mother had suggested that she go to London to get over her broken heart, Colette had agreed.

An angry honking of a car's horn at the Artane roundabout brought Hilary back to earth and real life. Thank God it wasn't directed at her, she thought guiltily. She had been driving on auto pilot, her thoughts way back, what was it, ten or more years since the days of their giddy early twenties? And now both of them were married, she to Niall who had indeed phoned her to arrange a date, and Colette to Des, a London-based financier whom she had married in a fairy-tale wedding in Rome.

Both of them married, both of them mothers, she to Sophie and Millie, Colette to Jasmine. And both of them with very, very different lives, Hilary reflected as she stop-

started her way to work. Colette was such a complex character, it was a wonder their friendship had lasted as long as
it had. She was one of the most competitive people Hilary
knew. She *had* to be the centre of attention. Had to have a
bigger car, better job, sexier boyfriend than any of their circle
of friends. But Hilary knew that behind the confident, smug,
superior façade lay a young woman who was plagued by
insecurity. Hilary was one of the few who knew the real
Colette. The Colette who was generous to a fault, the Colette
who would cry buckets because of a broken heart, the
Colette who had longed to be 'ordinary', just like Hilary
and her sister Dee, and have a mother who was waiting at
home when she came in from school, who would be interested in hearing about her day, and who would have a
yummy dinner waiting for her. Even though her friend
could drive her mad with her selfish, thoughtless behaviour, Hilary could never stay annoyed with her for long,
because she was a big softie and she knew Colette's vulner-
abilities and she knew that Colette thought of her as the
sister she'd never had.

Colette wouldn't be stuck in traffic, doing the school run
and the bumper-to-bumper commute to work though.
Hilary couldn't help the pang of envy, knowing that her
friend had a nanny and housekeeper in her luxurious
London flat. She wouldn't come home to breakfast dishes on
the draining board and a hastily swept kitchen, or a moun-
tain of clothes in the linen basket that had to be washed,
ironed and put away, like Hilary would. Their lives had
always been dissimilar, even when they were little girls, but
their friendship, imperfect as it was, had lasted this long.

That in itself was an achievement, Hilary thought, amused, remembering some of their humdinger rows as she swung into the car park of Kinsella Illuminations, the showrooms of the family's lighting and electrical business.